BRIDGEWEST BRIDGEEAST

For Justine and family

Other Books

As Morgan James Allen

Tales of Ulidia: The Trinity Knot (2020)
Tales of Ulidia: Sword and Stone (2021)
Tales of Ulidia: Kingdom of the Norse (2022)

1

Soon there would be no one left to remember. No one to dispose of the dead. And if, miraculously, one person managed to survive, would they even recall that such a thing as funerals had ever existed? Or religion? An afterlife? Or a Void? No. People will eventually just give way and fall, their bodies decomposing on the streets of every town and village, scorched in summer, washed away by winter rain. And afterwards, the cities would be country once more, new pastures cracking through the streets, ivy strangling the proud citadels of steel and glass at their heart, shrouding offices and boardrooms into perpetual darkness.

Although death was inevitable, in the five years since the beginning of the Great Forgetting, efforts were still being made to reassure the citizenry that at least the memory of their lives would matter. While still possible those at the early stage of the sickness had been issued by the government a generous portion of Virtual Cloud, their own particular cul de sac on the information highway that had once been the

Internet, but which was now just a digital warehouse, an Ark of personal memorabilia, a mausoleum for future anthropologists to gape at in wonder. There they recorded the minutiae that comprised the sum total of who they were.

Later even that drifted away, replaced by the sale of last century Filofaxes of every shape and size, carried around like bibles on Sunday. One could never predict, they supposed, when the series of vital neural pathways that chronicled the particulars of a person's name, the name of their spouse or partner, next of kin, their home address, bank details, medical history, where they worked, or simply the location of their car, would finally disconnect itself from the synaptic traffic the brain had to oversee every millisecond. To them they added their more intimate data, the bric-à-brac of a person's lifetime of choices and experiences: their personality types, their hobbies and pastimes, their favourite sport, food, colour and so on. In short, anything one could think of that would isolate them from the common herd, individualise them, encapsulate their remarkable and vainglorious uniqueness.

Obviously, none of this mattered. There wasn't a day that went by that I hadn't spotted these leather-bound compendiums of scribbled half-truths and fictionalised facts, casually discarded on park benches, at shuttle stops, on railway platforms, or on the dashboards of abandoned cars. They tipped the tops of bins and scraped the bottom of landfills. They littered the verge of motorways and nestled in the copse of trees. Their owners having simply left them behind.

In the end, their minds would not be preserved. Like gazing down on the grids of a city at night, each one, its power source removed, blinking out its light.

I was one of the more fortunate ones. Before leaving my job at NeuralNet I had managed to acquire for myself several crates of the corporation's new inhibitor drug, Traxilene, known popularly as 'amber'. First trials of Traxilene had been promising in treating the early onset of dementia, but this highly sought-after placebo pill had little or no effect on those poor souls in the latter stages of the virus. That, however, did not prevent crime syndicates all over the world from profiting from its sale on the black market. And so those who could afford to do so squandered their savings on something that did not work, enriching cartels of overnight billionaires who would soon forget where their money was stashed.

I wasn't exactly sure why I maintained my own daily dosage. Perhaps it was how the tiny capsule of fiery fluid felt on my tongue before swallowing, how it fitted snugly into one of my uncapped molars, how it trapped the light, or how it tensed slightly between the pressure of my finger and thumb.

I knew, of course, it had more to do with Imogen, than any illusions of efficacy I had that amber was any cure for the carnage that Science or Nature had unleashed on the planet in the last half a decade. It was the image of my younger sister who guided my hand off the whisky bottle every night, who poured me out of bed each morning and into the laboratories of AT -Alzhimene Therapeutics -where I slaved for eighteen hours daily, only stopping for a quick lunchtime shuttle to the sanatorium where Imogen had been residing for the last three years.

Her eyes, I noticed upon arrival that afternoon, peered through me vacantly at first. Next, they flitted uncertainly, butterflies of confusion verifying my aura, before settling into focus on my familiar smile. She smiled too and, as always, I wondered if hers was more a reaction to my own, the kind two passersby share in a park, both straining with dogs on a lead, or dealing with a toddler's tantrum. A nurse, whose name was Janice, offered hers as well, a professionally restrained version that AT reimbursed at the end of every month. In a society where most workers had given up their jobs, a smile like hers had been the hard bargain I had insisted upon if my new employers desired my services. That and the care plan they doled out to paper over the cracks of a health service that was on the verge of collapse. Nurse Janice was probably on the same wages as a brain surgeon in better days. The absence of a ring on her wedding finger explained everything else.

‘She’s had a good long rest, doctor,’ she began, glancing down at the notes on a clipboard left behind by her colleague on the nightshift. ‘Didn’t wake once, apparently.’

‘No, I bet she didn’t,’ I replied, peevishly, having already made formal complaints to the sanatorium’s hierarchy concerning the number of sedatives my sister was having pumped into her arm daily.

‘Hmm, well,’ she answered, detecting my sarcasm. ‘I will give you both your *allotted* time.’ She looked around absent-mindedly, as though checking the temperature of the room, holstered a pen in her pocket and announced with an angry nod: ‘*Fifteen* minutes.’

‘Patrick,’ Imogen said drowsily when the nurse had gone. She was sitting up to manoeuvre a difficult pillow into place. I moved quickly to assist but she waved me away. ‘I wish you wouldn’t antagonise her.’

‘Me? Antagonise *her*? Don’t think for one moment I am impressed by her matronly façade, Imogen. These types are all the same. Buxom, maternal psychopaths masquerading as the milk of human kindness. Besides…’

‘…Besides what?’ she giggled.

'Besides...I hate the way she addresses you in the third person. As if...' I paused, searching for something with which to focus my attention on through our third floor window. There wasn't much except for a church steeple in the mid-distance towering above the jutted slate roofs of suburbia. A church whose bell never stopped sending out its clarion call, perfectly in tune with the Apocalypse.

'...As if I wasn't there?' she continued, finishing my sentence.

I sighed, shook my head, and began to chuckle. And so did she, the way we used to when we were children, the laughter that followed a joke that no one else understood. I was two years older than Imogen, so could never remember a time when she was not there. And yet to have her, physically in my field of vision, but at the same time not *there*, was something I didn't think I was going to be able to withstand much longer. She began to whistle. A melody we used to sing together from those times. And with it a memory of toy boats on a river.

'Are you still taking them?' she asked, having pacified me.

'Amber? Yes. For all the good they have done.'

'You haven't shown any signs?'

'No,' I answered. I collapsed into the armchair beside her bed and combed a hand through my hair. Looking up, I saw her now as she really was. Barely thirty years old but with all the tics and cues of someone decades older. Stretched skin around her cheekbones where elsewhere it languished under eyes and chin. Dark crescents had eclipsed her once brilliant eyes and her lush, blond hair smeared itself across her forehead like wet straw. As always, and just for me, she had had the nurse apply a thin shadow of cosmetic to conceal the pockets of least resistance to her illness. A crayon of rouge had been awkwardly daubed to a pout of lips. The problem, Dr. Andrews had said, was her inability to hold down her food. An unfortunate by-product of the new treatment that I had forced him to try. I would have to desist or she, Imogen, would never survive even Stage Two of the illness. And his recommendation? More drugs. The equivalent of playing dead and hoping the Grim Reaper would pass you by. Saying or doing idiotic things was an early symptom of the contagion that had afflicted millions. How to detect this alongside mankind's natural insanity was something even the experts had yet to fathom. I wondered if Andrews had tested himself recently.

'Anyway, don't worry about me, sis,' I said, dismissing my thoughts. 'I still know how to get to work in the morning.'

'I wish you wouldn't,' she replied, after a while.

'What? Go to work?'

'No.'

'What would you prefer? Join the tens of millions who have already retreated to their castles, drawn up the bridge on their lives? Or perhaps I should embrace religion? Enlist in a suicide cult? And what about the hedonists? Or the death squads that go around murdering innocent bystanders just for the sheer hell of it?'

'No, Patrick,' she breathed, heavily. 'You must work. Of course, you must. But not so much. And not for me.'

And there it was. The same debate. The same hot shame. The same vital minutes wasted. My stubborn refusal to allow a medical conundrum that had got the better of every neuro-chemist across the globe to deliver to me my first professional failure. Hand in hand with Imogen's guilt that I wasn't wasting the remainder of my hippocampus ticking off a bucket list of 'last places to visit before you die', praying my pilot didn't suddenly forget how to fly and steer my first-class airbus into the nearest vertical landscape.

And yet, could I really blame her? Who knew what memories of our sibling affection had already yellowed in the brain fog that was her past life. I was playing mental tennis with someone who didn't have strings in her racket.

'I'm sorry, Imogen.' I leant over and kissed her forehead. 'But AT are running new trials. They show promise. Less side effects.'

She grimaced and looked away to conceal her annoyance. From across the city, the church bells lamented once more. Further out, a muezzin was clearing his throat. The daily emotional air raids on the human condition were calling the faithless to repent.

'No, Patrick. I want you to stop,' she affirmed, summoning up the last reserves of her day's strength. 'Soon, very soon, I will be nothing more than your memories of me. Rest. For both our sakes. Settle down. That friend of yours. She was beautiful. What was her name?'

'Who?'

'Yes, she would make a lovely bride. Something old. Something new. Something borrowed…' But then the flat of an anonymous hand swept past her face and she was wiped clean once more. A tranquil, narcotised glaze alighted on her features. Footprints removed from snow. 'How are you?' she began again.

On the stairwell I stopped to take my third amber of the day, flashed my ID at security at the door, before crossing the road to the shuttle stop that would take me back into the city. There was little need to check for danger. The streets were practically empty. Our new National Assembly, most of which were made up of under fortysomethings from across the political divide, had prohibited all transport except for themselves, the corporate elites and emergency services. The rest of us had to endure long queues for irregularly timed shuttles or trains, the infrastructure of which had been unprepared for the tremendous increase in passenger volume since the early days of the pandemic. In the end, most walked to work and narrowed their circle of friends.

While those diagnosed at Stage One still retained the capacity to drive, it was impossible to predict when Stage Two would suddenly incapacitate its victim. The length of the different stages varied according to the individual. For some, it was years. For others, months. The progression between stages, however, was something akin to a bolt of lightning, or an old-fashioned heart attack. It could occur when you least expected it. In the weeks before the new legislation, and the release of self-diagnostic kits to every household in the country, there had been innumerable cases of train drivers, for example, hurtling past their stops, crashing through level crossings, derailing their carriages into fields of startled sheep, or even worse, into the lights of oncoming trains. There had been near collisions in the air before automatic systems overrode human error. And shuttles, if they didn't upend themselves onto pavements or shopfronts, had often jettisoned their bemused payloads several dozens of miles from their original destination. I had even read of a case where one old army veteran had taken a notion to drive his night service to a village several hundred miles north, to the very spot where he had first met his childhood sweetheart.

The sleeping cargo inside, ignorant of their driver's personal odyssey into the deep recesses of his own troubled mind.

Perhaps it was for the best, I reflected, as I crunched my boots atop the slush to the left of the waiting platform, my threadbare overcoat about as practical as a match struck in a hurricane. The line was at least three shuttles long and so I was beyond the sheltered altar enjoyed by those ahead of me. Instead, an awning of filthy cloud above was depositing large spores of sleet onto my bare head. Or was it ash, parachuted on the wind from newly constructed crematoriums to the west of the city? I shivered away the possibility, then sneezed, receiving an ugly glare from the person next to me. The stranger moved a pace away and adjusted his face covering. He was either an absent-minded surgeon, or one of the several million maniacs who considered the possibility that infected brain tissue could be transmitted through a person's nose. He shared a similar build to my own, was in his late twenties, but also like me, had probably not visited a gym in years. I held his look, removed my hands from my pockets, and dared him to make the next move.

Just then, a long, black saloon car homed into view. It sidled to a halt in front of me, a dark mirror of glass purring downwards.

'Dr. Bishop?' a voice enquired from within.

'Would you like to save the world?'

2

She became aware of herself. A different darkness.

Two golf balls of pain, she imagined, sat in sockets at the back of her eyes. Twin emissaries sent from the inside of her skull. She pictured her brain, an anvil at work, its dull rhythm dispatching warning signals to her optic nerve. She groaned involuntarily and for the first time sensed the presence of someone else in the room.

'Are you awake? Try to relax.'

A voice. Female.

'My eyes...'

'...I know. We have blindfolded you for your own protection. Try not to open them just yet.'

'Where am I?' she sobbed. 'My God, my head!'

'Did you hear that?' the woman asked, punctuating the silence.

'Yes,' another replied. A man this time. 'A good sign.'

She felt a motion towards her. Attempting to move, she realised her body was a dead weight, an anchor on the seabed. A moment later, a cloying scent filled the space around her, its wetness parting her lips.

Before losing consciousness later, she imagined the golf balls reduce themselves to the size of two grains of rice as they were driven off into the distance.

Over the next period, the man or the woman would ask her, upon waking, a series of simple questions. Questions that somehow seemed impossible for her to answer. For example, they began by wanting to know everything she remembered. The name of the country where she was born. Her occupation. What her parents did for a living. Whether she had siblings. And oddly, the age she was when she had died. The latter enquiry frightened her. She could not think of anything to say. She couldn't, she realised, even recall her own name. Soon, however, the word 'Helen' brimmed to the surface of her consciousness. A name without a face, but a name, nonetheless.

They seemed surprised when she confirmed her identity because she sensed an awkward silence and then somewhere a pen scribble and a page turn.

'What year is it?' the man would continue.

'I'm not sure,' she would mutter.

'What month? What day?'

'Day? I don't know. Please, I can't move...'

'...Guess!' the man would insist, losing patience. 'Tell me, what day do you think it is?'

'Sunday?' she replied once.

'Better!' the woman interrupted, the sound of something metallic being lifted from a tray.

'Perhaps,' the man replied when they believed their patient was asleep.

'You know it would be easier for you if you just tell us the truth,' the woman was saying now, as if she had just stepped back into the room. Her voice was different. Kinder.

'Please!' she groaned.

'You are not well, child. That is why you are suffering. You must listen to the voices.'

'What voices?'

'What day is it?' the same man asked again, from further away. She tried to clench her fist against the pounding in her head, but her fingers resisted the impulse. Like hooks at rest on a keyboard that would not play.

'I don't know!' she managed to cry. 'Monday? Tuesday?'

'Good,' the man encouraged. 'What month?'

'April,' she replied, drowsily.

'Yes, April. If you wish. April,' the man replied. 'And after April?'

'May.'

'Yes. As you say. May. And what year was it?'

'Year? I…I…can't remember.'

'You will. In time,' the man replied.

'Time,' a new voice declared, solemnly. 'A clock without a face. A face without a clock. There are no days,' the other man's voice soothed, a hand stroking her hair. 'Not anymore. No time.'

'No time,' she echoed, her words trailing off.

When she came upon herself again, it was if her skull had been removed, polished and replaced. Her brain unpacked. The brass section there had walked off the stage. A sun was shining somewhere in the world and her arms felt that they could stretch out in praise of it, a hazy warmth kissing her skin. She tasted a sticky residue on her mouth. Drugs again. Better drugs. But then she noticed the lightness of weight over her eyes. As if pennies had been taken away and spent.

She opened them to a wooden ceiling, knotted pine beams and a skylight framing a vista of blue. Managing to sit up, she noticed a bedside cabinet to her left, replete with a candlestick and new candle, a jug and a small cup. On the pillow next to her lay a straw hat and a pair of dark glasses. Straight ahead, a writing desk with a chair. In front, a scroll of parchment and a pen. There was also a wardrobe, a set of volets, a laundry basket, and a long mirror in the corner. There didn't seem to be a second door leading off to a bathroom or toilet.

Then, she took an inventory of herself.

Her name was Helen. That was what she had said. But what was her second name? She closed her eyes and threw a rope into the empty well that was her parents and family. The bucket returned empty. Those memories will come back too she assured herself. It was simply a question of time.

A question of time? The doctor, if he had been a doctor, had mentioned something about time. And there had been a woman too. A nurse? Who were they? And what was she doing here? Wherever here was.

Quickly, she examined her right arm; tanned, youthful enough, but evidenced near the shoulder a swollen lump of soreness. She pressed a finger. The deltoid muscle. How did she know that? Was she a nurse too?

She scrutinised her hands. No rings. Nails clipped and unvarnished. Pulling away her bedcovers, she discovered a young body, lean at the stomach with what seemed like a pair of shapely legs ending with two slippers of unpainted toes peeping out just above the hem of a nightshirt. Instinctively, she placed a hand on her left breast. Then the other. Several cup sizes smaller than before. But before what? In a panic, she clasped the top of her head. A thin, velvety nap of chestnut hair gave way beneath her fingertips. She stumbled to the mirror, her bare feet unsteady across the parquet floor.

The woman gazing back at her was an older, pastier version of the girl she seemed to remember. This counterpart was in her early thirties, perhaps a decade older than the impression she had of herself. Had she been asleep for that long? A coma? Had there been an accident? That would explain the headaches. The girl in the glass seemed to have lost several inches of height, more than could be compensated by any lack of heels. Make-up, jewellery and hair aside, accessories that could be adapted to the context of any given situation, the boyish facsimile that mirrored itself back at her was both her, and not her. Her eyes, but not her shape of eyes. Her lips, but not exactly her mouth. Not quite her nose, but a standardised, close relative of her nose.

What alarmed her the most, however, was the fact that the figure seemed colourless, haunted, a ghostly remnant or afterthought of a life that had ended badly. Perhaps, she *was* dead? Perhaps, this was the soulless carcass that was discarded when the divine spark of a person was snuffed out forever.

She tried the door. To her surprise, it was unlocked. Opening it slightly, she peered out. A sweltering blast of air overwhelmed her. She shielded her eyes, briefly glimpsing a grey mountain and a patch of sky providing the backdrop to a group of people idly chatting by a fountain. One of them was mounted on an animal shaped like a camel. Perhaps a dromedary, black with splotches of white. Its rider turned towards her just as she managed to slam the door shut.

She bit her lip and considered. Crossing

to the wardrobe, she inspected its contents carefully. Linen underwear, camisoles, coveralls, nightshirts, and leather sandals, all in white, were packed or laid neatly in order. Five of each garment, two pairs of footwear. She quickly dressed and, out of habit, checked her appearance in the mirror before leaving.

She looked like a worker-bride, somebody about to undertake a day shift in heaven.

Glancing over her shoulder, she remembered the hat and sunglasses by her pillow. Putting them on, she breathed deeply, and opened the door once more.

Wherever it was she had arrived from, it had not prepared her for the incandescent light and heat of her new surroundings. Her body liquified almost instantaneously, perspiration percolating through her skin, a wash and slide of electric eels. She staggered onto a veranda and found herself holding onto a hitching post. The strange, narrow face of the camel-like beast turned to stare at her. Her mouth had never been so dry and somewhere in her brain, her nemesis, the blacksmith, was once more sharpening his tools. The sound of raised voices filled her ears.

And then nothing.

A sip of sweetness. Then another.

'That's enough, Master Weaver,' someone said.

'Enough,' someone else intoned.

She opened her eyes to the face of a man,

the same man she had seen on the camel. This time she knew that she had not been unconscious for long. She was sitting, propped against a pillow. She recoiled, drawing her legs in defensively. He looked at her dispassionately, a dull shovel of a face, the same age as her own but older somehow. Leaning back, his companion emerged from behind. She studied them both. The two of them could have been mannequins in a shop window, animated into life, both selling the same outfit. Unlike the Weaver, the other was dressed in black overalls, not navy. Like his colleague, he sported a matching straw headpiece, akin to a Fedora. They were both of similar physique, not overly stocky, but not unaccustomed to hard labour either. The one who had spoken had removed his hat, revealing a stump of brown hair not too dissimilar from her own.

'Seer?' the Weaver added, questioning the silence.

'I will look after the Apprentice now. There is a loom, I have heard, that the Woodturner needs to fix?'

'Yes,' the Weaver replied, unable to move, his attention absorbed by the newcomer on the bed. Finally, his head dropped, noticing slowly a cup in his hand. He placed it back on the bedside table, took a rag from a pocket and wiped his face.

'Two suns, twice the day, Seer.'

'Two suns, twice the day,' the other replied automatically.

With that, the Weaver turned and lumbered off towards the door. When they were alone, the one who was the Seer faced her anew.

'Who are you?! What is this place?!' she cried.

'This is BridgeEast, Apprentice. I am the Seer. Do not be afraid. You are home.'

3

No mad man is an island. He lives in a city with other mad men. This one was old, his face as reliable as that of a grandfather clock, its time spent in careful and precise calculations. Brownlow's biography would have had opening chapters dedicated to breathable, wide country air and a diet of organic vegetables mashed with cow's milk straight from the udder of life. Later pages would recount the young adult, extracted from bucolic obscurity. How he enlisted and fought bravely through the proletarian ranks. How he allowed his accent to waver in order to grandmaster the subsequent peace and regulate the temperature of a new, cold war. And then, he would have hoped, an epilogue, the chance to exchange the soot of the city for the lay of the land.

But his script had been rewritten, the stage reset.

All this I would learn later. Then, the face which revealed itself behind the glass of his ancient Jaguar was that of a jovial septuagenarian, his eyes twinkling, in defiance of the dead fish stare shared now by so many of his peers. They took me back to a world of gerontocratic guarantees, where experience was accrued and distributed. Wise, silver hair and pensive pipes. Cosy chats with cats on laps and dogs on mats.

'My name's Brownlow,' he added, needlessly. Of course, like everyone else freezing in line, I had recognised immediately the avuncular charm of Arthur Brownlow, having watched enough late-night TV debates with him arguing the toss over arms deals gone awry and the latest puppet dictator who had gone native. A distant Jurassic period of menial concerns, before television had been encrypted, its cipher broken only for two daily news updates of line graphs, pie charts and histograms. The statistical analysis of life-death ratios.

'Save the world?' I replied. 'It's all I can do to get up in the morning.'

A door snibbed and from the front passenger side a stereotypical, sun-shaded bodybuilder in a dark suit approached, his hand addressing the vehicle.

'Would you get into the car, sir?' he snorted. And then, as if remembering something in his training: 'Please.'

I did as I was told, finding myself on slick, leather upholstery, behind soundproof glass and in front of another burly, snow-blind heavyweight, 'Dr Bishop,' Brownlow began, cradling a tumbler in one hand. 'Would you care…?'

'I don't mind if I do,' I answered, checking my watch. 'Bitter out there.'

'Indeed, it is,' Brownlow agreed, decanting a measure of whisky into a glass. 'Don't worry, Dr Bishop. I have informed your *current* employers that you will not be returning for the rest of the day.'

'I wasn't…' I said, as he caught my eye, his brow raised, just like the cube he had pinched from the bucket to his left. I shook my head, and he relaxed the tongs, releasing the ice back with a watery chink. '…worried, I mean.' I held the glass to my lips and sipped. 'Just checking that somewhere it's already five o'clock. India, probably.'

'I see,' he sniffed, giving me an odd look. 'Winston!' he called out, leaning forward slightly.

With that, Winston, our unseen driver, ignited the engine. We eased off slowly, sitting in silence for a while, obeying the twenty mile per hour speed limit, a slalom of mostly empty roads heading south. The whisky tasted good, some Highland malt or other, the product of decades of maturation within its arboreal host, distilled at a time when its acquisition hadn't become as rare as diamonds. Brownlow drank water instead, lost in reverie, his attention absorbed by the world outside. He could see it, but it couldn't see him, behind his one-way window, his camera eye flitting onto a scene of hunched-back hooligans, shuffling with plastic bags in large groups, past boarded up shop fronts, on their way to their local CRDP or Central Rationing Distribution Point. In this zone, the turnstiles of a stadium where football used to be played.

The city was a shell, a crater blast in broad daylight. Outside of my own work route, I had forgotten what the rest of it had become. What hadn't been looted or razed to the ground was left to rot. Crime, outside of the nightly drug trade, had plummeted. With nothing left to buy or plug in, no one to read your latest fashion statement or worry about how you conveyed yourself from A to B, life had shed its trappings, reducing itself to the collective prayer for daily bread. Even rent and mortgages had been frozen. People simply lived or squatted where they wanted. Those working in Health, Education and other essential services travelled to and from work via shuttles that operated between dawn and dusk, and which were supplied with armed guards just in case.

'Where are we heading?' I asked, as our car worked its way free of the shackles of the metropolis. We had just joined a motorway; an ambulance in front of us and the red dot of fire engine about a half mile behind.

'To the coast, Dr Bishop,' Brownlow replied. 'There are a few people I think you'd be interested in meeting.'

'Should have brought my bucket and spade,' I joked feebly, holding out my tumbler for a refill.

'I am afraid one will have to be your limit, doctor,' he smiled. 'You will need a clear head today.'

'A *clear* head? Very apt.'

'What? Oh, I see what you mean.' He chuckled, looking across at his armed sidekicks, neither of whom flinched. 'But that is exactly why you are here, Dr Bishop. Clarity of vision. Clear skies overhead. Better than having our head in the clouds, eh?' He snickered.

I put my head back and yawned. 'Just wake me up when we get there.'

An endless line of gargantuan turbines stroking the air, and through their blades, a lighthouse bedded in rock out at sea. A flotilla of trawlers beyond casting nets for cod and herring and no horizon that I could detect in the greyness. We were encapsulated. Landlocked. And yet, in foreign lands too, civilisation had fallen. It was all the same in translation.

'Back up,' Brownlow explained, 'to our generators.'

We had changed cars towards the end of our journey. A land rover better serving to trundle up a gravelly incline and then along a hazardous breakneck of road. A swipe of seagulls above and a series of telephone poles looping wires back to the nearest town. Down again to the seafloor and through a set of manned gates into a naval base where submarines used to moor in a forgotten war.

'What is this place?' I asked, taken aback, as we navigated past a desolation of warehouses, abandoned tidal berths and basins. The hulk of a rusting frigate, toppled ignominiously on one side, seemed to doze under the watchful eye of an enormous crane. 'It's not on any map I am aware of.'

'A century ago, Dr. Bishop, we had different enemies from the ones we have now. Now, we don't even have those. The dry docks there are no longer of use, of course.'

'Then what are we doing here?'

'An ancient piece of old-world engineering that absolutely no one outside of a small circle knows about. Certainly not those idiots in short trousers back in the city.'

'They have youth on their side, Brownlow,' I countered. 'Incidentally, aren't you worried...?'

'Ah,' Brownlow replied, teasing a finger at me, a wry smile playing on his lips. 'You finally have asked what I am sure you have wanted to ask as soon as you set eyes on me. Aren't I afraid,' he harrumphed, 'as a *man of vintage*, shall we say, of finding myself *indisposed* at short notice? In need of my marbles, so to speak.'

'The idea had crossed my mind.'

'But that is exactly why you are here, Dr Bishop. As for the science to how I have developed a spring in my step I will allow Dr. Hunter to explain. I am sure you speak the same language.'

'Hunter? Rachel Hunter?'

'Yes. You know her?' he asked.

'We both fell asleep at the same conference once. But, if Rachel is here…'

'…Do not fret, doctor,' he replied, reassuring me. 'We are only a few minutes out. All your questions will be answered then.'

His timing was impeccable. Very soon our vehicle was passing through another checkpoint where two grizzled-looking guards with sub-machine guns halted our progress. Satisfied with papers, they elevated an electric barrier. We appeared now to be leaving the base, but then, after a hundred yards or so, Brownlow braced himself and, on cue, Winston promptly delivered a sharp right turn. Another right followed a minute later after which a chalkface of high crag loomed into view above an inaccessible shingle of beach below. A vast, metal hangar door suddenly opened a mouth into the rockface, camouflaged to fool anyone within fifty yards that it wasn't there.

We slid through. Like a card into a magician's sleeve.

It had started life as a subterranean cave, Brownlow explained, but had been quarried inwards as easily as a blowtorch on solid ice.

Sections of the original limestone still prevailed here and there on external walls, but everywhere else was reinforced steel, fluorescent light and row upon row of computer hubs, boxed off into tiny booths. Four other levels of similar terminals administered the gaps between the ground floor and the false ceiling above whilst deeper below the vault of the cavern, I would soon learn, were housed the laboratories where countless numbers of white-coated technicians beavered away with centrifuges, test tubes and cauldrons of the latest witch's brew. Beneath our feet, spiralling downwards to the earth's core perhaps, were the residential zones, the seminar chambers, the nuclear-resistant bunkers, the vast stores of tinned supplies and bottled water, the gymnasiums, the solariums, the archives, the classrooms, the playrooms, the canteens and who knew what else.

Over the next few days I would encounter high-ranking representatives of the navies, air forces and armies of the major global powers; ex-presidents and current prime-ministers; world-renown physicists and poet laureates; minor kings and queens and assorted proxies from the world of music, art and film, some of whom I had been led to believe had died in the last decade.

But for now, it was all I could do but marvel at the sheer enterprise of the place, the scale of human endeavour required to continue what nature had started aeons ago. Monitors flickering indefatigably to the cicada of clicking keyboards while operators rushed from cubicle to cubicle, looking harassed, nursing essential papers or files.

'The best in their field,' Brownlow said, watching me closely. 'Hand-picked. The hard-drives process and calibrate the data accumulated below. 'Speaking of which...', he glanced at his pocket watch, a tokenistic, two-fingered gesture to the modernity around him, '...Dr Hunter should be coming to the end of her shift. Would you like to see her lab?'

'Why not?' I answered, trying not to sound too impressed.

A soundless, numberless elevator made it impossible to judge just how far below the labs were. It was obvious it did not stop off anywhere else. Brownlow widened one eye to the retina scan to the left of its doors before being granted access. After a minute or so, they hissed open again. He dismissed the security detail that had accompanied us with a simple conciliatory nod of the head. Stepping out, we left our two guardian angels to return to the surface and their next clandestine assignment.

I found myself in a long, wide service corridor adjoined by at least a dozen laboratories to my left and right, each one served by its own office and lab support and picketed with an armed sentry. The walls, floor and ceiling were perfectly sutured in white, panels of fierce LED lighting above guiding our progress.

'How many of these are currently operational,' I ventured, paying attention to the luminary on the wall beside me, offering me details on occupancy, temperature, and the energy consumption of the chamber within.

'All of them,' Brownlow replied. 'Twelve teams in all. At work on their own individual projects. Naturally, when they think they are onto something, the apostles all pull together.'

'The apostles?'

'Ah, yes, that was my idea. Numbers are a bit sterile, don't you think? Besides, it helps to remind us of the magnitude of our predicament. Your colleague is in 'Peter'.

'That's funny,' I replied, suppressing a smile.

'Is it? Why?'

'Scientists are at best agnostic, Brownlow.'

'These are different times, doctor. A little faith can't do any harm.'

'Hmm, if you say so.'

I followed Brownlow through our surly guard of honour, our footsteps tiptoeing in the silence, a dramatic change to the hive of activity above.

'It's very quiet,' I mentioned.

'The labs are hermetically sealed. There is another elevator just through those doors there. It's for the replacement shift. They'll be here soon. The volume will pick up then.' He approached the doors of the laboratory at the end of the passageway and slotted a laminated card into the wall as our machine gun toting attendant looked on. A tag on his sleeve: 'Cephas'.

'Cephas?'

'Someone's joke. Now, I'm sure Dr Hunter will pardon the interruption. She's been looking forward to seeing you again.'

4

‘Who are you?’ she repeated. ‘What do you mean? BridgeEast?’

‘I told you, Apprentice. I am the Seer. We are east of the Bridge. Here, I have something that will serve. Please. They will help you forget to remember. And remember to forget.’ He held out a palmful of tan-coloured confectionary with one hand and gesticulated towards the cup on the bedside cabinet.

‘I don’t want to forget!’ she shrieked. ‘I want to remember!’ She struck his hand, causing the pills to cascade to the floor. He ignored the pattern of their falling, keeping his eyes fixed on her. An overhang of bottom lip and a small, barely detectable sigh.

‘Everyone forgets,’ he smiled sadly.

She sat back on her bed. ‘My name is Helen. I remember that.’

‘You mustn’t say *that*, Apprentice,’ his voice quietened into panic. He turned to the door, but it was still closed. Outside, she could hear the sounds of a small community going about their daily business. The slop of something being upturned into a pail; the scrub of hard brush on wood; the snort and canter of a passing animal; the murmur of a conversation just out of range.

'Why not? Why can't I say my name?'

'It is for the Archives only.'

'The Archives?' Helen shook her head. 'I have no idea what you are talking about.'

'Of course, you don't. Not yet. That's how it should be. But soon, you will call it everything to mind.' She winced. A long needle had just tightened an agonising thread somewhere in her brain. 'Best if you put on your sun shades, Apprentice.'

She noticed the glasses once more on the pillow beside her. She put them on and had to admit to herself that they helped ease her discomfort.

'How long have I been here?' she asked.

The Seer frowned. 'Not long,' he replied, the words foreign on his lips.

'Then there can't be that much to remember. What about before here?'

'Before? You mean the pre-life?'

'The pre-life? Yes, the pre-life. Wherever I was before I arrived here.'

'The memories of your final incarnation are part of the reason you are not well. But they too will pass.'

'I don't understand.'

'Some...a small few...begin like you,' he replied. 'We call them Apprentices. They retain images of their final life...words...recollections.

That is why the Haven exists. It eases the transition where there should be no transition. At least not yet.'

She laughed. 'You think I am insane because I think I am sane. I am dreaming. I must be.'

'We are all dreaming,' the Seer agreed. 'Good. You are already getting better. Now, if you promise not to remove your glasses, I will take you to the Archives.'

'I am not going anywhere with you!' she snapped.

'Where you will begin your journey,' he replied, ignoring her. 'The others will be excited to meet you. Do not worry. They will mean you no harm. But…'. He paused, and with no change of intonation, added: 'Your designation is not a name. You are the Apprentice. *If* you wish to leave the Haven. Or perhaps you prefer to stay in this room?'

She slipped on her sandals and counted her toes. They did not seem her own.

A small crowd had gathered outside. The did not seem excited, merely curious. Helen, careful not to look up at the saffron wash of sky above, levelled her gaze and tried to differentiate one from the other, male from female.

Facially, there was very little difference. The same cropped hair. The same overalls in a myriad of colours. Different races, stripped of all diversity.

The men were all clean shaven, with squarer jaws and thickset eyebrows. The women, as far as she could tell, possessed more heart-shaped faces, with rounded corners extending down to the chin, lusher lips and yet, without makeup, it would prove difficult for the casual observer to tell gender apart.

She recognised the Weaver in front, a drop spindle in one hand, a length of yarn wrapped around his other. Next to him, a blacksmith, in grey, a hammer in his fist. Alongside, another dressed in white, a book under his arm. Behind him, a woman in green, one glove on her hip, the other on a spade. To her right, another with raised hands, offering bread. Perhaps two dozen in total. Each one, approximately the same age as the other. There were no children, she noticed. No elderly.

She smile weakly, but feeling it inappropriate, waved her hand instead. They looked at her, mystified. An awkward silence ensued during which she began to realise that the congregation had gathered not just to greet her, but also to display the tools of their trade. She remembered her outstretched hand with embarrassment and quickly placed it by her side. A memory flashed through her mind of some playing cards she had as a child. A doctor. A nurse. A teacher. A priest.

'This is the Apprentice,' the Seer declared. 'She receives your labour with gratitude. Later today she will begin her work in the Archives. Soon, it will bear fruit.'

A ripple of appreciation ran through the crowd like a cool breeze dissipating the tension.

'In that case,' boomed a strong voice, 'the Apprentice is welcomed!'

An invisible knife sliced downwards from the back of the crowd causing it to split into a V shape. Through its middle a figure in purple made his way, dressed in a cassock tied with a belt, a cape and a broad hat. Behind him, two hooded attendants in red. As he got nearer, Helen could sense even the Seer hesitate. Those in front lowered their eyes slightly, arms slack by their side. They adjusted their feet together deferentially and waited.

The new dignitary was, like the rest, in his early thirties, but something in his eyes suggested an older soul.

'Acolyte,' the Seer began, 'we are honoured! I did not expect someone from the Temple today.'

'And why not?" replied the Acolyte, his eyes fixed firmly on Helen.

'The situation in the West...'

'...is not your concern,' he answered, turning to the Seer, who did his best to look away, afraid, or unaccustomed, to holding the Acolyte's gaze. 'Besides, it is customary for an Acolyte to meet a new Apprentice. He stared at Helen, as if she were a book, too high upon a shelf for him to read. For her part, she examined him directly. A haughty tip of nose and a hint of ochre around the eyes. He blinked in confusion and took a step back.

'Are you sure, Seer,' he whispered, 'this Apprentice is ready?'

'Of course, Acolyte. The chemistry of her mind will soon reassert itself.'

'Excellent. The Council will be delighted.' He leaned forwards. 'As of course will be the Advocate.'

'His Holy Name, Acolyte,' the Seer said, closing his eyes.

'His Holy Name,' the Acolyte repeated. A moment passed as the two men appeared to commune with something, or someone, either within themselves, or without. They dabbed their fingers to the centre of their foreheads, the hand returning to their sides with a flourish. When they had finished the Acolyte tilted his head to one side and shot Helen a dissatisfied look. 'Make sure the Apprentice learns our protocols first. Even the newly wakened must not be exonerated for long.'

'Of course,' affirmed the Seer.

The Acolyte smiled, turned, and raised his arms. 'In all of BridgeEast, there is no village with which we are not more content. The Temple is at peace with Ceres. Continue in your duties and follow the vision of your Seer. Two suns, twice the day!'

'Two suns, twice the day!' the villagers parroted.

With that, the Acolyte departed with his small retinue. After retracing their steps through the crowd, Helen noticed them ascend into a vehicle resembling a sort of long barouche, pulled by a quartet of the same strange-looking beasts she had seen before. Only when it had disappeared into the hazy distance did the assembly disperse.

'Who was that?' Helen asked, when they were alone again.

'The Acolyte,' the Seer answered. 'Fourth of five.'

'And the Advocate?'

The Seer recoiled, placing an open hand on his chest. He appeared to be muttering an ablution, cleansing the space between them.

'You mustn't say His name.'

'Fine, Seer, or whatever it is you wish to be called. I've played along so far but it's time for me to return to wherever it is I have come from. One thing is certain. I don't belong here.'

'Where do you belong, Apprentice?'

'I belong to…to…somewhere where they don't have temples and where you are not named after your profession.'

'Profession?'

'Your *work*,' she explained. 'What a person does.'

'Good. 'Profession'. A word I do not know. At least good for now.'

'What do you mean?'

'The Physician has helped to restore some

of your memories. From your pre-life. To help you realign. Yours are the most vivid I have ever known in a new Apprentice, but they too will fade. That is why they, and everyone else's, must be archived. In the end, however, you will remember everything.'

'You mean soon I will not remember my name?'

'You should not know it. Not yet. But that is why you will be a gifted Apprentice. Perhaps, a Master one day.'

'But what about everyone I used to know?'

'You remember them too?'

'No, not yet,' she admitted.

'The nature of things is such that no memories of the pre-life continue. For Apprentices, it is different. From what we have learned from the Archives, it is much better this way. So much pain. Separation.'

'Then why store them at all?'

'They are not stored. They are compiled and then sacrificed to the Great Unseen.'

She thought about this for a moment. She was sure that there had been beliefs held by many in her previous incarnation that heralded the promise of a second life. A better world. And yet, this place, this reality, seemed to jar with whatever creed or philosophy she had forgotten or had yet to remember.

'Come,' the Seer said, suddenly. 'Let us walk. The Archives are not far, just north of the Village.

The others will be waiting for you.'

They crossed a central marketplace dominated by a fountain and surrounded by two and three storied adobe buildings. There were no signs as such; it was obvious by their facades what each interior space entailed. In most cases, the work carried on inside spilled over onto the dusty thoroughfare in front. A farrier hunched over, busy amidst fireflies, sparking off iron; a stall with unidentifiable, oily fish glistening on ice; a wheelwright lining up an axle; a butcher at his block; two sweating hulks loading sacks of grain into a cart; lumber being guided through a circular saw; the scent of candles and spices from somewhere merging with the smell of hard shit that patted the ground as large and hot as dinner plates in an oven.

Some atavistic impulse made Helen push the slide of her hands into the imaginary pockets of her overalls.

'Money. I don't have any.'

'The one before you said the very same. There is no currency of exchange here. Every villager contributes to the general commonwealth. As long as you work, you will have shelter, Apprentice.'

'In the Archives?'

'Yes.'

They passed through the centre, following a grit trail, into an open area of dazzling white domed structures. It was only then the full measure of the sky showed itself to her, unfolding its insufferable blanket of heat; brushstrokes of gold and bronze emanating from a high sun, much larger, in her mind, than it should have been. Further to the east, another orb shimmered, closer to the horizon, its corona barely discernible in a bowl of light. Between the afterglow of both stars, the sky paled into a potpourri of greenish blue.

'There are two…'

'…suns. Of course. We are blessed.'

'And the West?'

He pointed to a slither of darkness in the distance. 'Beyond the Bridge is the land of eternal night,' the Seer replied, solemnly. '*They* have never seen our suns.'

'This Bridge, it is a barrier between the east and west of this island?'

'A barrier? Yes, in a way. It is the releaser of the souls that make their journey here.'

'So, that is where I came from?' she asked, stopping to shield her eyes. A murky grey wall of gloom appeared to ascend from a mascara line of black. It was impossible to tell how high the wall was. 'So, it is always night there?'

'Night?'

'There are no suns there.'

'In BridgeWest, they have the dying suns. Too weak to light their sky.'

'Moons,' she said to herself.

'What did you say?'

'Nothing,' she replied, quickly.

'The Bridge separates the Island,' the Seer continued. 'But all souls incarnate at the Bridge. Would you like to drink?'

'Sorry?'

They were standing by a cluster of wells in the midst of sleepy, desert plain, populated with trees, their large lilac leaves cupping the sky. The domes peppered the landscape, each one with an entry door and four windows of curvilinear shielded glass.

The Seer handed her a ladle. She took a sip. Whatever it was tasted sweet, thicker than water, thinner than syrup.

'This is where the Village sleeps during the Tides.'

'The Tides?'

'When the waves rise against our eastern coast. This tells us when to rest.'

'But this is not where I will sleep?

'Your home is the Haven,' he reminded her.

'Seer,' she asked. 'Where are the children? The old people?'

'There is no young or old here, Apprentice. No time.'

'But then, how…?'

'…What is unseen remains unseen.'

They continued in silence. Helen found it difficult to match her stride pattern with the Seer in front, his sandals marking footprints in the dirt for hers to fill. Even though she had just quenched her thirst, she realised she needed to drink once more. She looked around for another well but nothing except a sweep of scoured dirt and gravel lined her vision in all directions. A mist of mountain range loomed large to her right, jealously safeguarding its shade.

'Are the Archives far?'

'Beyond the next ridge.'

'Why couldn't we travel by those camels I saw earlier or that vehicle the Acolyte used?'

'The desert-walkers are not for Apprentices or Seers. Neither the chariots. Your body will adapt.'

'Oh? Then why is there a desert-walker heading towards us?'

'What?'

The Seer narrowed his eyes. Up ahead, the vaporous outline of a quadruped and its rider was making slow but patient progress towards them. Behind them tracked a second desert-walker.

'The Master Apprentice,' the Seer scowled, for the first time a thin trace of annoyance in his voice.

5

I might have time-travelled into the future, a lunar module cast adrift on the Sea of Tranquillity. The mellow glow of highly advanced technology at ease with the muted Georgian cerulean of the surrounding walls. Rachel Hunter straightened, a coil of blonde visible beneath her hairnet, tinted with more grey than the last time we had met. Square goggles over tired, green eyes. and a pristine starch of lab coat that hemmed at her knees.

I thought back to our first meeting eight years before -a symposium at the university where I had just completed my PhD. She had distracted me from my notes, daring me to bear witness to her arrival from the tiered seating of the lecture theatre I was sharing with my fellow eggheads. All of us, gathered together to make a messy, weekend omelette out of current research on the use of AI in early detection of frontotemporal dementia.

Perhaps it was the way she had parted her hair then that had first attracted me. Long soutane wings to the small of her back, a style she maintained from her bohemian student days, she later told me. Or maybe it was her matronly tweed skirt and thick stockings. Her high blouse and knitted cardigan. Or the way her forehead creased when she sucked on a pen, thinking no doubt of how much she disagreed with whoever it was that was speaking, *ex cathedra*, insulting her intelligence from the high stage of smug, scholastic orthodoxy.

Or was it the manner with which she had later transformed herself at the post-conference party. From prissy, bespectacled academic to vampirish bird of prey who later that evening had tipsily spilled the contents of her whisky sour down the front of her sleek, little black something, offering me the opportunity to leap gallantly to her rescue. A dizziness of paper napkins proffered like promissory notes.

And now, here, was this very same woman, surrounded not by box files or male suitors, but by genetic analysers and integrated sequencers, thermal cyclers and multi-spectrum microscopes. She removed her goggles like binoculars from the brow of an Arctic explorer, and slowly unrolled a pair of latex gloves, a striptease of naked arms and hands, before dropping them casually into a bin by her feet.

'Dr Bishop,' she began. 'A pleasure to see you again.' She extended a hand which I shook, and nearly kissed. 'This is Doctor Knight.'

'Bill,' a friendly voice echoed from behind the open door of a refrigerator to my left.

Upon closing, it revealed a long-haired, bearded beatnik in his late twenties, a surgical mask cradled beneath his chin and an earring in the shape of a crucifix dangling from one ear. I caught a glimpse of a demon-skulled T-shirt between the flaps of his lab coat as he offered me his hand. A tattoo peeped from its cuff. It looked recent. 'No one calls me William. Not even my dear old mum.'

'I'll try to remember that,' I replied stiffly, finding myself frustrated that my reunion with Rachel had been interrupted by someone who evidently had more of a relationship with the woman of my dreams than I had ever had during my one-day stand.

'Hey,' he continued, taking a step back. 'You're a Bishop! And I'm a Knight!'

'Oh?'

'Chess,' he explained. 'Don't you play? I'm the piece that looks like a horse's head. I get to jump. And cut corners!' he added, bringing his hands together in a moment of self-delight.

'I see,' I managed to say, looking across at Rachel who seemed indifferent to my discomfort. She had removed her coat and turned to wash her hands in a nearby sink.

'Now, Dr. Bishop, don't let Doctor Knight fool you with his repartee,' Brownlow intervened. 'All a façade. You'll discover that he, like everyone else here, is at the top of his particular field.'

'And what field is that professor?'

'Huntington's Disease,' he replied, warily, sensing my coldness for the first time.

'The errant gene,' I replied. 'You think that Huntington has gone rogue on a global scale.'

'It's a possibility,' Rachel answered, drying her hands on a paper towel. 'It's an inherited problem. Perhaps, what we have here is a legacy that has been handed down beyond the white picket fence of the individual family.'

'So,' I replied, defensively, 'is that why I am here? Cure Huntington's, cure the world?'

'Only if you have a Messiah complex,' she quipped. 'I would start on saving myself first though.' She reached for something in her inside pocket and threw it at me. I snapped whatever it was out of mid-air -a small vial of transparent liquid with a bubble of air trapped beneath its lid. 'A few drops of that on your retinas twice a day will give you more than just 20/20 vision, Patrick.' She smiled, smugly. 'Save you destroying your insides with that amber of yours.'

'Trials?' I enquired, holding the vial up to the task lighting above my head.

'Phase Two,' Knight replied, suddenly serious. 'A couple of hundred subjects. Most people here.'

'Which is why they come, I suppose,' I replied.

Knight looked away, preferring not to commit himself, especially not against those paying his wages.

'And also why,' Rachel continued, 'you have

been wondering about Mr Brownlow. Arthur is our most senior case study. Isn't that so, Bill?'

'Yes, of course,' Bill replied, slightly hesitant.

'Delighted to be of service,' Brownlow chimed in.

'Did you...?' I began, then hesitated.

'...Did I succumb to the contagion?' he suggested, helpfully. 'Not yet, fortunately, but I wouldn't be a 'senior' if I didn't still have a few 'moments' now and again.'

I smiled. 'What about Phase Three?'

'Not yet,' Rachel replied, folding her arms. 'The other apostles...teams... have redoubled, tripled their efforts. MRI scans, biomarkers, animal research. The usual.'

'No improvement, but no degradation either,' Knight piped in, annoyingly over-familiar. 'Production blockers, tau aggregation inhibitors, nasal sprays, hormone therapies, anti-cholesterols, blood pressure meds. That little vial is our best hope at the moment.'

'I don't understand,' I admitted. 'As far as I am aware none of our victims worldwide manifest any of the movement or psychiatric disorders normally associated with HD.'

'Yet, cognitively, there is a connection,' Rachel countered. 'And, of course, there is transmission. The question of hereditary information being passed from cell to cell.'

'But there is no evidence that there is a genetic link with our virus. And we still don't know how anyone contracts the disease.'

'And yet, you see the evidence for yourself. I can show you Arthur's neuropsychological differentials, before and after trials. There are none,' Knight insisted.

I looked at Brownlow, grinning inanely at me. It wouldn't have surprised me if he suddenly began tap dancing right in front of us to prove the agility of his quickstep.

'Okay,' I replied. 'But there isn't any cure for Huntington's either. So how...?'

'...I had been close to finding one in the year leading up to the epidemic,' Knight answered. 'Even had my own lab. I just didn't have the funds...'

'...and now you do,' I interrupted, flattening a hand on the polished top of an incubator. I thrummed a few fingers there while I took a moment to think.

'So...and for the purposes of the uninitiated,' she added, with a nod at Brownlow, 'what do we know?' Rachel began. 'Well, we know each human cell has twenty-five thousand genes and most of those have twenty-three strands of DNA or chromosomes. The 'huntingtin' gene is attached to chromosome number four. It produces the huntingtin protein which is needed by nerve cells in the brain. The problem is...'

'...the problem is when the gene doesn't behave,' Knight continued, 'it causes a mutation due to trinucleotide repeat...err...', he caught a glimpse of a dumbstruck Brownlow, '...I mean... due to too many genetic sequences being repeated. This causes the build-up of amyloid plaque between brain cells. Just like in dementia cases. I had managed, or *thought* I had managed, to synthesise a drug which could slow down the rate of these sequences. It's only since I have been working with Arthur here that I could test the drug on patients with our disease.'

'Hmm, and so it also acts as a preventative.'

'We think so.'

'So, why am I here?' I asked.

'Perhaps we can discuss that over lunch,' Brownlow interjected. 'The canteens here have the best food still available in the country.'

Another elevator, large enough for about a dozen people, seemed to move us sideways, then upwards, if the minor momentum beneath my soles was anything to go by. Knight must be a bit of a lab rat, I thought unfairly. His stale odour had not been deodorised by a shower break any time in the last few days and the heating system located somewhere in the walls of the lift wasn't doing much for his armpits. We stood like four corner pins in a bowling alley waiting to see which one would be the first to swoon and keel over.

When the elevator doors slid open, we found ourselves in a wide-open, glistening hangar, sectioned off into various cafeterias all serving a wide selection of different food: Chinese, Japanese, Thai, Nigerian and Indian options vied for popularity, interspersed with pizzerias, fondu pitstops and fast burger outlets. Vegan, vegetarian, gluten-free and Keto-friendly alternatives were being offered in each one and for those in need of a caffeine fix only, a choice of espresso takeaways or sit-downs. Central zones of Formica-topped tables and chairs greeted the arrival of exhausted shift workers, delighted to let off steam for a few hours before bed.

'Don't see any booze?' I ventured.

'Ha! That dram earlier will be your last drop for quite a while,' Brownlow replied, with a giggle.

'That's *if* I agree to work for you.'

Knight ran a hand through his long, greasy hair. '*If*', he repeated, incredulously. 'You hear that, Rach? He still thinks he has a choice.'

I shrugged, though Knight was right. No way was Brownlow ever going to let me return to civvies after having seen this post-apocalyptic land of make-believe.

I settled back and decided to relax. The noise and smell of the bistros and restaurants brought back different times. Bright summer evenings spent trawling the cobbled terraces of city centre pubs, inspecting chalkboards for food and drink combos, amidst the shift and sway of optimistic, continental colours, the ethnic pungency of turmeric and coriander. But most of all, the expectation Friday had for the weekend.

Or was my mind already beginning to play tricks on me, embellishing the past with gentle brushstrokes, editing out all the pain. The boredom of the weekly launderette, the jostling, daily commute, the ant-like weight of insufferable burden.

'Your choice,' Rachel was saying to me.

'Sorry?'

'What delicacy would you prefer this evening, Dr. Bishop? Didn't you tell me once you had a penchant for French? Or was that a weakness for the wok?' She looked at me, her face suddenly overcome with tinkling laughter. As eight years before, Rachel seemed radically altered, as if crossing the threshold of her lab into the world beyond had stripped away her false decorum. I felt like grabbing her hand and pulling her into my memory. Instead, I flushed slightly, a warm tattoo of skin raising the hairs at the back of my neck.

'Oh, I don't mind.'

'You shouldn't have said that doc!' Knight declared, shaking his head. 'Hunter here has a preference for *bulgogi*. 'Fire-meat', I call it.'

We chose a table and within a moment a waitress appeared out of nowhere; a pencil doubling as a hair stick quickly drawn from her bun and a notepad slung from the pocket of her apron. Upon recognising Rachel, she smiled.

'The usual, doctor?'

'Yes, Marie. Two extra tonight.'

'You always order for each other?' I asked when the waitress had left. 'I'm not sure if I like Korean beef.'

Rachel nodded. 'It's our way of making sure we are always on the same page,' she replied.

I thought about this and then about the waitress who I could see stabbing our order slip onto a long knitting needle of other orders at the counter. She was young, perhaps not yet twenty-one.

'The waitress,' I began, 'and the other staff here. They are not specialists, I presume?'

'No, but they all have one thing in common,' Brownlow said, tearing the paper off his chopsticks. 'They are orphans. Homeless. Discovered on the streets and offered the chance of a lifetime. More than a chance. They get their eye drops too.'

Our food arrived, served with side portions of rice, egg soup and *kimchi*. The sliced strips of pork sizzled on a raised grill in front of us. Marie poured on a little extra soy on top at Rachel's request. The meat spat out once more in retaliation.

We ate in silence, each one of us alone with our thoughts. The food was spicy and nearly brought a tear to my eye. Brownlow handled his chopsticks with remarkable dexterity, and I wondered if he had spent a long sojourn on the Manchurian front, karate-chopping and high-kicking the locals to the bargaining table. Knight wolfed everything in front of him as if it were his last supper, a bit of maggot rice trapped in the toilet brush of his beard, while Rachel chewed slowly, separating each mouthful with a cooling sip of water.

'So,' I exhaled, reaching for a napkin, when I noticed we all had finished. Marie hadn't returned with a dessert menu, even though I could have murdered a brandy, or even a cigar. 'Why exactly do you need me?'

We all looked at Brownlow who was wiping sauce from the corner of his lips. Rachel took the opportunity to answer instead.

'It's about your time at NeuralNet.'

'Oh?'

'You left, having only spent six months there?'

'Alzhimene Therapeutics came along and offered me the chance to do some *real* research into our problem.'

'And what?' Knight snorted. 'You took a pay cut; twenty times less than what Henry Mayer was offering?'

'You ever play poker with matchsticks, Knight? Or roulette with blue chips? They're only bits of wood and plastic if you can't convert them into gold. The end of the world plays havoc with exchange rates.'

'Why did you leave?' Rachel persisted.

'I just told you…'

'…The real reason, please Dr Bishop,'

Brownlow interrupted, pushing away his empty plate, an obvious dismissal of my explanation. It scraped the surface of the table, somehow fanning my anger.

'Listen!' I snapped, suddenly irritated. 'I don't have to tell you anything! Now if you don't mind, I think I'll be running along!' I shuffled out of my seat and was just about to stand up when I felt a strong hand on my right shoulder. Turning around, I found myself once more face to face with the chiselled jaw and low forehead of one of Brownlow's well-groomed Neanderthals. His albino eyes concealed behind glasses, his attire suggesting he was still en route to someone's funeral. Where his accomplice had disappeared to, I didn't know. Nor did I care. I pushed his hand away. 'Who the hell do you people think you are?'

'We know, Dr Bishop,' Brownlow continued, waving his subordinate away with a sashay of wrist, 'that Henry Mayer employed you to work in R and D. We also know that he has been using Artificial Intelligence to sift through vast amounts of personal, medical data.'

'Which is something that you and your government cronies should have stopped him from doing years ago,' I retaliated.

'Don't be such a boy scout, Patrick,' Rachel said. 'It's the world we live in, or used to live in. Anyway, Mayer had you working on speech monitoring, visual indicators, medical image analysis, genetic analysis etc...The most advanced systems his money can buy. Since Henry Mayer is one of the world's one percenters, that's an awful lot of tech.'

'So, you want me to help you apply what I know of that technology to Knight's little application? All a bit cloak and dagger, no? Besides, it wasn't just me. There was a team. At least ten of us, I think.

'Twelve,' Brownlow replied. 'Your own group of disciples.'

'Ok, twelve. So?'

'So, Dr Bishop, any ideas of how many of the twelve currently walk this Earth?' Knight asked.

Something cold formed a pit in my stomach. 'No. Should I?'

Knight smiled. 'Are you sitting comfortably, Dr Bishop? It's quite a story.'

6

The figure and the animal it rode rippled like water where there was none, soft shadows gradually becoming edged as they drew nearer. Helen bent her ear to the windless distance between them while the higher sun above seemed to hum instead, a great solar pulse gyrating its heat to the life below. Desert jade, sage, cacti and feather grass marked the gaps between them as the desert-walker lurched forward. Soon its hooves and laboured breathing were audible and with it the face of its driver.

The Master Apprentice was dressed in a whiteness transfigured by the ferocity of the sun's glare. The peak of his hat indicating some kind of higher authority. He strained against the reins that looped around the beast which was, as it turned out, unlike anything she had ever seen. Its neck was longer and its hump less pronounced as she had first thought. A camel-llama hybrid of some sort.

The Master Apprentice looked down at Helen. Something in his eyes established a connection between them, a familiar recollection of shared experience. For the first time since her arrival in this strange world she considered the possibility that she might have known this man before. Was that how it was, she wondered. Certain individuals or soul groups in pre-life resurrecting their acquaintance after death?

He nodded knowingly, before dismounting. 'Greetings Seer,' he began.

'And to you also, Master Apprentice,' the Seer replied. 'It is…*unusual*…to see you so far from the Archives.'

'Is it?' he asked.

'Forgive me, Master Apprentice…' the Seer continued, a hint of alarm in his voice. His eyes shifted to the desolate wasteland of sand and brush as though he were at immediate risk of being overheard. '…is it not customary for the Seer and new Apprentices from Ceres to journey to the Archives on foot?'

'*Customary*?' the Master Apprentice replied. 'You speak, Seer, of a *before* and an *after* as if there is something other than this *Now*.' His eyes narrowed, and he raised his eyebrows slightly in surprise. Upon removing his hat, Helen noticed the line of a thin welt of skin, a centimetre below the dark buzz of his hair. He had an aquiline nose and it seemed to squint as if the Seer had stepped on something foul.

'Master Apprentice, I did not mean to suggest…'

'…Yes, of course, Seer. What is important is that the Apprentices protect BridgeEast from the lineal and temporal entrapments endured by those in the pre-life. We ingest that pain and then offer it as a sacrifice to the Great Unseen. This is our role. Yours is to act as guide. but I wonder…'

'…Wonder?'

'…if the Seers are not sometimes at risk of contamination while with the new Apprentices.'

'I can assure you…'

'…Yes, I know.' He stared at the Seer thoughtfully. 'I remain assured. For now,' he added. 'But, and this must not go further, this Apprentice's recollection is different, Seer. Perhaps, even special…'

'I see,' the Seer replied, surprised.

'The Advocate has instructed me to bring the Apprentice to the Archives personally. And… something else.'

'Yes?'

'She will receive guidance from another. And remain at the Archives.'

'But no Apprentice has ever…' the Seer began, before correcting himself.

'I have already spoken to your Master Seer,' he replied firmly. He turned to Helen, acknowledging her as if for the first time. 'Are you ready, sister?'

'Yes, I think so,' Helen replied, a little dazed. 'But I don't think I can ride this thing?'

As if to reassure her, the second desert-walker lowered its neck and sniffed her hand.

'The bond is made,' the Master Apprentice declared. With that the animal's front legs curtsied, genuflecting its torso downwards. A wooden box saddle invited her upwards. The beast had no stirrup or rigging so Helen had to heave herself into position with only its reins. It waited patiently as she manoeuvred herself into comfort before lifting itself up to full height. The Seer gazed upwards, still somewhat stunned. Smaller than Helen now. In height as well as stature.

'Two suns. Twice the day, Apprentice,' The Seer said in parting.

'Yes,' Helen replied, surprised by the sudden movement of the desert-walker. She jerked forward, her sunglasses nearly coming off her nose.

'Do not try to lead it, Apprentice,' the Master Apprentice advised. 'It will lead you.'

The desert-walkers touched noses before sullenly switching their necks and heads around to face the trail ahead. Helen turned her head back momentarily but the Seer was already making his way back to his Village.

For the first few minutes or so she felt her back and sides rock against the raised saddle. But the Master Apprentice was right. The desert-walker did not need much persuasion. Its thick, black and white pelt was perfect for the climate while its slit nostrils and long eyelashes operated as deterrents against the sand. It trundled alongside its partner, keeping in lockstep, and soon Helen began to feel more at ease with its plodding rhythm. A canister attached to the side of her seat contained more of the saccharine liquor she had tasted before. It quenched her thirst but also energised her as well.

'Don't drink too much,' the Master Apprentice warned. 'Give the *amrita* time to work itself around her body.'

'Amrita?'

'Yes. It is the 'not death' which sustains us,' he added. He looked skywards. 'It never rains here.'

'You mean there is no water?' she said, understanding.

'No.'

'Then how do we survive?'

'I told you, Apprentice. The amrita is all we need.'

'But there must be water in the amrita. No human being can survive without water,' she protested.

'It never rains,' the Master Apprentice repeated.

'But this is an island?'

'Surrounded by an ocean of amrita.'

'Then,' she continued impatiently, 'how do you know that such a thing as water even exists?'

'From the pre-life. Just like you.'

'You remember the pre-life?'

He pulled the reins of the desert-walker and brought the animal to a halt. Without encouragement, Helen's did likewise. 'That is why I am the Master Apprentice. I have yet to forget everything.'

'So, you…you at least remember your name?' she asked, excitedly. 'Mine is Helen.'

His eyes widened. '*That* is for the Archives.'

'But what is…I mean…*was* your name?'

The Master Apprentice closed his eyes momentarily. 'Who we were is not important. It was never important. We are what we do. In the pre-life, and the lives before it, this was the way until the way was lost. We were called after our work once. The potter, the smith, the wright, the fletcher.'

They rode on in silence. Not sand under the hooves of the walkers but a type of grit that sparkled in the light of the suns. To her left and right, Helen could pick out more of the cupola-shaped outposts, but no sign of any other living creature. The suns too had not moved in the sky. They seemed anchored there, casting the same, unending length of shadows across the gnomon of trees and domes.

Soon, over the brow of a dune, a large, white-washed blister of a wall become visible scaling about a thousand feet into the air. It curved out of range making it impossible for Helen to guess the size of its circumference. She thought about asking the Master Apprentice the origin of the structure but something in his world-weary stoicism prevented her from doing so. Whoever she had been in her previous life Helen was not someone who liked to over rely on others. She was also quite stubborn. That too she felt instinctively.

'The Archives,' the Master Apprentice announced proudly. 'For the entire Five. The largest known structure in BridgeEast. Apart from the Bridge itself of course.'

'The Five?'

'The five Villages. Yours is called Ceres. The others are Occus, Pares…'

'…and five Acolytes?' she guessed.

'Yes, one for each of populated zones of the island. Five Apprentices also. Five Weavers. Five Woodturners.'

'But *one* Advocate.'

'In *BridgeEast*,' he clarified, immediately.

'One Archives?'

'Yes.'

'Five years,' a voice came suddenly from within her.

He glanced across at her, a dark cloud crossing the featureless sky that had been his face. 'What did you say?'

'I don't know. Something I heard once. Before. It lasted five years.'

She sensed him try to read her eyes but unlike him she still needed the protection of her tinted glasses. Could he read her thoughts, she wondered. If so, there wasn't much to read. Not yet. Scattered vocabulary, wisps of phrases, an assortment of images. High buildings and even higher mountains. Grey and green counterpoised. Rain on her face and a kinder sun on her skin. But no faces. Definitions of heads but with their features pixelated in a kaleidoscope of colours like the dance of a flame on a bed of wood.

'Remember it. For the Archives,' he counselled, gravely.

The terrain sloped into the valley, the padded knees of the walkers supporting the strain of the gradient, the splayed toes of their hooves finding the necessary purchase to prevent themselves from keeling over and cartwheeling their loads down the face of the mountain. As the topography dipped, the sheer size of the Archive walls loomed headily above, a dizziness of height as Helen looked up.

'It's amazing.'

'They are,' the Master Apprentice replied, a soupçon of pride in his voice. 'Every thought ever thought, recalled, and transcribed for the Great Unseen.'

'My memories…?' she began, hesitantly.

'The Physician has done all he can. He tests all those who show promise. You will begin your journey through the Circles.'

'The Circles? What are they?' she asked.

A loud commotion from inside the walls of the Archives prevented him from replying. The Master Apprentice stared ahead as a huge stone door, approximately fifty feet high, was being opened on two sides. A tiny slither of inner light appeared from within.

'Quickly!' the Master Apprentice urged. 'Use your heels. We have to get inside. Now!'

'What is it?'

His eyes sailed upwards. 'A mara! Move! Now!'

'What is a mara?' she asked, stabbing her sandals into the flanks of her desert-walker.

'A nightmare. From the dark West.'

7

Bare olive-green prison walls closing in on my nightmares, held in check by the buffer of a single, grey bunk, table and chair. On the table, a laptop connected by ethernet to underground servers deep beneath the planet's surface, Wi-Fi as far out of range as a radio signal from Andromeda. The glide of a panel revealing a clothes rack, mostly lab whites and slip-on safety toes. In the far wall, a WC built as an afterthought to convenience. Blinding light or pitch darkness at the flick of a switch. Soft pillows and a mattress that provided little relief for the stiffness in my joints.

Home Sweet Home.

Things had moved fast. It had only been two days since I had paid my last visit to Imogen. Hours before that I had swiped my work credentials through the security reader in the foyer of Alzhimene Therapeutics and commenced what had turned out to be my last day shift at the coalface of their grey matter research. One kidnapping later and here I was: trapped behind bars I couldn't see, and now, it seemed, all for my own protection.

Given enough time to adjust, a person can become accustomed to almost anything. Even the end of the world could be reduced to an apocalyptic tiptoe if wrung out slowly over a suitably long period of adjustment. The entire human race was on death row, after all, waiting for its last-minute appeal to science, religion or extra-terrestrial deliverance to save the day. And in the meantime, people got married, divorced, and cared more for their pets than for each other.

And yet an entire jury of twelve had been discharged since my time with NeuralNet, an identity parade of half-forgotten faces that had borne witness to the alleged crimes of global business magnate Henry Mayer. All had suffered an earlier-than-anticipated demise: nine after the global outbreak and three before.

The trio who been spared the indignity of oblivion had died in the space of three months of each other. They had been the most junior members of our baker's dozen. Still in their late twenties, they had managed to either commit suicide, involve themselves in a motorway pile-up or drown a mile out at sea.

The other nine had had more 'reasonable' deaths, associated with the Stage Two or Stage Three stages of the virus.

Curiously, all twelve had died in the year following my departure from Mayer's corporation. Even stranger was the fact that our team had disbanded within weeks of my leaving.

'So, any idea why Mayer would want to silence an entire group of elite scientists, Dr Bishop?' Rachel had asked me, as I reeled from the revelation that every one of my ex-colleagues was no longer around to talk shop about the good old days -which were never all that great in the first place.

'The time frame is not conclusive,' I fired back, struggling to convince even myself. 'The nine deaths subsequent to the spread of the contagion will not have had the usual post-mortems and the three before...'

'...Alan Wilson had a wife and two young children. One newly born,' Knight reminded me. 'Threw himself off the top of a block of flats. No suicide note. Audrey Lee's mangled car was discovered en route nowhere near her home or place of work. Heading west. No one knows why.'

'And Dickie Armstrong was a veteran swimmer,' Brownlow added. 'Conditions at sea on the day of his death were calm according to meteorological reports.'

'So, you think that Mayer has conspired to rid the world of a coterie of the world's leading authorities on neurological disorders at a time when the very same world needs them the most? His reason being?'

'Why did you leave?' Brownlow insisted, his mask of wizened cordiality finally slipping. 'What was it you saw that made you want to resign?'

I waved the question off with a light chuckle. Brownlow's face darkened. I looked at Rachel and Knight. They seemed deadly serious. 'Saw? What do you mean?'

'Look, Dr Bishop, we all know Mayer's reputation,' Knight replied. 'Billionaire recluse. Widower. Rarely been since in public since all this madness began. His corporate henchmen have acquired, by fair means or foul, the patents for every new neuro-drug on the market in the last two decades. AI. Computer software. Christ, there was even talk of his financing a manned mission to bloody Mars not so long ago!'

'You know, Knight, one of the best things about the fall of the Internet is the end of all those absurd conspiracy theories surrounding people like Henry Mayer.'

'You have to admit, Patrick,' Rachel intervened, 'these deaths are a tad coincidental.'

I shook my head. 'I crunched the data, Rachel. Was rarely in the research lab. You know AI has always interested me. Hell, that is where we first met, remember? At the conference.'

'What was your success rate?' she asked, ignoring the memory of our first encounter.

I exhaled loudly. 'After comparison with the standard memory tests, our machine learning algorithm was able to prognosticate with up to eighty per cent accuracy.'

'Impressive,' she replied. 'So why did you leave?'

Over Rachel's shoulder, our waitress Marie was balancing a tray of steaming dishes in the direction of three exhausted-looking young males in white coats, former post-grads probably, plucked out of the promise of burgeoning careers and new mortgages. They looked miserable, deflated, unlike their hostess who was counting her blessings along with each of the bowls of miso soup she was setting down in front of them. The two women, Rachel and Marie, just over half a decade apart in age, competed for my attention momentarily. Unlike the men, neither of them had given up. Not yet at least. Each one instinctively performing a duty of care -on hugely different scales admittedly - one a mere pawn, the other a queen, but both with their own role to play. With a whisky out of the question, I suddenly felt the need for a post prandial cigar -which was strange as I had never smoked. Nothing beyond a few marijuana puffs at college. Perhaps, psychologically, it was the need to tear down my own temple before the arrival of the imminent earthquake.

'Imogen,' I began. 'She was diagnosed in her early teens.'

'Of course, Patrick,' she faltered. 'I'm sorry.'

'No need,' I replied, as jollily as I could. 'Funny thing is, what we are currently dealing with seems to have put her schizophrenia to bed. At least for now. Anyway, she was going through a bad patch and needed looking after. And as we have no other family…'

'…You don't need to explain, Patrick. Not anymore,' she added, throwing Brownlow a look of warning.

'The AI…' Knight persisted.

'Bill!' Rachel exclaimed.

'It's ok,' I replied. 'You all need to know. But, believe me, there is very little to tell.'

'Go on,' Rachel encouraged.

I exhaled. 'I probably knew the least about the AI side of things but was keen to learn though. I provided the genetic data to Armstrong. He was the real guru – a bit of a geek, really. IT background. Knew all the jargon. The speech analysis of the trialists was overseen by Audrey. Smart cookie. Spoke about six languages and probably the leading phonetician in the country.'

'And Wilson?' Knight asked, leaning forward. Just in range of a solid left jab I thought to myself.

'Alan? Oh, he worked on eye movements -tell-tale signs of cognitive dysfunction.'

'And the others?' Rachel enquired.

'The usual stuff. Prepping the paperwork. Readying the equipment.'

'What? The admin was all done in house?' she asked, surprised.

'Sure. My supervisor…'

'…Who was he?' Knight interrupted, excited.

I whistled. 'Hmm…I only met him once. He was on my interview panel. What *was* his name? Levy! That was it. Eliot…no…*Elias* Levy.'

'Anyone else?' Knight again.

'Two others. Both female. Williams? Williamson? The other was from the sub-continent. Her name, I can't recall.'

'Not to worry,' Brownlow said, producing a notebook from his inside pocket and scratching down the names. 'Easily checked.'

'Anyway, half the team had non-medical backgrounds. As I say, Jimmy P...'

'Jimmy Peterson?' Brownlow asked, pausing his pencil.

'Peterson, that's right.' I clarified. 'He was the hardware man. Armstrong the software. A couple of others compiled the lists. Those with dementia and the volunteers. All vetted of course. Gloria something or other…'

'Cooke?' Brownlow helped, reading from a list.

'Yes, that's right. We joked about that. Gloria stirred the pot, salted the broth.'

'Oh?' Brownlow asked, looking up.

'She worked on the pharmaceutical application. Yes, Gloria…attractive…' I stopped, a thought emerging.

'What is it?' Rachel asked.

'She was friendly with Audrey and the others.'

'Wilson and Armstrong?'

'Yes,' I replied. 'They were the only ones who I think met socially. That was frowned upon by Levy. We weren't supposed to divulge details of our private lives to one another.'

'Bit strange,' Rachel replied, her brow knitted

in thought.

'You think so?' I rubbed my chin. 'Maybe. I think Levy and the company were worried that well-known researchers dining out in public might attract the curiosity of corporate spies.'

'Hmm,' Rachel responded, unconvinced. 'What made you think the four of them knew each other outside of work?'

'Oh, just something Gloria let slip. And it might not have strictly been outside of work. She was talking to Audrey about a tracker of some sort. Her back was turned to me, and she hadn't noticed my arrival in the lab. Audrey hushed her up a bit too quickly if you know what I mean.'

'The tracker's name wasn't Localis, was it?' Knight asked.

'Localis? Might have been,' I replied. 'Is that significant?'

'It's a subdermal implant that allegedly can be used to send a signal to a database, alerting you to any pressing health concern.'

'What kind of database?'

'Could be anything. A wristwatch even.'

'You think NeuralNet found a way to apply this to Alzheimer's?'

'If anyone can, they can,' Knight replied. 'Would be worth a lot of money. Especially now.'

'No,' Rachel countered, pouring herself another glass of water. A prop, I thought, in the absence of a mobile phone or a cigarette. She was buying herself time to think. 'It must be something bigger than that, to kill all those people.'

'Or they simply died. A lot of people *are*, you know. Dying.'

She gave me a withering look. 'What you have just stated about Audrey and her male counterparts has confirmed our suspicions that something else is going on. Besides, there's also Gloria.'

'What about her?'

She took a breath. 'She was the fourth of your team to die. Overdose.'

'Overdose?' I repeated, an icy shiver tingling down my spine. 'How?'

'Downed a bottle of sleeping pills.'

'Lots of people did, Rachel.'

'On April 14th? Five years ago?'

'The day the world ended?'

'Yes. Which begs the question. How did Gloria know things were going to go south so quickly? If I recall, governments were informing us that we were dealing with some kind of brain flu which would only affect the elderly. Have you forgotten all the hype about a cure-all vaccine already in the works?'

'So, either Ms Cooke knew something serious was on its way,' Knight added, 'or Mayer was tying up loose ends. Keeping a proverbial lid on the situation.'

'I still don't believe it,' I declared, with all the

conviction I could muster. 'Anyway, what does any of this matter now?'

'Patrick,' Rachel began, softly, just in case the post-grads a few tables away might have their attention dragged away from their fishbowls. 'We're not going to make it in time. Everything we are doing here...it's not enough. Have you seen the new statistics?'

'I stopped watching TV when they stopped making television programmes, Rachel.'

'I'm not talking about the crap they spew out on those nightly reports, Patrick. You know, the ones with the computer-generated graphics of a virus we haven't even isolated yet. No, I mean the *actual* numbers. We're talking five seconds to midnight on the doomsday clock.'

'How long?' I asked.

'A few more years. Unless a miracle happens.'

'Like raising Lazarus from the dead?'

'Or,' Brownlow interrupted, 'finding out exactly what Henry Mayer is up to in the high tower of his?'

'You think he has a cure?'

'He has *something*, Dr, Bishop,' Brownlow continued. 'At the very least the final piece to Knight's little puzzle. The question is *what*. And *who*.'

'What do you mean *who*.'

'The someone who is going to organise a meeting with a certain Elias Levy and ask for their old job back.'

8

There were about a dozen of them, huge patches of billowing Cimmerian blackness that eclipsed the lower sun as they arced skywards. From a height, they were like ship sails that had loosened from their masts, shadowy sheets of laundry flying in formation. On closer inspection, the talons of the mara which had nearly snatched Helen from her saddle had burnished, midnight claws extending from sinewy forearms half the size of its upper limbs that were welded beneath its wingspan. A humanoid body of sorts, surrounded by a layer of translucent skin, veneered in a red light which pulsed slowly, a warning signal offered when it was too late to avoid the danger. Helen had just enough time to paint a picture of its scaly, robust thighs and stretched ribcage before ducking beneath its grasp. It circled, or perhaps it was its accomplice which span inwards. A razored, face-sized bill that squawked to reveal a top row of jagged glass and a ribbon of tongue as taut as a windsock caught in a prevailing wind.

They were moving fast, quicker than Helen believed they could on such plodding behemoths; powdery specks of dust and sand assaulting her mouth and nostrils, crystallised to the exposed parts of her legs and feet.

'Keep your head down, Apprentice!' the Master Apprentice shouted from slightly ahead. 'Don't look at their faces!' he warned. But she already had. And it had already stirred some emptiness within her, a spasm of something from before. 'Head straight for the opening!' the Master Apprentice bellowed again. 'I will distract them!'

He veered off to the left while adroitly removing something from the veil of his gown. It looked like an old-fashioned pistol of sorts, flared at the muzzle. A blunderbuss, perhaps. He directed it skywards just as her desert-walker galloped past. An instant later an undercurrent of energy seemed to charge the air with static. It pulsed momentarily with an eerie, turquoise light at her side. She surfed its wave towards the still opening doors of the Archives where a group of attendants were beckoning her on, their arms windmilling through the storm of sand targeting its walls. She didn't dare to look back, but something assured her that the maras overhead had been purged somehow.

The Master Apprentice appeared then, suddenly to her right, racing her to the finish line as their spectators looked on. They crossed the threshold together as the doors boomed shut behind them, filling the vacuum within.

Their desert-walkers slowed down gradually,

cantering to a standstill, hooves clipping loudly on a wide, wooden passage between a set of rails which narrowed in the direction of a trough filled with husks, plants and seeds. They knelt forwards to relieve themselves of their burdens before turning to dine immediately, a couple of young hands in brown coveralls rinsing them down with more of the amrita. It wasn't just for drinking Helen thought.

She steadied herself, slightly overwhelmed by the shift to solid ground. She stepped off the raised platform and felt a soft hand around her waist.

'Gently,' a woman's voice soothed. 'One step, then the other.'

Helen looked up and into the chartreuse eyes of someone attired entirely like herself. 'Apprentice from Ceres Village, I am your neighbour from Tempus.'

The surface beneath Helen's feet cooled her soles, grey slate stretching out as far as her eyes could see.

'Thank you,' she managed to reply. 'This is the Archives?'

'Yes. The other Apprentices are at work. The Master Apprentice,' she bowed her head slightly to the latter, 'thought it wise if I show you the way. I am to be your guide.'

'What *were* those things? Were they trying to kill us?'

'Kill?'

'The mara,' the Master Apprentice explained, 'prey upon our new arrivals this side of the Bridge. They come from the West, feasting on your old memories...while you still have them. Your dreams of the time before. The worst kind...'

'My nightmares.'

'Yes, good. Your 'nightmares'.'

'They were horrifying. So ugly. One had a huge beak.'

'Oh?' the Master Apprentice replied, his curiosity piqued.

'It brought something back to me. An image.'

'Something you once dreaded. Or feared. The mara has a different appearance for each newcomer. Without the stones to protect you they can...'

'...You mean they don't appear the same to everyone?'

'Yes,' he replied.

'Then how did they appear to you?'

He ignored the question and looked away so she thought it best not to persist. She wanted to ask what exactly the Master Apprentice had seen when he had first encountered the mara. What *his* visions had been. But it was too early in their relationship for such questions -if indeed people on the island had relationships. The souls here were either automated singletons slaving away at their own menial tasks, or their sense of identity had been crushed, lost in the fabric of some overarching collective. But perhaps kinship within the group was possible. The Apprentice from a neighbouring Village had been the first to display any feeling of warmth towards her, a genuine concern for her well-being. The touch of her hand in the small of her back had stirred something deep within. But what was it? Love. No, certainly nothing as potent as that. She was beginning to understand that love was an unknown commodity in this world, as if the very concept of it had been drained away through the gap that separated the heart from what it once had been. Friendship then? No, not that either. So, what had it been? And then the thought struck her. It was compassion she had sensed, a wave of empathy activated as sure as it had been through a switch on her back. A flash of feeling, but different to those induced by the chemical changes swelling around inside her. It had derived from another place.

She looked behind her, expecting her fellow Apprentice to have disappeared, but she was still there, her head lowered in the presence of her Master.

'Why do they attack us?' Helen asked instead.

'It is in their nature,' the Master Apprentice replied.

'Are there others like us? In the West?'

'Not like us,' he responded firmly. 'They are vile, twisted aberrations of what they once were.'

'You mean before?'

He looked at her, and then through her. An arrow piercing its target.

She looked away, and for the first time, allowed herself the time to breathe in her surroundings. They were in a cavernous vault, the ceiling of which melted into darkness above. The huge compound where the desert-walkers were being brought to rest impersonated the world outside. It stretched off in one direction as far as her eye could see, low heat lamps warming the surface of its earth and vegetation with a warm, red glow. The needle of her compass angled itself elsewhere, towards looming colonnades that tipped away in what she could only assume was a circle around the vast emptiness enclosed within: the fall of one would have caused the collapse of the one next to it. If there was a light source, she could not find it. A crepuscular semi-darkness balanced itself overhead, blacker the further it scaled the height of the vestibule. Mixed with it a golden torus of cloud that hung in a layer of sky which she could have touched with an outstretched hand if she had wanted to. It glittered a gossamer gauze; motes of light, alive like fireflies, lining a path towards a huge arch. Along its curvature were engraved deep-chiselled glyphs and runes while the space between was large enough for several desert-walkers eight abreast to saunter through unperturbed.

The Master Apprentice placed his hand to his

forehead before turning and walked off into the brooding dusk. The click of his heels heard long after his physical form had immersed itself into the shadows.

'Come, Ceres,' the Apprentice from Tempus said. 'I will show you where you will be working.'

'Ceres?'

'Yes. Your name. We Apprentices are granted that honour in the Archives. After our Village. You may call me Tempus.'

They walked together through the arch, a retinue of four following them two male and two female. Helen did not ask who they were, or what purpose they served. They were dressed in white too, a seraphic quartet of lesser Apprentices perhaps. There was a hierarchy to this world, she had discovered. A Master Apprentice. An Advocate. A ladder of sorts, but not one that could be scaled. You entered on a particular level but, since time appeared to have no meaning, you remained there forever, perhaps as a reward for whatever it was you had achieved in the pre-life.

She considered the five Villages. They couldn't be very large, at most offering living space for a hundred or so inhabitants. If that were true, then where were all the others who had ever enjoyed or suffered a pre-life? Were they the only ones to be saved, the select few to be reborn? Or were they in the West, crammed together in a half-world of despair and rejection? But how was that even possible if you considered everyone who had ever been born?

They passed through into a void, speckled with tiny pinpoints of light like stars. If it were not for the flattening touch of her sandals on the surface of the floor beneath her feet, she would have imagined herself floating in space. They were surrounded by a deep purple but directly above a gilded crown of light hovered, following them like an umbrella in rain. Helen realised suddenly that in this part of the Archives, and due no doubt to the tremendous space and distance involved, light was apportioned to only those who needed it.

'It's like the night sky.'

'You remember that?' Tempus asked. 'It's how we remember it. The darkness. As you are probably aware now, it is always day here in BridgeEast. The same day. But the night is sometimes beneficial. It helps us to appreciate the day.'

'Where are we going?'

'To the First Circle.'

They continued, blindly, with no point of reference ahead or behind them. Tempus seemed drawn however, gravitated along the length of an invisible rope cast into a bottomless well. Finally, she spotted something, perhaps a hundred metres ahead, a full stop of whiteness on a page of black.

'What is that? It's getting bigger the closer we

get to it.'

'That is the Circle where the most recent Archives are maintained.'

'How many Circles are there?'

'No one knows except...' she stopped, her face a mask of serenity and awe, her hazel eyes wide in reverence, her shaven skull haloed in a nebula of copper mist.

'...except the Advocate,' Helen guessed.

'His Holy Name,' Tempus said, automatically. 'As you progress through the Circles, you forget the ones you left behind as what is recalled is absorbed into the Archives.'

'Is the Advocate like us?'

'We must not speak of Him,' Tempus stammered, genuine fear in her voice.

'Please, just tell me a little more. Is he a natural being like us?'

'Natural? Yes. His Holy Name is the Book of Final Testament. The Book at the centre of the Archives.'

'So, he was the first person on the island?' Helen persisted.

But Tempus had already moved on, quickening her step towards the light ahead, which had doubled in size. Helen counted her steps, each time her left foot touched down was another pace. Fifty. One hundred. Two hundred. The dot became a ball, then a moon, then, acquiring definition, another arch. As they neared, she noticed out the same language as before inscribed on its lintel.

She thought about the sunglasses she had placed into the front fold of her coverall but realised as she approached that her eyes had already acclimatised to the gradual brightness to which they had been subjected.

The circumference of the white had reached the limits of their vision and they were enveloped in a bright, white fog. A series of jolts reverberated through her temples and finally softened into a flutter of electricity as though these points of her had just been interfaced with something vastly larger than herself. She felt herself float, and out of the whiteness, a slithering snake-like movement shimmered, one end of which appeared to pause in front of her face, a twisting hose of tiny granules to which her brain tried to give a pattern -perhaps the head of some intelligent and self-aware being. It bulged to the size of a fist, hovering in front of her, before pouring itself into her nose and mouth, her eyes and ears.

Involuntarily, her limbs began to extend, her body coming alive, a hive of a million bees busy at work inside.

'Do not worry,' Tempus' voice echoed inside her head. 'It is always like this the first time. The Archives first need to read you. Then, you will be ready to read them.'

An image began to form, its contours emerging from the light. It was that of a person, of similar height and build as her own, standing behind a veil of lactose luminescence. The figure began to gain solidity as the haze began to clear and then, all of a sudden, it drained away, as if down a hidden sinkhole. What remained was a woman, attired after her own fashion, in blouse, skirt and boots. Her skin was fresh, alive with colour and as Helen moved, the woman moved with her, perfectly symmetrical.

‘Who is she? Helen thought, the words booming in the space between her and the woman. Helen ran her fingers through her scalp of hair while in return her counterpart ran hers through a beautiful mane of lush, chestnut, wavy hair.

‘She was you,’ Tempus voice replied to her, aware of her thoughts. ‘From just before.’

‘Her name was Helen,’ she said.

‘You remember your name in the pre-life?’

‘Yes, of course. What was yours?’

‘I don’t…I don’t know.’

9

The land NeuralNet Incorporated had annexed to the north-west of the capital had been previously occupied by the ruins of an abandoned airport once used, it was said, by long-since-dead celebrity millionaires: actors, sports stars, and musicians returning to the country in the dead of night, seeking privacy from hordes of adoring fans. It had had two landing strips, strewn side by side in an area of ancient fen that had been drained a century before and around which a forest of trees had been newly planted.

Before the airport, the area had been the headquarters of an ancient religious order. It too had taken advantage of its classified location, a few miles from a wedge of perilous coastline that dropped headlong into the ocean. The novitiates had constructed a large manor there, replete with turrets, crenellations, and meditative gardens. The building had survived the demolition of the air terminal and hangars and operated now as the NeuralNet's regional, administrative hub.

Henry Mayer had also had enough political

clout at the time to have had a tentacle of the metropolis' shuttle service extend itself another fifty miles to his new headquarters, a solitary line servicing only those employed by NeuralNet, with no other stops along the way.

Not that I had made use of it. Brownlow had chartered a helicopter for me with a pilot pepped up on the former's latest memory pills just in case. We alighted onto a field, several kilometres away from my old stomping ground. A car awaited me there. The same one in which I had been picked up before. Driven by the same chauffeur. The man Brownlow had called Winston. Or at least I thought it was the same Winston. Dark glasses and a peaked cap notwithstanding, I guessed he was ex-military, if the milky cicatrice on his right cheek was anything to go by. He seemed a lot younger than I had originally thought. An officer of some sort, judging by his posture. He probably kept a pistol up his sleeve, an heirloom passed down from father to son through several generations of military service.

The mansion in the distance was swathed in mid-morning fog. I sauntered along the verge of a main road, stopping along the way to give my eyeballs two further shots of Bill Knight's magical snake oil.

The NeuralNet complex was surrounded by a state of the art, twenty feet tall electric barricade, mounted with watchful cameras that kept track of my progress as I ambled, briefcase in hand, towards the main gates through which I had driven on so many occasions. The guard at the security barrier was new, of course, but he smiled in expectation as I showed him my letter of invite from Elias Levy. He shouldered his rifle as casually as if it had been a bag of golf clubs.

That too had been new.

I was directed towards a small, motorised cart where another helmeted guard sat primed at the wheel.

'My colleague will take you to the Abbey.'

Yes, the 'Abbey'. How could I have forgotten? That's what we had called the large estate where NeuralNet had based its offices. It had a large residential wing where it was rumoured Henry Mayer himself sometimes bivouacked.

Deposited within its cloistered walls, I found myself in a gravelled courtyard. A gardener was clipping a privet hedge nearby but failed to notice me as I scaled the marble steps up to the entrance door. I had never set foot inside the Abbey itself since my team had been allotted for our research one of the three futuristic glass and chrome tower blocks over a mile away to the south of the compound. The eave of a small medieval church jutted into view just behind the residence as I approached. That too had been off limits during my time at NeuralNet.

There was no one to greet me at reception. Instead a couple of empty sofas perched idly in front of a table of unread magazines. I found the lift and took it to the third floor.

Elias Levy shook my hand cordially as I entered his large and neurotically clean office. No bookcases or cabinets. Hardwood floor and empty cream walls. A solitary keyhole desk, two chairs, a coat stand and a sizeable bay window from which hazy light petered in from a watery sun. He was sitting by a computer terminal, tapping away busily, but stood up as soon as he saw me, smoothed down his crisp three-piece suit and offered me a slender hand. On one finger, I noticed a signet ring, gold with diamond encrusted letters: NN intertwined in curlicue font.

'You have Wi-Fi?' I asked, noticing a router, among his piles of neatly stacked paper.

'Oh, yes,' he replied, proudly. Email *and* Internet.'

'Internet?'

'World governments have theirs,' he smiled, offering me a chair. 'And global corporations, like NeuralNet, have ours. We need to keep in touch.'

'Not much in the way of porn then?' I jested, already beginning to feel myself becoming annoyed by his smug, sanctified air. He belonged in a clerical collar, I thought. A tall, thin greying vicar standing by a prize pumpkin at a village stall. Perhaps he had been at the Abbey too long.

'So,' he continued, a manicured finger resting on a high cheekbone, a thumb under his chin. It was the same pose as the one he assumed at my interview, humming and hawing enigmatically as if contemplating the endgame before a single chess piece had been moved. 'You mentioned on the telephone to my secretary something about the possibility of returning to work for NeuralNet? You know, of course, your former project is no longer operational.'

Secretary? I thought. I hadn't seen one. Apart from my armed escort I hadn't encountered a single other soul. The Abbey had felt maintained but uninhabited. Plush, pampered, white carpet, very little in the way of furnishings, and bare walls. A few chandeliers slung from the ceiling in the corridor outside but saving on their electricity bill.

'Yes, Mr Levy. The team split up, didn't they? Quite soon after I left, wasn't it?'

He considered his response, an explorative pawn teetering on the verge of a new square.

'Mr. Mayer decided to take the organisation in a new direction,' he replied, finally.

'Yes, I had hear NeuralNet had gone skin deep.'

'And then the epidemic befell us,' he replied, ignoring me, making a show of surrender with his hands. 'But I have heard you too have opted for that side of things as well?'

He had done his own homework I thought. No doubt as soon as his underling had informed him that I had approached NeuralNet with a view to getting my old job back. Worse still, he didn't seem too concerned about my reference to Localis.

'AI? Not really. More of a hobby than anything else, quickened for the most part at what I had witnessed here. No, I'm a test-tube and microscope kind of guy. Not like Dickie and the others.' I paused, watching Levy for any sign of reaction. There was none. As impassive as a priest in his confessional.

'Dickie?' he said, thoughtfully.

'Dickie Armstrong. The head of the team,' I explained, with a smile. 'Champion swimmer, by all accounts.'

'Oh, Armstrong. Richard Armstrong. Yes, I interviewed him for the post. Never met him much afterwards. Well, I wouldn't, would I?'

'I suppose not.'

He adjusted his signet ring, as if on the precipice of a decision. 'Shame what happened to him. Drowned, didn't he?'

'Did he?' I replied, slightly taken back.

'I believe so. His death got lost with all the others. The only reason we learned of it was because of his widow. He took out a small pension with us. You did too if I recall.'

'Yes, but I'm still alive,' I replied, pointedly.

He looked at me, as if a tennis ball had just dropped within the line of his back court and gone out of play.

'I'm not sure, Dr. Bishop, that our current work here at NeuralNet would suit you,' he continued somewhat prissily.

'What is the nature of the work?' I asked.

'I am afraid I am not a liberty to say.'

'Top secret then?'

'You should know not to ask. Our team of employees sign non-disclosure agreements. Just like you once did.' He splayed his fingers on the desk in front as if to lever himself once more to his feet. If I didn't say something quickly, this interview, or whatever it was, would be over before it had even started.

'Just the *one* team?'

'What do you mean?'

'Quite a few empty spaces in the car park I noticed. In my day, it was nigh impossible to get a bay.'

He glanced briefly down at one of the drawers of his desk. Something in his look made me think there was probably a gun inside. 'There's a lot less drivers,' he replied. 'These days.'

'They stay here then, I suppose. Monks in the monastery.'

He grimaced and dabbed his ring absentmindedly as if sending out an SOS in code. 'We here at NeuralNet are working on something altogether different from before. We really need someone with more than a passing flirtation with Artificial Intelligence.'

It was Levy's turn to study my face. I had poked the bear and the bear had come out of the woods, his claws newly sharpened. I wondered momentarily if NeuralNet, and all the resources at their disposal, had not already seen right through me. They had feasted on enough dubious government contracts in the past to take the necessary precautions against possible infiltration. Especially if what they were currently working on was of such earth-shattering significance. They probably had their latest drones do daily fly-bys over Brownlow's cloak and dagger operation. Knew exactly what he and his cronies were up to in their base underground. Perhaps I too had overplayed my hand.

I coughed and crossed my trouser legs, affected a wry smile and thought about what a proper spy would say.

'Ha! You know scientists,' I answered, merrily. We all have rather considerable egos. I, on the other hand, like to underplay my talents. No, I have been continuing my AI research with Alzhimene. It *has* proved worthwhile.'

'Oh?' Levy replied, stifling a yawn.

I reached inside my jacket pocket and pulled out the small vial of clear liquid I had almost half-finished. 'A few drops of this on your eyes, Mr Levy, is a hundred times more effective than Traxilene.'

'Oh? He repeated, his indifference really beginning to annoy me. 'And what may I ask is that?'

'The...the... Huntingdon gene,' I stammered.

'My research indicates...'

'...*Your* research?' Levy intoned. 'A sugar pill, Dr Bishop. Nothing more. NeuralNet have already been down that route. It goes nowhere. A couple of years added to your prison sentence. Nothing more.'

'And yet, I discovered this by use of the *latest* AI systems.'

'I doubt that, Dr. Bishop.'

'It's a start,' I replied, my neck beginning to stiffen.

Levy rotated his ring once more and drew his hands together in supplication. He then angled them towards me, the tips of his fingers forming a closed triangle.

'There is no cure, Dr. Bishop,' he noted, gravely. 'At least, not in the way you think of one. If there were, we would have discovered it.'

'Then what may I ask has NeuralNet been doing while the world has gone up in flames?' I asked sulkily.

'Again, I'm afraid that's not anything I can help you with. You know our protocols better than most, Dr Bishop.'

'Yes, but...'

He stood up and smoothed out a crease in his suit jacket. It looked as though it had never been worn before. Levy himself appeared freshly laundered as if he could have been popped onto a coat hanger and sidled into a wardrobe.

'...I am afraid your journey has been a wasted

one,' Levy announced, definitively, extending his hand once more. 'AI has moved on dramatically since your time with us, doctor. That is no disrespect to your...achievements in the field. But NeuralNet is currently working with the greatest minds in the world, all of whom have been engaged at the cutting edge of AI their whole careers. Most scientists consider themselves fortunate to be at the top of their field in any one discipline.' He shook his head. '*Two* in a lifetime is a trifle more difficult. I hope you understand.' He held out his arm.

'Yes, of course,' I managed to say, accepting his wet plimsole of a hand. There was very little else I *could* say. As brush offs went, this was subtler than most. I turned to leave but then, my curiosity piqued, faced Levy anew.

'Do you mind if I ask, Mr Levy, why you saw fit to see me today if there was never any chance of me re-joining the ranks of NeuralNet?'

Levy frowned, his eyes suddenly looking for something over my left shoulder, something to light his way out of the dark. Then, suddenly, his lips levelled and upturned slightly.

'It's always good to know what the competition are up to, Dr Bishop.'

'Alzhimene Therapeutics don't provide much competition to NeuralNet, Mr Levy.'

'AT? Oh no. They don't, Dr Bishop. *They* most certainly don't.'

He flicked or pressed something just beneath

his desk and immediately the door opened behind me. My military friend was standing there, grim-faced, to help me retrace my steps to the lift.

Outside, as our golf cart returned me to the main exit, I snatched a quick look at the three high rises of mirrored steel that had formed the epicentre of my former life at NeuralNet. Thirty floors of offices and labs, they faced each other like monoliths in a stone circle. Each with an area of artificial verdure and picnic tables where I would often grab a sandwich and fresh air with the others on break. Today, in the broth-filled air that separated me from them, I sensed an absence of life from them, in the same way one does when they know they have just walked past a haunted house.

Behind me, decreasing in size, were the gables of Henry Mayer's gothic abbey where I realised his brain trust of elitist experts slaved away inside under the eye of Elias Levy and his weaponised goons. As we shaved a bend, it veered into view once more. On its fifth and top floor, from a balcony, two shadows appeared to be standing side by side. One taller than the other; the smaller one I knew instinctively to be female. They were close enough to establish some kind of intimacy. Not of lovers. Perhaps one of doctor and patient. Or father and daughter.

10

Had she been beautiful? In a world where everyone's identity conformed to a single image, like that of a monarch on a coin or a dead politician on a bank note, it was difficult to evaluate grandiose concepts such as beauty. Aberrations in coloured attire apart, Helen looked no different from anyone else she had encountered in BridgeEast. She wore the same mass-produced mask that had been moulded onto the faces of every other islander. For the rest it had simply required an approximation in weight and height, an androgynous haircut and a visit to the same tailor.

Since being read by the Archives, more of her pre-life had bled through to her. Not just hers, but the prior existences of so many others; an unsettling, heaving brew of flashbacks. A carousel of faces, foreign vistas and fragments of broken conversations all experienced through eyes that were not her own.

And yet eyes were the mirrors of the soul they said. In this place, only a person's eyes bequeathed any nuance of separation from the collective, their level of wisdom indicative of the age or knowledge base acquired by the individual at the time of their departure from the pre-life. They captivated somehow a distillation of everything that had once been important, a shade of self-recognition she perceived in others and which she had sensed in herself.

The woman, Helen, who she had glimpsed in the Archives, was both her and not her. She had brimmed with a colour and vitality she only now was beginning to realise that she had lost. This was what the Archives did, Tempus had explained. It produced a final facsimile of the entity you once were, an over-exposure that would fade gradually behind your eyelids. The download from the Archives, along with the drugs she had received, would maintain her memories just long enough for her to record them into the hard drive that was their beating heart.

The other Helen's flesh had been lighter in tone. Her hair with a vibrancy all of its own. Her lips had been fuller, redder, and her eye sockets, nose and chin more pronounced. And then there had been the other's breasts. Heavier and contoured by the blouse that partially concealed them and which revealed only a whispery finger of cleavage. They were more than the dried mammary glands she now possessed, shrunk behind the tight band of her regulation camisole. She knew they had harboured more than the biological imperative of suckling mewling infants.

And while she had examined every detail of her counterpart's physical form, she too, she sensed, had been a mystery to the other. But the other Helen was simply a copy, an imitation of every gesture and muscle twitch she could think of. Tempus had watched on, an audience to their weird, symmetrical dance.

In a matter of moments, or hours, the cloned version of herself had begun to lose physical integrity, the background behind her synching with the foreground as she faded away. Soon the other Helen was transparent, an apparition, a phantom of photons to be dispersed into the nothingness from which she had come.

'Tell me,' Tempus had enquired. 'What did you think of her?'

'She was beautiful. And I think…'

'Yes?'

'…that her appearance mattered to her.'

'Does it matter *to you*?' Tempus asked.

Helen closed her eyes and tried to organise her thoughts. If indeed they were her own. 'It did matter. To me. Then. I could feel how it was important to her. She used her beauty as a veil behind which to hide.'

'Hide?'

'Her intellect. She was intelligent. I am sure of it.'

'From whom did she hide her intelligence?'

'Someone. Someone she was frightened of.'

'And how does that make you feel? Do you still sense this fear?

'A little.'

'And how about pride?'

'Pride?' Helen had replied, taken aback. 'No, I don't feel anything like that. I am the spirit of the woman she once was. The physical trappings this Helen once had are meaningless to me now.'

Tempus smiled. 'The Archives give and also take. You have gained a reawakening of sorts, into the person you once were, but it has also acclimatised you more to the true nature of your existence. Here. With us.' Helen thought about this. She *did* feel different. What had seemed unreasonable or unnatural before her symbiosis with the Archives now seemed more reasonable, less open to interpretation. 'You have been offered a glimpse of who you were in your pre-life,' Tempus continued. 'Now, you must isolate those parts of yourself from everyone else you used to be. Only then, will you be ready.'

'Ready for what?'

'Reunion,' she replied, excitedly.

'Reunion? What is that?'

'You will know soon. But I will leave you now. All you have to do is try to recall a memory of your past lives. The Archives will create the space for you to do that and record everything that you see and hear in that space. In doing so, you will file away the memories of all those with whom you ever came into contact. Or ever were. You will know when it is time to move on.'

'Move on?'

'To the Second Circle.' Tempus turned to leave.

'Why can't you remember your name?' Helen asked, suddenly.

'We remember them all but not the last one. Not until we reach the final Circle.'

'Please. I feel…perhaps… we might have known one another. Before.'

Tempus raised a finger to her lips. 'No more. That is sacrilege,' she warned, angrily. 'You were not part of my soul group.'

Helen stepped back, shocked by Tempus' sudden outburst.

'Sorry. I didn't mean…'

'…It is of no consequence. But you must not speak like this during your time of transit.'

'What happens when you reach the end of the Cycles?' Helen asked, but Tempus had already moved off. The four minor Apprentices had gathered around her and together they had commenced a kinhin of slow heel and toes, in no particular hurry, in no particular direction, through the cloud that had encroached around them, concealing them from view.

Helen, for the first time since waking up on the island, was alone. Just as then, she felt something stir in the pit of her stomach, a small parasite of fear emerging from the darkness, reaching out, exploring her chest, back and legs, a cold numbness submerging her. And yet, unlike before, it was not fear of where she was and the strange inhabitants she had first encountered that was troubling her. Now it was altogether different. What she felt was a deep unease of being apart from the others. The dread of being cut off from the whole. From the island. Something had changed since she had arrived in the Archives. An affinity had been established with this world. What had been extraordinary was now merely rudimentary. The minority part of herself was now becoming its majority.

She was beginning the process of forgetting and remembering.

She looked around. The mist had somehow drawn nearer to her, a living curtain all around. There was no sign of the serpentine creature that she had been exposed to. All was silent. She became aware of her breathing, a quick staccato of warm air matching the temperature of her surroundings. And then her heart, a rising bodhran of nerves, began to thrum and then to beat, as the tall avalanche of whiteness threatened to overwhelm her. The haze thickened as it approached, reaching the toes of her sandals and, without a period of adjustment, she was immersed, disembodied, just a floating series of thoughts. The vessel that had bottled her consciousness had uncorked and out had poured its genie, dispersing itself into every corner of the blank canvas that was now her reality. Instantaneously, she recognised herself, without frontiers, limitless in scope, a drop in a vast ocean of formlessness over which she had immediate control. She could shape and mould it into whatever she wanted. Go anywhere. Review anything. She just had to think the thought and it, whatever *it* was, would materialise in front of her.

And so, she picked up a brush and began to paint.

Firstly, in her mind's eye, she began to rerun some of the images she had witnessed with the help of the being with whom she had just communed. And as she reflected, the wedding veil in front of her began to lift. A full palette of vibrant colours swirled and swayed into definition, gradually forming the objects to which they belonged. The world that she had summoned to attention.

Soon she was a point of perspective, cornered and gazing down at the backs of a congregation in prayer. A fly on the wall of what looked like a church, mahogany pews separated by a draughtsboard of black and white tiles. And as soon as she thought of herself as a fly, she was in flight, careering off on unsteady, invisible wings. Or perhaps she hadn't moved at all, and it was the ancient chapel that had veered itself sharply to her left, allowing her a better view of the conclave, as seen now over the preacher's shoulder, his hair reaching down to the small of his back and over which he wore a dark ankle-length cassock.

She had been here before, she knew. And yet not in this time. The scene to which she was privy was taking place centuries before. And then the year revealed itself to her. 1786. How could she possibly know that? A voice in her head -a head which she no longer seemed to have, answered. 'Time is meaningless.' As meaningless in her former life as it was in the one that followed. It had always been so, but only now could she really see it. Truly understand. The Archives, it seemed, were an anthology of all the experiences and memories of everyone who had ever existed and who had made the interdimensional voyage to the island.

The church, however, was significant. She had been there before.

She navigated herself closer to the back of the solemn figure in black, locked at a pulpit, his arms a flurried windmill of fists and elbow. In front, the faces of the congregation were ashen. Tight collared men and women shrunk in fear, children with faces like corpses barely able to comprehend the molten fire of words that were being rained down on them.

The scene continued soundlessly and so she thought about volume. She wanted to hear what the minister was saying to hold his audience in the grip of such fear. But his words did not come. Something in herself was impeding her from hearing them. She tried to move her sense of awareness forward but wherever she positioned the essence she had become, it rebounded against a glass wall on all sides, refusing to allow her to see the face of the pastor.

She returned then to the audience. She was invisible to them, of course, but she could see them all quite clearly. They were familiar to her. Recognisable. This one was an uncle. That one an aunt. Others were cousins. Still more, friends of her family. How could that be possible, she thought, if the year was 1786? And then again, she called the truth back to herself. There was no time.

In the back pews were those whom she had known as colleagues, people with whom she had shared her working and recreational life. Names did not come to her, but the faces formed part of a collective a group of people who had intimate knowledge of her. She tried to shout out, but she had no mouth with which to scream, no arms to wave, no legs to kick.

And then in the front pew she noticed someone with whom she felt an even stronger affinity. Tight-lipped and frail, with a high-buttoned black jacket and skirt, the woman wore her hair tied back, over which had been fixed a sombre, broad-brimmed hat. Like all the women there, her face was pale, without make-up. The men likewise were dressed as if for a funeral. Perhaps what she was witnessing was exactly that but looking around she couldn't see a coffin.

The woman was looking up at the pastor, watching him intently. And then Helen noticed. Unlike those standing alongside her, the woman's face was not one of fear mixed with reverend awe. No. Her face was full of hatred, a barely contained venomous loathing. The woman looked down, to her right side, and following her line of vision, Helen noticed the face of a small girl. The girl was holding the woman's hand. Obviously, it was that of her mother's. But it was the face of the child that drew Helen's gaze from all the others. It was one of sheer happiness, a ray of sunlight touching the waves of so much despair. The little girl, regardless of her dark pinafore and patent leather boots, was unfazed by the dry, sepia demeanour of her fellow congregants.

And then something else dawned on Helen. She was astonished that she hadn't noticed it before.

The little girl was looking directly at her.

11

Our journey back avoided the city which by early evening had already begun to glow with pockets of sporadic fire in the distant gloom, thin strands of smoke rising into a pink haze of sky above. The power grid was down again it seemed and, judging by the darkening motorway we drove on, the issue was spreading to the surrounding countryside. The entire nation seemed to be blacked out as if expectant of an aerial threat overhead. Winston motored on regardless, sometimes swerving at the last moment to avoid the odd abandoned car or lorry. The dead traffic on the lanes heading in the opposite direction of the capital were worse still: lumbering, ghost-ridden hulks of shadow that had expired through lack of fuel, their desperate inhabitants venturing onwards on foot. Within a dozen miles their frost-bitten bodies lining the routes north.

Once, Winston's headlights veered sharply, lighting up a signpost doused in red paint, directing motorists to 'HELL!'. As if hell wasn't everywhere.

Rachel greeted my return to base with a smile

I had hoped would suggest more. Meanwhile, Knight looked every inch his smug self, although he had changed his T-shirt to a Zombie on a motorbike, clad in leather, its face splattered in blood. I got the feeling, not for the first time, that the end of the world suited people like him. They had been in rehearsal for it their entire lives.

Brownlow, on the other hand, did not join my small welcoming party. He had had an 'off-day' Knight had explained in an off-hand way as though our glorious leader was simply suffering a bout of the blues.

We were in Rachel's quarters, the exact replica of my own, a prison cell without the bars. She, at least, had attempted to domesticate her surroundings. Some flowers in a vase, a couple of pastoral prints on the wall and a few paperbacks which included, to my surprise, a bible.

'I didn't know you were a believer?' I asked, running a thumb through its wafery-thin pages.

'I think we *all* are, Patrick. At least, until we find a cure.'

'Hmm. I suppose.'

'Would it surprise you to learn that Bill gave me this?'

'Oh?' I replied, genuinely surprised. I appraised Knight anew. He shuffled his feet sheepishly.

'Well, the fact that you are here suggests Levy didn't take the bait?' he asked quickly, moving the conversation along.

'Levy is fishing in different ponds,' I replied, attempting a modicum of wit to dispel the atmosphere in the room which was beginning to weigh heavily over our heads. 'Different oceans.'

'What do you mean?' Knight asked, his fingers moving absent-mindedly to the little crucifix that drooped from his left ear. It seemed to be aggravating him for the area just around it was enflamed.

'Honestly? I think Levy knew I was coming.'

'Of course, he knew you were coming, Bishop,' Knight piped in. 'That's how interviews work.'

'No, I don't mean that,' I replied. 'I just got the feeling that he was expecting the sort of questions one doesn't normally come up with at an interview.'

'What did you ask him?' Rachel interrupted, her beautiful curtain of hair revealing the stage that was her face, lit up by two spotlights of green for eyes. As she was off duty, she was wearing jeans and a simple, blue sweater which complimented her figure perfectly. I felt myself blush. The potential demise of the human species and, like a typical male, I was being waylaid by my own libido. I thought of Rachel's bible: 'Go forth and multiply…' the words encouraged. But surely not before we saved the world first.

'I mentioned our dead swimmer,' I replied. 'Levy didn't even flinch. In fact, he himself brought Armstrong up soon afterwards. Then I threw in the Localis angle.'

'And?' Knight interjected eagerly.

'Well, if NeuralNet are working on implants, it's small fry to them.'

'Could have been an act.'

'If it was, Knight, it was a good one. But I don't think so.'

'Oh?' Rachel asked.

'It wasn't an interview, Rachel. There was never any job. Whatever they are focusing on, it's beyond my levels of competence. I am a mere dilettante by comparison with the people Levy must have around him now. He virtually told me so.'

'Which is probably why you are still alive, Bishop,' Knight suggested.

'Perhaps.'

'You mean you believe us now, Patrick?' Rachel asked, sitting down on her bed. There was a measure of relief in her voice which sighed with the impact her body made with the mattress beneath her.

'Levy was definitely hiding something. And there's something else.'

'What's that?' Knight asked.

'He knows I am not working at AT. I even tried to distract him with your little concoction. Showed him the vial. Suffice to say, he wasn't impressed.'

'More fool him,' Knight replied, peevishly.

'But that's not what I am getting at. I think

Levy and NeuralNet are aware of Brownlow's set-up here. The whole caboodle.'

'That's not possible,' Knight declared.

'Oh? And why not?'

'Because…look I've been here longer than both of you and I know most of the folk that have arrived here in my time. No one leaves this place, Dr Bishop. Where would they go to? There is no email. No Internet. Just a basic intranet for the troglodytes here to communicate with each other when they can't be bothered to hang out.'

'I don't know, Knight. Brownlow and co. must have some way to get in touch with other government projects across the world. Even Levy had access to the web. He said all corporations, if they are large enough, do.'

Knight was silent. The zombie on his T-shirt looked a little bit more pathetic than before. He touched his earring again and dug his hands into his lab coat.

'So, you think NeuralNet have someone in the inside here?' Rachel whispered.

'I am almost sure of it. I am also aware of the obvious fact that I ought to be the prime suspect. After all, I used to work there.'

'No, not you,' Rachel replied. 'I know you.' Now it was her turn to redden slightly. She looked away as if deep in thought.

'That's how espionage usually works, Rachel. Look, I am not the mole, but I really do believe there is one. The person must have access to

Brownlow's systems. Might be an idea to let the old man know. Maybe, sweep the entire place for listening devices.'

'That'll take a while,' Knight reflected. 'But your reasoning is sound, Bishop. That is, of course, that you yourself are not the one working undercover.'

'You forget, Knight, it was Brownlow who picked up this particular chess piece. Not the other way around. And since I am no longer of any use to NeuralNet,' I stood up to leave, 'it follows that I am of no use to Brownlow either.'

'That's not how it works!' Knight snarled, blocking my way. He had puffed out his chest the way a pigeon does when encountering a rival to his hard-earned crust. He had a few years on me, of course. More than I had cared to admit. But something about his laid-back, heavy rock persona completely at odds with the dogmatism required of his choice of career had grated since our first meeting. It all seemed a bit forced to me. Overplayed. And yet there was strength under that T-shirt, perhaps even a flat pack of six little square muscles. I noticed the beginnings of a snake tattoo coiling up from his wrist as the sleeve of his lab coat slipped up his arm. Maybe he worked out? I was more fast-food flab and whiskey nose than gym-rat, but I still fancied my chances of survival if permitted a first strike at my prey. The problem was I think I had telegraphed my first punch days ago.

'How does it work then, Knight?' I spat back regardless, my anxiety heightened by my desire not to lose ground in my hopeless pursuit of Rachel. The look of disgust on her face told me that I already had. I wonder if Knight had picked up on my schoolboy infatuation. Probably. Another reason for him to stick the boot in.

'I don't know, Bishop. That's up to Brownlow. But one thing's for sure: there's no way you'll be allowed to leave. You know too much.'

'Too much about what? Your extract of sweet FA. Levy's been there and has already shat all over that, Knight! Let's be honest, your drug is just honey to attract the bees to the hive. Rich donors being the bees and this place being the hive.'

'We only have *your* word for that, Bishop!' he countered. He took a step closer. I thought about a karate chop to the back of his neck. In my mind's eye I had already unleashed a guillotined arm and reduced him to a cowering mess at my feet. In reality, my only option was a toecap to his nether regions. A woman's ploy. Could I really do that in front of Rachel?

In the end I didn't have to. The door to Rachel's room opened, heralding the arrival of one of Brownlow's sun-conscious goons, supporting the same dark shades on the bridge of his aquiline nose. By his side was Winston, sporting a surgical mask on his nose.

'Mr Brownlow would like to see you, Dr.

Bishop. Alone,' Winston said.

'Oh? I thought he was under the weather?' I replied.

'His condition has improved in the last few hours,' the bruiser to Winston's left answered, as if he had practised the line. He looked at Knight in the same way Knight had been looking at me. With contempt. He never gave Rachel a first glance, never mind a second. She was completely under his radar, no doubt like the rest of her species.

'Well, in that case, I'll pay him a call. I am a *doctor*, after all.' I winked childishly at Knight but regretted it almost instantly as I caught Rachel's disapproving eye.

Brownlow's boudoir was a valley away underground. Unlike Rachel, who had a modest-sized apartment with kitchenette, Brownlow had gifted himself, or been gifted, a penthouse in comparison. Two floors of sweeping carpet, linked by a narrow, metal spiral staircase which he was obviously able to negotiate in spite of his years. On the ground level, a three-piece button leather sofa with a fauteuil sat next to a small coffee table on which were perched a teetering tower of paperbacks. Fiction mostly, he explained, as he sometimes enjoyed the odd, low-brow potboiler. But he owned non-fiction too, he added hastily. Biographies, history tomes, atlases, DIY manuals and survivalist brochures amongst so much else. The latter a more recent and less recreational pursuit.

These adorned the shelves all around the walls, their hard stems glossy and neatly stacked. Brownlow's bodyguard, whom he christened Henney upon our arrival, ran a thick fingertip along their binds, as if checking for dust. Or maybe he was trying to calculate their weight. He stood moodily by one bookcase, a silencer no doubt secreted away in his suit pocket, surveying my movements.

'Henney,' Brownlow repeated. 'I said, you can leave us.'

'Sir?'

'Where's McKenna?'

'Asleep.'

'Why don't the two of you grab something to eat before he goes on shift? Breakfast for you, supper for him?'

I stared at Henny's square jaw and boxer's ears. He looked tanned, no doubt the result of some clandestine government operation abroad. In the first year of the virus, there had been a serious grab for oil, gas and rare minerals amongst the leading nations. This had threatened to spill over into full-scale nuclear meltdown. 'Don't make the epidemic academic!' the protest placards had read at the time. It took a while before the first wave carried off those politicians old enough not to care.

When Henney left, Brownlow, informal in a

silk, dressing robe, crossed over to a trolley void of alcohol and poured himself what looked like lemonade. Ruddy hell, I thought. The bugger's done that on purpose.

'I normally prefer gin in my tonic,' I quipped. Brownlow smiled.

'Clear heads,' he replied.

'Hmm. So, you said before.' He made a gesture with his glass, but I shook my head with disdain. 'I heard you had taken a turn for the worst.'

'Did you?' His eyes narrowed, the egg of his head tilting to one side. He offered me the sofa but I preferred to stand even though I was dog-tired. Brownlow was the director of this little scene, and I was loathe to play the part of a helpful extra. He sat down and rummaged for something in the pocket of his gown. A pipe, of course. Its bowl must have been pre-filled for soon the tobacco was alight, Brownlow sending smoke signals across the room.

'I suppose you heard my visit to NeuralNet went awry?' I asked.

'Oh, they were never going to employ you, Dr Bishop. But I knew Mayer would be curious enough not to pass up the opportunity.'

'Mayer? You think he was at the Abbey?'

'The Abbey?'

'What we and the others called their inner sanctum,' I explained.

'The Abbey,' he repeated, thoughtfully. 'Interesting.'

'Is it?' He puffed on his pipe and crossed over a leg, lost in the pleasure of the moment. A smell of plum reached my nostrils. I sensed a tickle at the back of my throat. Pointless, I knew. If he hadn't offered me a drink, he was hardly going to pass me his peace pipe. 'You think Henry Mayer was there?' I asked again. 'At the Abbey? He's not supposed to be in the country.'

'He's there all right.'

'How do you know that?'

'The same way, Bishop, that he knows everything about our little operation here.'

I massaged a knot of muscle at the back of my neck and decided to take Brownlow up on his offer of a seat. From my new vantage point, I could see the end point of his winding staircase. It levelled off onto a landing which led, I was sure, to his private chambers. On sentry there was a medieval knight in full armour, a lance propped alongside.

'So, I went there on some sort of recce?'

'We needed to know that Levy was still Mayer's number one man. He's been dark for months, so we had to know what was going on. Whatever Mayer is working on, Levy doesn't know or is being prevented from telling us.'

'You mean Levy is your man on the inside?' Brownlow didn't reply. 'Well, he certainly had me convinced,' I added, somewhat shocked. 'Does he know the name of their agent?'

'Agent? You've been reading too many spy

thrillers, Dr Bishop. But to answer your question: yes, we know that Mayer has someone relaying data back to NeuralNet. What we have yet to find out is who that someone is.'

'You thought it was me, didn't you?' I asked, the thought suddenly dawning on me. 'You knew about Imogen's schizophrenia all along but couldn't guarantee that was my real reason for leaving NeuralNet. That's why you brought me in?'

'Levy was sure of you. Believed your motives were pure. But it's a dirty world, Mr Bishop…for all we knew Mayer was using you as bait. Let you leave so we would pick you up down the line.'

'And that's why you contacted Rachel?' I realised. 'You knew we had met.' Brownlow looked away. 'So,' I continued, 'all that nonsense about *me* providing *you* with insider knowledge was just that. Nonsense.'

'We had to protect our source. Mayer was beginning to suspect something. Levy was getting scared. You have no idea, Dr Bishop, the type of man Mayer is. In any case there is not a room in that Abbey of yours that isn't bugged. Including Levy's. He has left a wake of dead on three continents. He's a megalomaniac. A religious nutcase. He leads some kind of cult. Even has his daughter signed up.'

His daughter, I thought, remembering the last image I had seen of NeuralNet. The two figures on the balcony.

'So, you already know what happened to Dickie Armstrong, Alan Wilson, Audrey Lee and Gloria Cooke?' He nodded. 'Through Levy?' Brownlow nodded again. 'That being the case, you also know *why* they had to die?

'Cooke was the problem,' Brownlow began. 'She was onto Levy. Probably shared her suspicions with the other three. Levy had to persuade Mayer to look elsewhere. So, he set up Armstrong. Problem was Mayer's paranoid tendencies are such that he ended up getting rid of the others including Cooke. Levy never thought Mayer would actually resort to murder.'

'So how come he let me live?'

'You were already gone by then. Levy had to insist that our supposed spy was still operational. Then the pandemic hit.'

I whistled and tried to alleviate the knot of pain in my neck and shoulders.

'You alright, Bishop?'

'Just an ache in my neck.' I moved my head from side to side and then tilted it back for relief. As I did so, Brownlow's stuccoed ceiling gazed down at me, a pattern of roses, alternating in shape and size from east to west. 'So, if you don't suspect me, you must have your eye on someone else?'

'Levy confirmed knowledge of our new trials to you. That was him letting us know that the flow of information was still active. Unfortunately, *our* mole is reporting directly to

Mayer.'

'He thinks it's Knight, doesn't he?'

'I think so,' Brownlow replied.

'What do you think?' Brownlow didn't answer. His pipe had taken the opportunity to let itself go out. Brownlow placed it on his lap and set about the task of hunting around his pockets for a lighter or box of matches. He took his time. No doubt hoping for me to move on. I paused a few moments before giving in. 'I knew there was something shifty about that bastard,' I snapped, delighted that Knight had somehow become the villain of the piece. 'Would explain his sudden medical breakthrough, wouldn't it?'

Brownlow fumbled in his pocket for his tobacco pouch,

'What Levy said was true, wasn't it? There's nothing particularly remarkable about Knight's research, is there?

'Just keep an eye on him for the next day or so while we dig a bit deeper,' Brownlow replied.

'We don't exactly see eye to eye, Brownlow.'

'Good. The perfect cover,' he replied, standing up, his newly lit pipe in one hand, a finger raised in the other. 'Just be careful,' he warned.

I made to leave but then turned. 'Rachel? Does she know any of this?'

'No. And we'd like to keep it that way, Dr Bishop. For now.'

12

The little girl she had witnessed in the church had been aware of her. She was more convinced of this than anything else she had seen in the Archives. But more than this, Helen knew deep within the normally unapproachable recesses of her soul that the girl was her. A younger version of herself who had sensed her aerial presence overhead, had appeared to know where she was at all times. To the child, she was not a transitory moment of non-locality, a brief stepping out of causality and time that others might induce with pharmaceuticals or ancient botany. The girl had been seduced by a passing daydream, the object of which she could not detect, but which left her with the uneasy feeling that she was not who she thought she was.

Helen had felt the same. On countless occasions. This feeling of disconnect. But staring into space as she so often had, lost to everything around her, how could she have known that she was picking up a thread to another plane of existence, holding hands for a fleeting moment with her Higher Self, a unique expression of a Whole, communicating with its poor corporeal relation?

The congregation in the church, she would soon learn, had been all the members of her soul group, gathered together in one space, at one time. A visual metaphor of all those with whom she had shared each reincarnation through the countless lives she had lived. They had been her personal spirit family, and like her, had inhabited diverse bodies, male or female, in various periods of history, with different interrelationships and roles.

In one existence, she discovered, she had been a father of four. In another, one of her very own children had assumed the role of her mother in her next incarnation. She had passed a lifetime as a poor farmhand tilling the soil of a medieval estate, but then had been a rich landowner lording over the very same demesne. She had died in her teens countless times, even more at birth, and once had incarnated at hundred and twelve years old. She had been all manner of ethnicity. Had had affairs with those of the same sex. Had spoken dozens of languages all of which she could now understand.

And that had simply been her human life.

She had also been a variety of lifeforms from a myriad of other worlds, scattered across a number of different galaxies.

The names of her fellow travellers hardly mattered. Neither had their physical trappings. It was simply the sense of Beingness she felt each time their ship reached its final docking place after each transformation. And then, there would be another departure. A new lifetime of adventures, a new set of hopes and fears. Challenges to be overcome, love to be rekindled again in new bodies.

But now it seemed all had come to an end. She was moving through the Circles as she had once through lifetimes, aggregating everything and everyone she had ever known to a vast, limitless depository. Her vessel had never before reached the shores of the Island. But she had returned alone. The others had not finished their Circles yet.

And there was something more: the identity of one of their numbers, first embodied in the Archives as the pastor in the church. She had yet to discover the mysteries of that particular soul.

Once, it had lived as a hermit, eking out a solitary existence on the edge of some forest or other. In another time, it had been the out-of-reach member of some royal family -just a name, whispered in fear and awe by the peasant class to which she had belonged. It had been a celebrated author or musician, a vicar and an evangelical preacher. Their nation's leader, but next time around, its greatest enemy. A world-renown inventor. A billionaire altruist. A sadistic dictator. A ruthless tycoon. It had been a serial killer and then later a monk. It had even been the first to leave their planet's atmosphere.

Unlike Helen and the others, the pastor had always been either famous or infamous, someone to be loved or feared in equal measure.

There was no pattern to any of it. Helen leapt from life review to life review, an immediate download of energetic composition which somehow she fed into the Archives. Not just from her own perspective but from that of everyone with whom she had ever been in contact. All the love she gave and had received. And all the pain she had felt and caused others to feel. Her consciousness, each time, seemed to funnel and pass through a pivotal point in the centre of her physical manifestation that some called 'the third eye'.

The other impediment, beyond that of not being able to recognise the face of the pastor, was the fact that her most recent lifetime was closed off from her. No doubt, this was a discovery waiting for her at the final Circle. The closest she had got to her pre-life was the lifetime before - one led as a field nurse, at a time in her nation's history when it was at war. Traumatic scenes of human life being sacrificed on scarred, shell-pitted fields had overwhelmed her -a merciless slaying of the youth and potential of an entire generation.

Helen spent the interim between Circles at rest, in deep contemplation, comparing a mental ledger of all her memories. There was no judgement, no sense of right or wrong. Nothing she did or hadn't done was her fault. All of it was simply a by-product of being nearer or further from Source. And that Source was the Island and the Great Unseen.

Throughout it all, Tempus had been her guide.

'I've had so many names,' Helen said to her once. 'So many. And yet I can't remember being 'Helen'. How long before I reach the final Circle, Tempus?'

'You know better than to think about it in those terms, Ceres. For example, how long have you been here? In the Archives?'

'Not long. But also, seemingly forever. I feel both are possible.'

'Yes.'

'But it will soon be your time of Reunion?'

'Again, your thoughts begin to stray, Ceres. The Archives do not exist to serve you. You exist to serve them. You may reach the final Circle before me. It is also possible we have both already arrived, or not even begun our journey. Everything is happening at once. Once you remember yourself, in all your incarnations, you will be ready to archive everyone else. Those who can't remember for themselves.'

'You means the ones here who are not like us.'

'They are the strangers that populate your memories. When you focus on one of them, they come alive to you, and you live their memories for them. Then, after that, you will reach the end.'

‘So this will finish?’ Helen asked.

Tempus sighed. They were sitting cross-legged on a short wooden jetty that overlooked a flowing river. On the other side was an area of dense woodland, thin tall trees clustered together as far as the eye could see. They swayed to a dance of wind, their branches following the current of the river which led Helen’s gaze, as it always did, to a huge, snow-capped volcano smouldering before a purple sky. It was Tempus’s favourite power-place, somewhere from a previous life where she had felt most at peace and which she could conjure up at will. Once you had relived a memory you could return to it as often as you wished in the Archives.

‘Yes, after you have gone beyond. Then, you will remember the lesson you finally learned that has brought you to the Island.’

‘And after that you return to the Great Unseen?’

‘Our natural state. Infinite, non-vibrational consciousness everywhere at once at every time. Or nowhere. At no time. But those are only words. They cannot express what it is really like. Only the Advocate can.’

‘None of the others I journeyed with are here,’ Helen replied.

‘They are not on the Island, or they have already sublimated already. That is all.’

Helen looked up. The thread of smoke from the volcano in the distance seemed thicker than before. Darker. It was daylight but there was no sun visible. There didn't need to be. 'And that is why you don't know your name, the one you had in your final life?'

'Yes, but that too will be revealed.'

'But you saw yourself when you first entered the Archives.'

'Yes, of course,' Tempus replied.

'Why is it then that I can remember my name?'

'That I don't know. Perhaps it was the manner of your death. You are sure you remember nothing?'

'No.'

'You are not the first Apprentice I have guided. And once I was guided by another. It is *unusual* for you to remember your name. Strange for the Seer not to bring you to the Archives. Strange for a new arrival not to remain at the Haven after each visit to the Archives.'

'I don't think the Seer was happy with the Master Apprentice.'

'Our vibrational form on the Island is higher than in our pre-life. But it is still nothing compared to the Great Unseen. These emotions do still exist. When they arise, they must be controlled.'

'Does that explain how we appear on the Island?'

'Yes, it prepares us for our state of formlessness when we are all One.'

Helen thought about this. She tried to

remember the shock she felt when she first became aware of her appearance back at the Haven. She thought about the cloned version of herself that had been the gatekeeper at her entrance into the Archives. All her initial feelings of curiosity, excitement, jealousy and so on had dissipated. Nothing remained of them but a hole, not a hole that represented the absence of something, but a hole that had always been there. It had been the same with the life reviews. As soon as they had been relived, from every conceivable angle, the memories left her, merging with the Archives. 'Forget to remember, remember to forget.' That was what the Seer had said. A perfect self-perpetuating circle. She remembered merely to forget and ultimately there would be nothing left but the confrontation with her pre-life.

Who knew how many lifetimes meanwhile had passed on Earth? Or perhaps it had only been a matter of months. And yet, sometimes, she sensed a restart, a pausing of what had gone before. Tempus called this period of repose 'the Tides' which synced with the waves that reached and withdrew from the Island's shores. They came and went with rhythmic regularity, like a menstrual hiatus when her body yearned for rest. Helen never knew when she would be carried away by them, or how long they lasted. She didn't feel refreshed after them, or tired before them. But she accepted them, nonetheless.

It was after one such reawakening when Tempus approached her with the news of her Reunion.

'It's my time,' she announced, a quiver of fear in her voice.

'How do you know?' Helen asked.

'I've been to my pre-life.'

Her eyes were different, the same green colour but with greater depth as if they had just stared over the edge of an abyss. They were in one of Helen's oldest memories, as far from her own pre-life as she had ever been. She preferred this memory to any place her mind could conceive. A colonnade overlooking a pristine garden in the middle of which stood a small temple. A cloudless sky above and the smell of brine from a line of azure far in the distance. Her former self had been happy here, a servant girl called Akila whose only occupation was to prepare a daily sacrifice to a god called Nekhbet. Her mistress had been kind and she had lived a long and simple life.

'I could live here forever, Tempus,' she replied. 'Do you see her? There in the white vestment?' Helen had long since learned to project an astral image of herself into her memories. She directed a finger towards a girl carrying wood to a blazing furnace high up on an altar upon which stood a gigantic, stone vulture. 'Only sixteen at the moment but she lives to an old age and has many grandchildren. How does she spend this worldly existence? Worshipping a bird!'

'Ceres, there's something I need to tell you,' Tempus began, projecting her form directly in front of Helen. Once more, Helen registered the change in Tempus. She was no longer a puzzle searching for its final piece. She seemed whole. Complete. But with that had come a price. A dramatic upheaval in her psyche that had etched itself across her once serene features. Helen didn't recognise this new Tempus and didn't want to. She lowered her head.

'I know. You are leaving. To the Great Unseen.'

'Yes, so *they* say. Ceres, this place. The Archives. The Island. It is not what you think it is. I remember how I got here.'

'Your death in the pre-life?'

'My death? Yes, in a way...and I remember you.'

'We were friends?'

'No, not friends. But not enemies either.'

Helen closed her eyes and Akila, the temple, the whole vista of ancient memory dissolved into whiteness.

'You knew me?'

'Yes, but only in the pre-life. Ceres...Helen...'

'You are using my pre-life name. That is not permitted...'

'...Listen, Helen, please. I do not have a lot of time. I shouldn't be here. All my memories will disappear soon.'

'What is it, Tempus?' For the first time in a long while Helen felt afraid, an ancient, exquisite sensation in the pit of her stomach.

'When I departed the pre-life, I was still a young woman.'

'You were murdered?'

'No, not exactly.'

'Then, how did you die?'

'Your father...'

'...My father? I don't remember my father.'

'Helen, he is the pastor you first saw in the Archives. The one you told me about. The one who has remained hidden from you all this time.'

'He is my father in the pre-life?'

'Yes, Helen. He is an extremely dangerous man. Very powerful. It is your father who is responsible for everything!'

'What do you mean? I don't understand.'

'No, I am not dead, Helen. Not yet, anyway.'

'What do you mean, Tempus? If you are not dead, then how can you be here?'

'Your father *brought* me here.'

'How...how is that possible? Who is he, my father? Who am I?'

'Your name is Helen Mayer,' Tempus replied.

13

I had stopped taking Knight's drug. If he was working for Mayer then who knew what alchemy he had mixed into his supposed restorative? In the week that followed my tête-á-tête with Levy I had suffered a migraine of epic proportions. Electricity enflaming different parts of my brain, setting my synapses on fire.

I tried to remember if I had started feeling unwell as a result of Knight's libation or whether my symptoms had started earlier. Perhaps there was something in the food being dished up in Brownlow's canteens and we were all part of some elaborate trial, an inner circle of elite survivors that was really just another outer ring orbiting the actual spider at the centre of the web.

Or maybe Brownlow was right and I had read too much spy fiction.

As it turned out, there hadn't been any need for an electronic sweep of the base. Brownlow, though, conducted one anyway. Secretly. When everyone designated with work tasks were at their assigned stations and when those rich enough to ride out the Apocalypse were at their duly appointed blackjack table and wheel of fortune. Not to remove the bugs, of course, but merely to locate any blind spots where his army of minuscule operatives might potentially have already been unearthed. They were as omnipresent as house flies, it seemed, but they came with the small print. Once you signed your Faustian pact with Brownlow, your civil liberties went the way of the dinosaurs.

But, in the end, everything was in its rightful place. If Knight was the mole, then he was deep underground and finding some other way to get his messages through to Mayer.

I realised, however, that for all intents and purposes I was living in a surveillance state. As bad as the one above our heads. We were still getting the nightly broadcasts. Shelves in the shops, according to the latest reports, were rapidly emptying. Imports had ground to a halt and even if there had been foodstuffs like wheat or pasta entering the country there were precious little people left willing to drive the trucks needed to bring it in.

The numbers reaching the latter stages of the virus were reaching an all-time high. Even the production of amber was on the slide. In the last few weeks, suicides, assisted and otherwise, had risen alarmingly. Doctors and patients alike had taken to throwing themselves off hospital roofs.

I kept my promise to Brownlow and said nothing to Rachel about Elias Levy being

Brownlow's stool pigeon. Who knew? Maybe she was under suspicion too. I also kept close watch on Knight as he persisted with his own research. There were other work teams, probably dozens more, so Brownlow could afford to have him waste his time on a drug that had no hope of ever ridding the world of memory loss. Perhaps, if Knight was on the level, he might actually surprise us all and make some progress.

Rachel and I meanwhile were given our own corner of the lab and tasked with looking into Localis and whether the implant that may not have indirectly caused the death of my former colleagues was an avenue worth pursuing.

It suited me to have her close by. I didn't trust Knight or anyone else and I had enough old-fashioned idealism to find myself strangely protective of a woman who I knew was more than capable of looking after herself. The truth was I was still unerringly drawn to Rachel and if I could keep both her and Knight under close scrutiny -albeit different types of scrutiny -then so much the better. Besides, there was every chance Localis could turn out to be a gateway which led to something even bigger. Whatever NeuralNet were currently working on had yet to yield anything in the way of progress. Levy had said as much. But that didn't mean Mayer wasn't up to something with potentially even more dire consequences for mankind.

I didn't see much of Brownlow. Suffice to say,

he had his own people above him, pulling the old man's strings. We were inhabiting a pyramid of power, and the base of this particular pyramid, I soon realised, stretched out for miles, perhaps across several counties. The perfect project to waste taxpayers' unwitting monthly donations. It had been planned years in advance of our present predicament and was much more than just a place where efforts were made to save the world. It was also a new world to replace the one that couldn't be saved.

All this time I couldn't stop thinking of Imogen. Brownlow had agreed to have her carers updated on the 'important research' that I was carrying out for the government. The thought that she would forget, or not understand any of this, tormented me. Brownlow probably had over-egged the pudding, had made me out to be some kind of hero, a hero she would not recognise in her brother.

In return I had been promised regular feedback on my sister's condition. And yet, it had been over a week since I had seen Brownlow and reports on Imogen's current condition had not been forthcoming. The well had run dry. I couldn't bear the possibility that Imogen would think that I had abandoned her. Perhaps it might have been better if her illness was allowed to run its course and that she yielded up her past and everything related to it.

Better for her, or better for me, I wondered.

'You know you are behaving like a child?' Rachel whispered to me one afternoon. She had just nicked a wrinkled fold of skin from the hand of our latest subject and was preparing to inject a RFID chip a quarter of the size of a grain of rice. Within seconds the transponder would relay a PET scan of the patient's brain to a monitor on her right. Each implant had its own unique reference number which provided a complete medical history of the subject but, most significantly, an algorithm which would alert us, day and night, to any irregularities or 'tipping point' in the accumulation of amyloid in the brain, the first sign of the virus.

'Excuse me?' I whispered back, swivelling around on my chair.

'You heard me,' she replied, with an affected smile to our volunteer. 'You are up and running, Joseph,' she said to him. 'You might have difficulty in making a fist for a while, so not boxing, eh?'

'Yes doctor,' the young man answered. He looked about eighteen but was probably slightly older. An undergraduate in his former life with an overdraft he would never have to worry about again.

'What do you mean, Rachel?' I asked, as soon as we were out of listening range. Knight was on a break and two of his team were taking advantage of his absence by grabbing a quick coffee and a chat from a dispenser in the far end of the lab.

'The man on the inside. You think it's Knight?'

I inhaled and thought about what to say next. Useless, I knew. I was a terrible liar and could be read like an open book in large print.

'And you don't?'

'No.'

'Why not?' I asked churlishly.

'He's not the type.'

'Oh? What *is* the type?'

'*If* we knew that, Patrick, Brownlow wouldn't have just turned this place upside down. Tell me, what did you and Brownlow chinwag about last week? More than that, where the hell is he?' I turned back to face my computer screen and pretended to analyse the map of Joseph's brain that had just appeared there, shaded in various colours of red, orange and green. We would soon all have these implants I thought to myself. Better than the daily grind of MRI scans which represented thirty minutes of wasted downtime each morning. Our student looked like he had just entered Stage Two. 'Patrick?'

'Rachel, you have to see this…' I began.

'…Never mind that,' she replied, harshly. She had a temper to match her green eyes. I wondered if she had ever been a redhead. 'What did Brownlow say to you?' she barked. 'I've waited long enough for you to cough up the details.'

I held her look a while longer than I should have. 'He thinks it might be Knight,' I said, finally.

'And I'm telling you it's not him!'

'Ssh. Keep your voice down,' I whispered, worried about being overheard if not by Knight's team then by Brownlow's tracking software. 'How can you be so sure? Come on, Rachel, the tattooed hipster profile is all a bit desperate. Besides, it's new.'

'What is?'

'The latest ink engraving on his arm. I caught a glimpse of it the other day. I'm telling you, Rachel, the whole character is borrowed.'

'How do you know if that tattoo is not just a more recent addition to his overall bodily paintwork. I happen to know he has tattoos all over his arms and legs.'

'How do you know that?' I couldn't help but ask.

She sighed deeply. 'It's not him,' she repeated. 'It's far too obvious.'

'A double bluff?' I said, losing ground.

'He's arrogant, Patrick. I give you that. But he's too one dimensional to be a spy.'

I smiled, the child in me placated.

'So, who is it?'

'Not here,' she said, looking around her, nervously.

'Tell me.'

She shook her head. 'First, you tell me what

you know. *Everything* you know.'

'I will. But not here.' I nodded to Knight's assistants who had finished their coffees and were returning to their workstations. 'Tonight. At dinner. Bulgogi for two?'

She shook her head. Her emotions cooling into a smile. If anything, she admired my persistence in that moment, her drawbridge lowered slightly for suitors courageous enough to scale through the gap.

'Alright. But you won't believe me, Patrick.'

'No?'

'No. Not without proof. And that's on the other side.'

I was about to ask what she meant but Knight chose that moment to breeze back into the lab. 'Hey!' he yelled across the floor. 'What are you two lovebirds gossiping about?'

It was Marie who alerted me to the possibility that Rachel had gone missing. I had sat for nearly an hour over a glass of carbonated water that was rapidly losing its sparkle when the waitress first approached me. I must have cut quite a pathetic figure, running an absent-minded fork through my *kimchi* hors d'oeuvre, for the young woman flopped herself down in the chair opposite me, a hand cradling her anxious frown. Something was wrong she pouted. Rachel was the punctual type. Never late. She had dropped by earlier, she told me, and had asked her to prepare a secret dish of steak and chips for me instead of the usual Korean fare. She had even managed to procure a half bottle of cabernet for our first date. Those were Rachel's very words: 'first date'. Marie repeated them for my incredulous ears. There's no way she would have gone to such trouble and not show up. That was at 6.30, two hours ago, and she was still in her work clothes, Marie added. The restaurant wasn't busy but there were enough people there to corroborate her story. Even in her lab kit Rachel was still the type to turn heads, Marie continued, without even the remotest hint of jealousy in her voice.

'Was Doctor Knight with her?' I had asked.

'No. She was alone. She would have noticed him, she explained. *He* wasn't difficult to miss.

I thanked her and immediately began hunting for Rachel. I tried the lab first. The night shift were already on duty. Just Knight's team and some friendly faces I recognised from my own. I tried a few other labs, restaurants and a couple of the recreation suites on our level but Rachel, it seemed, hadn't been seen all day. Convinced now that something was really amiss I tried her quarters but was met by a deafening silence each time I knocked on her door. No sign of life within.

I was about to take the elevator to Brownlow's level when the doors opened to reveal the man himself, accompanied on either side by his armed escorts, Henney and McKenna.

'Where is she?' I began, my voice beginning to fail.

'You know?' he asked, his eyes narrowing.

'Course I bloody know! I have just been waiting for her for an hour in her favourite food court!'

'And she didn't show up?' he whispered, looking all around him. There was nobody about. We were in an open atrium, leading to doors and corridors against which the residential areas were soundproofed.

'No!' I replied. 'How did *you* know?'

'Let's go to your room. We can't talk here,' he said.

'So what's going on, Brownlow?' I began as soon as we were inside. I gave both Henney and McKenna a questioning look. Their boss was keeping them close. Unlike before, they weren't going anywhere.

'Rachel has definitely disappeared.'

'How do you know? This place of yours is as large as a middle-sized town. It spans two counties. You couldn't have checked everywhere. Not that quickly.'

'Like all of you lab rats, Rachel is a creature of routine. Besides…'

'…Besides what?'

Brownlow looked at Henney who reacted immediately by pulling up a chair for his employer. McKenna, meanwhile, crossed over to my kitchenette for a glass. He filled it half full of tap water, took a sachet from his pocket, tore it open between gritted teeth, sprinkled and mixed its contents before offering it to Brownlow. I watched the choreography play out, a well-drilled sequence, a new audience to what felt like the same old scene. It was the worse I had seen Brownlow. His face was ashen, and his silver hair had lost its sheen, more slate grey like well-trodden snow. It seemed he really was sick.

'What's that?' I asked rudely, more interested in any potential antidote than the state of Brownlow's health.

'Never mind,' Brownlow replied, waving the question away. He gulped his medicine down and passed his glass back to McKenna.

'Ok, we will leave *that* for now. You were saying: besides…?'

Brownlow inhaled deeply, his school master's face as pale as blackboard chalk. 'Besides…?' he began, before casting a frustrated glance at McKenna. McKenna relayed the look to Henney who completed the circle by launching an angry dart at me. Brownlow had not only lost his train of thought, but the train had already left the station. 'Besides,' he said again, with greater authority, gathering himself as best as he could, 'we see as well as hear, Dr Bishop.'

'Meaning?'

'Meaning,' Henney intoned, 'we slipped a bit of nanotech into Knight's vial when he wasn't looking. It goes into any new intravenous solution or pill.'

I looked at Henney, stunned, not sure whether I was more astonished that he had spoken than by what he had actually said.

'But Localis…?'

'Localis,' McKenna continued, 'is more complicated. It works over an indefinite period of time. Our trackers are simpler…sat nav for the human body. They get flushed out eventually.'

It seemed McKenna, Henney's tag team partner, was much more than the sum of his muscular parts as well. I stared at him and reminded myself never to judge a work of art by its comic strip cover.

'So, Rachel's tracker is no longer showing up on your radar.'

'Something like that,' Brownlow said. 'She's off-base. Her biometrics were last picked up a mile from here. Seems they got out via an old mining shaft east of here.'

'They?'

'You were right, doctor. Before going dark, the other signature read as belonging to Doctor Knight. He's gone too.'

14

Tempus had been a traitor, the Master Apprentice had said. Sometimes, on rare occasions, certain entities in the West were able to intervene at the Bridge and hijack a soul as it made its crossing from the last life, immerse it with the twisted remnants of themselves, the broken, shattered residue that normally found itself cast out for all eternity on the other side of Day.

'I don't understand,' she had replied.

And so, she had been allowed to return to the Haven, leave the Archives until such a time that her thoughts could readjust.

'No, but you will,' the Master Apprentice had said, his voice comforting, a smile threatening to corner at both sides of his mouth. It had all been a terrible mistake, he had told her. Unforeseen. Even by the Advocate. His Holy Name was furious that the incursion had been allowed to occur, that one of His precious Apprentices had been preyed upon in such a way.

He passed her some amrita which she gratefully accepted, its energy revitalising her.

Newly invigorated she steered her desert-walker left, back once more onto its own tracks, the circuit which led to and from the Haven.

'But why me? Why did she choose me?'

'You are special, Ceres. Those in the West realised that. Our mistake was we in BridgeEast didn't realise *how* special. The mara was a warning -a warning that was not heeded.'

But the Advocate was omniscient, she had been informed, but knew better than to say. And hadn't the Master Apprentice been the one who had decided to use Tempus as her guide?

'How long will the Seer of Ceres remain in exile?' she asked instead.

'As long as he continues to refute the charges made against him. His own Master Seer will see to his replacement.'

'And if he doesn't repent?'

'He too will be thrown into the River of Sorrow that flows beneath the Bridge. That is the final death. He will never reunite with the Great Unseen.'

Something inside Helen cried out at the Master Apprentice's words. The Seer had been the first to welcome her to the Island. She had believed him wise, but he too apparently had played his part in the conspiracy to destroy her soul.

'But why am I special? Is it because I remembered my name?'

'Yes. That and other things.'

'What other things?' she persisted.

He did not reply. Instead he reached into a leather pouch that formed part of the desert-walker's saddle, took out his sun shades and put them on.

'The suns are stronger today,' he replied. 'A good sign.'

'Who was Helen Mayer?' she asked.

'She was a lie, Ceres.'

'But I have seen her, Master Apprentice. The Archives revealed her to me, and I *will* relive her memories when I reach the centre of the Circles.'

'You will never complete the Circles, Ceres, unless you rid yourself of this...pollution.'

Two suns twice the day. That was what the people of the Village said upon greeting one another. And yet the expression made no sense. There was no day without a night to follow or precede it. The suns shone high and low in the same unchanging sky and the Master Apprentice set his gaze on each one of them in turn. His eyes had long since grown accustomed to them. Two chips of blue ice that would never melt. The shades he wore, however, which he put on during each of their desert rides, were his way of drawing the dialogue to a close. On each excursion she inched their conversation along, in her own mind a little further each time, but it always finished the same way. As soon as she asked about the name she had had in her last life -Helen Mayer -the Master Apprentice would shield himself from her, as if the intensity of the question outshone the two golden orbs that were pinned in the sky above.

The identity of Helen Mayer also been the driving force of Tempus' final words to her. Words she had had to keep from the Master Apprentice. Her questioning of him was simply a way to find out how much he already knew.

And instinct told her he knew everything.

Immediately afterwards, when Tempus had been removed from her presence, and after the inquisition which she thought would never end, Helen had chosen to retire for a while in the memory of her life as Akila, the servant girl who worshipped the avian deity known as Nekhbet. She had needed to rest for a time in the presence of the version of herself she had preferred the most.

The Master Apprentice had visited her often there. He had arranged it so the Archives would allow her to dwell in the memory of this particular lifetime for however long it took for her to recover. And so she traced once more her young predecessor's journey as she matured, got married, had children, grandchildren and then eventually died. The Master Apprentice agreed with Helen. Hers had been a good life. Nothing special. But simple, natural and with purpose.

And now once more Akila had died.

'Was any of it real?' Helen asked, as their

spectral, invisible forms gazed down on the elderly woman's withered remains as they were being prepared for its funeral pyre. Her grief-stricken children were washing their mother's corpse with natron salt while her grandchildren readied a roll of linen.

'Of course, it was real, Ceres,' the Master Apprentice had replied. 'Doesn't their grief look real to you? You know these people. Each one of them has shared an infinity of lifetimes with you.'

Helen looked down again. It was a cool summer's evening. The family had gathered on the roof top of Akila's small mud-brick house, and the zodiac above gaped down at them in all its mythological glory. A half-moon there provided ample light for the ceremony that was taking place. Two small children stood in the centre of them all, bravely holding clay bowls filled with oil that had been set aflame. She recognised them, of course. A boy and a girl. Nephi and Nenet. In this life they were Akila's great grandchildren. She remembered their births and her feelings of love for them threatened to overwhelm her.

'But why is the pastor not here?' she had asked.

'We have spoken of this, Ceres. It is because he is not a part of your soul group.'

'He is!' she exclaimed. 'I can feel him. Or her. Each time.'

'In this life you believe he is a Vizier. You told

me that yourself. Do you really think someone of such significance would have anything in common with a poor servant girl. Would attend her funeral?'

Unlike Akila's family she had been spared the sight of her friend's death. The Master Apprentice had simply reported that Tempus had been thrown into the Sorrow which either meant that, unlike the Seer, she had not repented, or she had been punished with greater severity since her soul had never vibrated with the higher energies of the East. She had been darkness masquerading as light, the Master Apprentice had said. The Seer's soul, on the other hand, was still not beyond salvation. There was still a chance that it could be salvaged, freed from the malign influence that had corrupted it.

Helen, however, had lived through the remembrance of enough lifetimes to know that the last thing a human being relinquished, regardless of the circumstances, was its integrity. Its sense of right and wrong. Even when faced with certain death, some cause, sense of moral purpose, familial or romantic love, was all it took for individuals to sacrifice themselves willingly on the altar of a higher purpose they could not understand in one lifetime alone. As a result, she could not shake the feeling that if Tempus was dead, then she had died because everything she had said had been true or she had convinced herself of its truth.

Regardless of how much the Master Apprentice tried to persuade her otherwise, she believed that this was an equation that balanced perfectly on the very pivot on which her own soul rested. She had known it from the very beginning. Her connection with Tempus on the Island was a pale afterglow, she was sure, of how their lives had intertwined in the life before it.

She thought once more to her final meeting with her friend. It had taken place too in her memory of Akila -the real reason why she so often returned to it now.

'My father brought you here?' she had asked her.

'I had got too close,' Tempus had replied.

'Too close to what?'

The garden temple with its colonnade shimmered in the moonlight as Helen looked across now from the roof of Akila's dwelling, replaying the scene once more in her mind's eye. It looked desolate, an empty stage, but she could almost see herself and Tempus at that earlier moment, two actors surveyed from the perspective of an unseen audience. She wished she could call out to her past self and tell it that she believed. That she now understood. That she had just needed time. The irony was not lost on her. She had needed time in a place where time was an illusion.

'Too close to the truth. Helen,' Tempus had replied, clasping Helen's hands with both of her own and holding them momentarily to her breast. 'This is not real.'

'Of course, this isn't real,' Helen had replied, releasing herself from Tempus' hold and casting her own hand through the air as if she were sowing seed. 'Nothing seen in the Archives is real. They relive only what once *was* real.'

'No, I don't mean that. I mean the Archives themselves are not real. The Island is not real. You are not real.' She knelt down and picked up a handful of dark soil from a flowerbed which formed part of a perimeter around the sacred temple where Nekhbet towered from its lofty plinth. 'Here, take this.' Tempus forced the dirt into Helen's hand. 'Feel it!' she exclaimed. 'It seems real even though you know its very consistency, appearance, smell and so on has been forged by your communion with the Archives. In this space you are a projection of photons, of hard light, and so is this.' She pointed at Helen's hand. 'That is how you can interact with it.'

'I don't understand what you mean by photons,' Helen replied, confused. 'The function of the Archives is to bring to us the memories of our past lives. It records every lifetime our soul has experienced and helps us strip away the emotions that arose with those memories. In doing so, we find the golden thread that runs through them all.'

'You don't understand, Helen. The Archives

are a dream within a dream. There are no Archives because there is no Island.'

Helen threw the dirt to the ground and turned away. She stepped through the garden towards Akila and the fire she tended. She could feel the sensation of its heat prickle the hairs on her arm.

'If this is not an Island, then where are we?!' she exclaimed, turning around. 'What are we doing here?!'

'It is difficult to explain,' Tempus said softly. She approached and stood next to Akila.

'Why?'

'Because you have not lived through your pre-life.'

'Why is that so important Tempus? Tell me, what horrors did you see that have caused this turmoil in you?'

Tempus smiled sadly. 'Have you ever wondered why you cannot remember your very last life. It is because it is only in that life that the technology exists to create this world. You accept the Archives as a sentient lifeform. Remember the being that you encountered? How it was made up of tiny fragments of metallic, light-filled dust? It overwhelmed you, activated the memories of your previous lives. That entity is simply a thought projection used to explain what the Archives really are.'

'But I saw it!' Helen argued.

Tempus sighed. 'It was simply a veil, a trick of the light to convince you that this place has been conjured up by someone else and reigned over by the one you call the Advocate. But even he is not real.'

'I don't understand! I don't want to understand!'

'Look at Akila there,' Tempus said, pointing at the young servant girl who was now sitting on the steps of the temple and humming a tune to herself. Her beautiful auburn hair cascading down the small of her back while her bronze legs tapered to feet buckled into leather sandals. Her face in private awed worship of the sun overhead, a wide smile opening her lips. 'If she were to die and find herself on this Island, do you think the Archives would reveal itself to her in a form similar to the one it did for you? No. For her, in her time, with her innocence, it would probably be a talking bird like the one she makes sacrifice to every day. You remember your last incarnation before your pre-life?'

'Yes, I was a nurse.'

'A nurse who knew human anatomy. Has heard of molecules and atoms. Was aware of viruses. Could understand the principle of something intravenous invading her body.'

'So, who was I in my pre-life? This Helen Mayer? And how did you know me? You are not part of my soul group.'

'No, I knew *of* you in my pre-life. But I met you just once.'

'And my father brought you here? How?'

'In that life, you were a scientist, Helen. So was your father. Only he was more than just that. He was a man with aspirations beyond those of normal men. The world was broken, and he tried to fix it. In his own way. I discovered what he had done and what he was going to do.'

'And his name was Henry Mayer?'

'Helen, he is the pastor that never reveals himself to you. The one from whom you have never been able to break free. He held dominion over you in your last life and reminds you of it each time you visit your former selves in the Archives. But that is not your story, Helen. Akila never existed. None of the previous incarnations you have met ever existed. All of this is his fantasy. A fairy tale written by Henry Mayer. Your father and the creator of this world.'

15

I wasn't sure what I was supposed to do.

I handed Henney a jerry can, meanwhile keeping a close eye on McKenna's right hand, two fingers like chopsticks around the most dangerous cigarette I had ever seen. There had been a hole in the can and fuel had spilled over the proud bodywork of Winston's car, forming the beginnings of a puddle by his rear left tyre.

As predicted, every petrol station on the journey north lay abandoned, their attendants long since fled with everything they could carry by way of food and water. The pumps had been drained dry and the nozzle of their guns pointed at their heads, a row of strange, collective suicides. Elsewhere, cars and trucks were scattered on the forecourt like a child's toys. Forgotten.

'How many of those cans did Brownlow give us?' Henney asked, trying his best to guide as much fuel as he could into the dark mouth of the car.

'Six,' I replied, looking back inside.

'Six!' McKenna exclaimed, sucking gravely on his cigarette, 'my lighter has less chance of running out of fuel.'

'Dunno know about that, McKenna,' Henney replied. 'Not the way you smoke.'

'Ha bloody ha!' McKenna retorted, tossing his cigarette end mercifully onto the grassy verge of the motorway.

We had been on the road less than two days and already, free of Brownlow's influence, two distinguishable personalities had already begun to take shape in the hitherto unified tug of war duo that had been McKenna and Henney. Minus their sunglasses, they surprised me with eyes of varying colour: blue for the former, brown for the latter. Their hair, however, had been buzzed similar shades of brown. McKenna, for his part, was a couple of inches taller in his suit with more prominent cheekbones. Henney, on the other hand, maintained a lower centre of gravity and liked to rock on his heels like a boxer. McKenna, if he fought his friend, would have had a longer reach, preferring to work on the outside. Perhaps he was the cleverer man as well. I didn't know. They liked to bait each other, snipe at one another's failings and yet, I knew, that if I or Winston dared to join in on the fun, the pair would realign their allegiance sharply, establish an impenetrable wall which no outsider could scale.

Not that Winston, our taciturn driver, would ever think of anything so indulgent as conversation. He drove, ignoring everything except the soothing tones of his satnav, a jazzy, female vocal that threatened to break into song at any time. McKenna sat alongside, while Henney and I made up the rear. It was obvious that although Winston and the others were all on Brownlow's team, they were opposing parts of that team, decompartmentalised adjuncts surviving on differing scraps of food from their Master's table. McKenna was quite obviously keeping watch on Winston. Henney, meanwhile, wasn't letting me out of his sight.

I had told Brownlow that Rachel might have guessed the identity of our spy but also that she had been convinced it wasn't Knight. Somebody, probably the real mole, must have got wind of this and prevented Rachel from passing on her suspicions to me at dinner.

'If you were overheard,' Brownlow had replied, 'that means it must have been someone with access to our tracking systems. That requires top level clearance.'

'Or they simply got through by some back door or other?' I had countered.

'Impossible. Besides, if Rachel was right, and Knight isn't our man, then what the hell is he doing eloping with her to God knows where? Unless...'

'...Unless?'

'Unless they're working together.'

'Working together?!' I exclaimed, the high octave of my voice quivering a notch.

'Maybe, they picked up the trail of the real spy and have gone off in pursuit?'

'No way!'

'Why not?'

'She would have told me. She had planned to tell me.'

'Hmm…something could have happened, and they had to work fast. Who knows?'

'No, that's not it.'

But perhaps it was. At any rate, I replayed this conversation over and over as we made our way first to Knight's and then onto Rachel's apartment in the city. Having no luck with either, we ventured further afield to their family homes, both of which were far north into the wasteland of bleak countryside that had once been the bread basket of the country but which now even the birds tried to avoid.

Both residences were empty, of course.

Knight, according to Brownlow, had only a mother still alive. On arrival at her home we were immediately discouraged: the grass in her once manicured lawns had filled with tall weeds while a toppled bin had splayed litter all down her drive. Some of the lead in her roof had been purloined and birds had taken to nesting in one of the bedrooms below. The furniture downstairs was either missing or broken. It was clear the old lady was either already dead or in one of the end-of-life sanctuaries that only the very rich or very well-connected could afford. These 'havens' were a notch above the smaller sanatoriums available in more densely populated areas but even a quick recce through the ones in the local area had proven futile.

Rachel's parent's home, a smaller town house in what was once in the middle-class suburbs of a pretty, coastal village, had been looted, ransacked, graffitied and boarded-up as efficiently as if it had journeyed on a conveyor belt gone backwards. Once more, there were no signs of her parents or any of her remaining family in the area.

It was clear to us that the daily news reports hadn't done the state of the nation justice. Going out after curfew was a death sentence, we knew, but now gangs of youths roamed the streets in large hunting packs during the day, preying upon the living, pick-pocketing the dead. Those, without family support, who ran the gauntlet of trips to food outlets, were usually too far gone to defend themselves by the time they arrived there while corpses lay as carrion for seabirds and urban pigeons in the high streets, jellied eyes displaced by dark, sightless holes.

On two occasions our car was nearly hijacked. It had taken McKenna firing a volley of rounds from his semi-automatic to disperse the thugs. He hadn't been aiming above anyone's heads either, I noticed.

All the time, amidst our bickering, Winston's deafening silence, and the lefts and rights of our disembodied navigator, I maintained an earnest needle on the groove of my own thoughts. What had Rachel meant by the proof being 'on the other side'? What other side I asked myself? Had she meant our political divide? That of rich and poor? Of infected and non-infected? The phrase had meant nothing to Brownlow either. But to me it had become a mantra, something to hold onto, a desperate hand raised above the surface of a tumultuous sea.

The truth was I was worried. Not just about Rachel, but also about myself. I had sensed my own awareness start to drift. Just for moments at first, and then maybe for a second or two longer. Time was beginning to stop, and then restart, and between the two a veil had begun to descend over my consciousness. To an observer I must have looked like a clockwork toy that had somehow ground to a halt. As for myself, it was as if I were awakening from a very short daydream. I had crossed a gap in my memory without having lengthened my stride to do so.

I was entering Stage One of the virus I feared. I recognised the symptoms. Brownlow too had succumbed, a mile or so ahead of me on the road to oblivion. And in front of him, Joseph, the student whose MRI scan had leapt to Stage Two in half the time it should have normally taken. That had been one the things I had wanted to discuss with Rachel. It was clear to me that something or someone had expedited the virus back at Brownlow's base. Or perhaps it had simply mutated. But I wasn't convinced by the latter. The timing was too coincidental.

If it were a race, the stakes were getting high. I had tried amber and Knight's vial. I had also learned of alternative approaches: Localis, and whatever elixir Mayer was working on. And now, suddenly, a newcomer to the pharmaceutical sweepstakes -the powder Brownlow had taken to ingesting every six hours. Henney called it 'sherbet' but knew nothing of its chemical composition nor even its real name. Neither did McKenna. And Brownlow had refused to talk about it. So, like an addict looking for a different high, I had asked him for a week's supply of his sachets of crystallised goodness for research purposes. He had thrown me a knowing look but acquiesced immediately. I couldn't tell if that was a good sign or not. Hopefully, we would come across Rachel and Knight before the week ran out.

Being of scientific mind I had suggested to Brownlow that we split up and pursue two separate lines of enquiry. One for Rachel and one for Knight. The mobile network may have collapsed but the satellites above our heads had yet to crash land to Earth I had argued. Perhaps all we needed was a couple of phones to keep in contact? McKenna and I on one end and Henney and Winston on the other. But Brownlow had shot me down. We had to stay together he had demanded. The country was about to tip us and everything in it into the ocean he had said. If that was the case, it was only right we went out all guns blazing.

And so, it had been decided: a road trip through hell, running on fumes, and my mind slipping through the grate of a memory hole.

'So, what now?' Henney was saying now, doing his best to wipe the grease off his hands with an old sheet of newspaper.

'Well, we've tried the obvious and as predicted we've got nowhere,' McKenna replied, stretching himself out into the shape of a yawn.

'It had to be done,' I ventured, apologetically.

'Waste of time. First places we'd look. They'd have known that,' Henney said.

'So, where now?' I asked.

'Depends,' Henney replied.

'On what?'

'On which of the two is running the show.'

'What do you mean?'

'Not too bright for a doc, is he, McKenna?' McKenna smirked and cast an eye across the forlorn landscape of motorway and brush. It had started to drizzle, rain cold enough to send a shiver down your spine if you allowed it to. 'I mean, if the girl's in charge, then it's more than likely they're off to some hi-tech lab or other. If it's Knight...?'

'...It *is* Knight. He has kidnapped her,' I replied.

'Hmm, well,' Henney muttered, noncommittedly, 'if that's the case, he's taken her back to NeuralNet.'

'You think so?' I asked.

'Brownlow's not too keen on us going there though,' Henney said. 'For obvious reasons.'

'What reasons are those?' I asked, trying not to look too defensive.

Henney shook his head and smiled. He stepped closer. 'You think McKenna and me are just a couple of meatheads, don't you, Bishop? You think neither of us knew about Levy?'

'No, it's just...'

'...We've been with the old man since well before this fuck-up of biblical proportions began,' Henney interrupted. 'We're his conscience, doc. His good and bad angel. His perspective if you like. The last thing Brownlow wants is McKenna and me doing something as bloody stupid as barging into NeuralNet. All soft-headed and heavy-handed. Especially not with you. A civilian. How long, Bishop, before you spilled the beans about Levy under interrogation by one of Mayer's people. Five minutes? Ten?' Henney took another step towards me, a primed coil of vital, pent-up frustration about to be unleashed. I could smell the petrol off his fists, the last cheap shave off his chin. I looked across in panic at McKenna who was reaching inside his pocket for what I hoped, this time, would just be another cigarette. Through the rear window of the car, the back of Winston's dark, crash test dummy of a head failed to trouble the still air around it. It was leaning back, motionless. Our driver having chosen a great time to fake a nap I thought. 'They're all special ops too,' Henney continued. 'McKenna and me have probably broken bread with them overseas.'

'Listen Henney...' I began, hating the sound my voice was making, '...we are all very tired. Let's try and...stay focused...'

'...Right now, Bishop, I'm very focused. You know what I am focused on? Ripping your arrogant little head of its plinth.' Henney was so close now I could smell his breakfast. I glanced at McKenna again and wondered if that would be the last meal I ever thought of. Our stretch of motorway curved onwards out of view, empty lanes of slick greyness. A buzzard or two no doubt licking their lips behind a bank of cloud above. I felt my bowels move and a large moth flutter its wings in my throat.

'Henney?' I pleaded.

He grabbed my collar and raised a slice of hand. I was about to be karate chopped into the next world by a bacon and egg-breathed, cheaply scented, black-belted, ex-Neanderthal. My last thought should have been of Imogen, or at least Rachel. My dead mother or at least a childhood pet. But all I could think of was how ridiculous our film set was and what a silly way it was to end your days when millions of others were succumbing to far more serious fates. I threw

McKenna a farewell nod and watched him as he slowly removed a hand from his inside jacket.

Two smokeless fingers aimed a make-believe trigger in my direction. In front of me, Henney's face lit up with a flash of molars and incisors, through which gushed a bellyful of scarcely-contained barrelled laughter.

'Very funny,' I managed to say after Henney's well had run dry, trying my best to recover my composure. I readjusted myself, fingered my neck collar where my skin had flushed red, a hot mixture of anger and embarrassment.

'You thought we were going to take you out, Bishop? Brownlow's golden boy? No way! Brains like yours, even those brains that are on the slide,' he winked at McKenna, 'are of a high premium in today's world. Just remember though the skull around it is thin and vulnerable. Without us!'

'Gentlemen, we are losing light,' a new voice echoed through the frost-filled air.

We all turned to see Winston standing by the open driver's door of the car. I think it was the first time I had seen him standing on his own two feet. He was tall, taller than I could ever have imagined with a build to match that of Henney and McKenna. His chauffeur's cap did its best to sit atop its oversized perch, a strand of fringe escaping onto his forehead. He stood, two hands clasped behind his back, like an old-fashioned butler, the straight edge of his hat adding menace to his eyes. Even Henney and McKenna stopped in their tracks, appraising Winston anew.

'What is it Winnie?' Henney lilted. 'You found your voice at last?'

'Mr Henney,' Winston replied, with barely concealed contempt. 'I have a proposition.'

'You do? What? Here in the middle of the motorway?'

'I had occasion to collect Mr Knight from his laboratory,' Winston began, ignoring Henney and addressing McKenna. 'The first time he was brought to our base. The same task I performed for Mr Bishop.'

'Yeah, we know that. We were with you at the time,' McKenna snarled.

'Yes, Mr McKenna. You were. We passed by Mr Knight's old workplace when we were in the city the other day. The one where he used to work on that gene.'

'Huntington's,' I said.

'Yes. Well, I couldn't help but notice that it still seemed open for business.'

'You must have been mistaken, Winnie,' Henney scoffed, a note of warning in his voice.

'No, Mr Henney. I wasn't.'

Henney glanced warily at McKenna. Something was brewing. 'Go on Winston,' I encouraged.

'Well, I do remember hearing, from Mr Knight himself actually, the lab did indeed close down after research into the Huntington gene moved to the base…' he paused, apparently unsure whether to go on although I knew he wanted to.

'And…?'

'…It's just, doctor, that I couldn't help but notice a rather large police and army presence at the laboratory as we drove past.'

'It's probably been used by another research team, Winston,' I replied. 'It happens all the time. Besides all science labs are under tight security. Junkies everywhere.'

'Yeah, junkies with sub-machine guns these days,' Henney added.

'Hmm, I agree. It definitely is being used. For something.' Winston concluded with a wry smile.

A silence ensued. I noticed McKenna had slipped another cigarette into his mouth. Henney was glaring at Winston, a red rag to a bull. A cold breeze suddenly made me shudder, but I tried to keep myself in check, forcing myself not to dig my hands into my trouser pockets. Henney was right. I *was* just a brain, but I didn't want to lose any more ground to the trio of killers that stood before me. If anything, Winston had proven to have the measure of Henney and McKenna.

'How large?' I asked finally.

'More than normal,' Winston replied.

'So what are you saying?'

'I have no evidence, but I think Mr Brownlow's

new medication is being developed there.'

'Winston!' McKenna threatened, flinging his cigarette to the ground.

'What?!' I exclaimed.

Henney squared himself, a wild cat about to pounce. Winston, meanwhile, stared back at his aggressor with insolent indifference. If he had had a moustache he would have twirled it defiantly.

'You stupid bastard, Winston!' Henney cried.

'You really think Mr Henney, Mr Brownlow wouldn't bring me into his confidence?'

'So,' I began, trying to deescalate the tension, 'there has to be something to this new drug. Seems it's too important to risk working on at the base especially given the fact that Brownlow knew we were compromised there.'

'And if Mr Knight is working for the other side,' Winston added, 'then he might just want to find out more about it. Maybe acquire a batch of it for Mr Mayer.'

'But the lab's under armed guard. You said so yourself,' I protested.

'If we have our security vacate the premises, or pretend to, it might lure him into making a move?' Winston replied.

'He tries to get his hands on the drug, and we'll be there waiting for him?' I summarised. 'Well, it's worth a shot? What do you think, Henney? McKenna?'

But they had already got back into the car,

their shoulders frozen together in the back seat. Neither of them were the type to like to lose face. Or say 'please' and 'thank you'.

'Well then, that settles it, Winston. Buckle up. And on the way, maybe *Mr* Henney or *Mr* McKenna will bring us up to speed on this new wonder drug?'

16

What haunted her most, more than the constant screech and wail of the mara that circled the star-less blackness above; more than the screams of tortured, sleep-deprived souls trapped in their own private purgatories below; more than the wind-blasted caves and ocean-lashed cliffs; more than the writhing, shifting landmass of serpents and other foul creatures that surfaced from dank, underwater pools; the locust-filled air; the sea-demons that prowled the shoreline; the two watery, lactose moons that scarcely penetrated the night but wreaked havoc upon the Tides; more than any of this was the thought that she had not actually woken up. That she was not really in control.

The gash on Tempus' right arm, which she now cradled gingerly to herself, had bled profusely, overwhelming the pain receptors in her brain. Real or otherwise, they sent agonising signals to her own flesh, so easily stripped away beneath the talons of the mara that had attacked her. Even if the predator's claws *were* a synthesised mesh of angled, razored photons, it mattered very little if the skin on her forearm was comprised of the very same interference pattern of light. The feeling was no different than what it would have been in the material world.

She looked up. Her assailant, the one that could read her thoughts, was directly overhead. She could sense its presence in her mind, an umbilical, invisible connection like the brushed finger of a blind child over braille. She knew its meaning in the darkness. Its intent.

Without words, she had only her thoughts. These too she would have to overcome.

Her mara, and she supposed everyone else's in BridgeWest, was surrounded by a pale aura of light, allowing Tempus to differentiate it from the rest. A thin reddish halo that appeared to be the only colour permitted on this side of the Island. The landscape was otherwise bleached and featureless, except for the rocks, the curious standing stones and the mountains of shale and slack that gave way beneath your feet. The sky beyond the mara kneaded a relentless pattern of fast-moving cumulus that developed and dissipated at the same alarming rate and kept pace with a never-ending gale from the western coast. There, a constant buffeting of amrita was whipped up from the sea, gulped down by those hungry enough to open their mouths to it.

BridgeWest, the side of the Island to which she had somehow arrived, was indeed an eternal damnation, the sort of horror only the most crazed, fundamentalist preacher could have ever imagined. And one thing was for certain: Henry Mayer was insane. Of that, there could be no doubt.

She had met him, of course. Right at the end. At the precise moment the consciousness of the woman she had once been had departed the physical form that had encased it. Now, she could remember everything. Everything except her name. The exact opposite of Helen.

And then there had been the traitor.

And beyond all that, a lifetime of memories, of family and loved ones, colleagues and acquaintances. There had been the epidemic, the brain plague that had wiped out most of mankind. And the man with whom she had wanted to share a life. His face, like all the rest, lacking definition, that of a stranger in a crowd or a bystander in a dream; familiar, yet at the same time, unknown. One which stopped you in your tracks, a déjà-vu just out of reach.

But not Mayer. If he had hidden himself from Helen in every lifetime, he was very real to Tempus, a madman hellbent on creating his own pocket universe, populated by mindless slaves like the one she had once been. Why was his the only face she could clearly see? And why hadn't he simply had her killed? Why, upon awakening, had she been allowed the time to make contact with Helen, time to convince her that she too was asleep? And why was it that she trusted the daughter of Henry Mayer?

If the pre-life and its world existed independently of Helen's father, then she had existed in it too. Not as Tempus, but under a different name. She remembered, as that other person, reading the media reports of the estranged daughter of the multi-billionaire Henry Mayer. There had been some disagreement between the pair. Something or someone had come between them. If so, was that the reason that Mayer had included his daughter in his grand, virtual theme park?

These and other questions had tortured Tempus since the ceremony at the Bridge, prevalent among them all the interminable doubt that her newly discovered sense of awareness had been too fortunate. Too coincidental. And the fear in her soul, imagined or otherwise, was that she was still asleep, that she was perhaps not even real in any sense of the word. But merely the first player in Mayer's game to ascend to the next level of his virtual hellscape.

Things had been clearer at the Bridge.

What was supposed to have happened hadn't happened. At the centre of the Circles, as her pre-life emerged, Tempus had somehow reawakened, a newer consciousness overlaying the one that had gone before. Afterwards, the Master Apprentice, now vaguely recognisable to her, had had her returned to her Haven in Tempus, to the very room where she had spent her first moments on the Island. Later still she was taken to the Bridge. And with her, the entire populations of the five Villages: the Acolytes, the Seers, the Apprentices, all with their Masters in attendance; the Weavers, the Wood-turners, the Smiths, the Physicians. Those from her Village assembled at the front of the rest, standing forlornly, with lowered heads, as if bearing the weight of her guilt.

She had been placed on a proscenium on top of a ridge overlooking the River Sorrow, the Master Acolyte and Master Apprentice to her left and right. Her white Apprentice's livery had been stripped of her back and replaced with a rough, hemp pinafore that had barely concealed her nakedness. The colours of the villagers in the sand below fluttered like rags in the breeze. Before the ceremony commenced she had had just enough time to draw breath and take in once more the inconceivable wonder of her surroundings.

She had attended many ceremonies in the same place, at the conclusion of which a living sacrifice was conveyed on a litter each time, at the head of a cortège, to the huge, vaulted gate of the East Tower. The Tower was the enormous monolith which marked the entrance to the Bridge. Once inside, those from the Temple would *assist* in the subject's final passing. A pyre, composed of the remains of every previous incarnation of the soul, awaited at its summit. Later, at a second ceremony, the ashes of the body would be added to the sacred framework of the Bridge in the form of a brick, or 'stepping stone', the final one the initiate took and which led to the Great Unseen. The Tower's adobe walls were at least a hundred feet thick, locked together and vanishing into the heavens above where it was assumed the Bridge to the other side of the Island could be accessed.

As she peered across to the Tower that day, however, Tempus noticed that its gate was firmly locked. Hers would be a different fate. As for the Advocate, His Holy Name had not deigned to make an appearance. Staring down the scale of cliff into the fathomless depths of the river that separated the Island, Tempus wondered if there even was a river of amrita running a course below. If it couldn't be seen, why would Mayer even bother to include the details of one? Not that it mattered. All of this was mere pageantry, for the benefit of masses she thought. Her proper self was somewhere else, projecting all this onto the theatre of her subconscious mind. But even if she were absolutely certain that she was not there, about to be thrown to her death into a bottomless chasm, she would never be able to persuade her senses of this. She stood instead, hot ribbons of exposed skin seething under the double suns above and the weight of panic inside so unbearable that it took her breath away.

Several miles across, BridgeWest stood like a huge, black glass wall, the length of which, she knew, stretched from north of the Island to its south and extending high into the clouds above. A pillar of greater darkness mirrored the Tower on the eastern side. Beyond the wall, various shades of blackness betrayed flickering silhouettes as they passed along the spectrum of grey, purple and black; two tiny discs of blurred moonlight providing the only respites from the thickly folded curtain of night.

The light from the East seemed to halt sharply before this high berg of blackness, two worlds nose to nose, staring at one another. A collision of matter and anti-matter. And yet that wasn't true either. The light, Tempus could see, had already begun to deplete as it approached the West, thinning itself out as though drained, swallowed by the event horizon, the equivalent of black hole on the other side.

With a lifetime of newly acquired knowledge now to guide her, Tempus had, for the first time, not just the ability to explain away the Island in scientific terms but also the inclination to want to do so. Mayer, it seemed, had a dogmatic, over-zealous and highly simplified vision of good and evil. Each person had been cordoned off on either side of an imaginary island with the simplicity of a child manoeuvring two opposing armies of toy soldiers. Perhaps, only he chose who incarnated where. The poor fools staring at her at the bottom of the desert valley below could just have well awakened on BridgeWest.

But Mayer's version of heaven was really just somebody else's hell and no doubt why he had expunged every islander's capacity for rational thought. Like most fire and brimstone preachers, his imagination could not conjure up a more beatific vision of paradise. His was a simple cult, just another of those that had sprouted up like mushrooms after the beginning of the Forgetting. The only difference was Mayer had an endless supply of liquid income at his disposal and the technology bought and paid for to avoid the tacky business of actually having to brainwash its members. But who were all these people she thought? In the real world? Old business rivals? Criminals? Other members of his extended family?

Her train of thoughts came to an end when the Master Apprentice, transfigured in a dazzling white robe, held up her left arm and began to speak.

'Villagers of Ceres, Occus, Pares, Frontes, and Tempus. Attendant Masters and Acolytes. Two suns twice the day!'

'Two suns twice the day!' the crowd intoned.

'His Holy Name...'

'His Holy Name!'

'His Holy Name has decreed that the Apprentice of Tempus is an imposter, having had her soul defiled at the time of her departure from the pre-life. The dark, negative entity that now resides there has sullied what was once pure, has vanquished its light and condemned it to a Second Death into the Sorrow below. From that there can be no return.'

The Master Apprentice looked skywards, shielded his eyes against the suns overhead, and extended his vision to the furthest point of the East Tower, the moment where its walls disappeared into a small dot of nothingness miles overhead.

'She will never make the journey beyond to the Great Unseen. Nothing of the soul she was now remains. Best that this foul creature is destroyed forever than return to the ranks of evil from which it came. There!' The Master Apprentice pointed a finger out into the distance towards BridgeWest. 'The land of the lost!'

At that, the crowd below turned its head and faced the longitude of darkness that bordered the sanctuary that was their part of the Island. Some recoiled in fear, some fell to their knees, their arms raised to the Tower, their fingers hooked as if they wanted to reach up to the heavens and claw the deity that was the Great Unseen from His invisible pedestal beyond the clouds. Others appeared to collapse in a paroxysm of ecstatic joy or dread. Tempus couldn't tell which. Her legs had begun to give away and her arm ached under the fierce grip of the Master Apprentice. She hadn't been nourished with amrita since her capture and a strange, ice-cold fever raged inside her body while her flesh continue to sear under the remorseless heat of the suns.

The Master Apprentice waited deferentially for the effects of his words to die down before continuing.

'For those of you from Tempus and Ceres, the Advocate assures you that no blame be attached to your Villages. No censure can be attributed to the Village of Tempus, no more so than can be given to the disembodied essence that was, and should have been, the Apprentice of that Village whose spark was stolen before it could even light up our Island. As for Ceres, His Holy Name has decreed that the Seer of that Village be cast out until such a time that he acknowledges his guilt in allowing this immortal vessel to be besmirched by the vile energies of the West.'

A wave of relief rippled through the two large groups below, representative of Ceres and Tempus.

'The Seer will be allowed to wander the eastern coast of our Island and have free access to the amrita there. He will not,' the Master Apprentice affirmed, his expression changing, 'be allowed to enter any of the five Villages, not until such a time that he repents of the part he played in trying to debase the Apprentice of Ceres. Anyone who is discovered offering assistance to the Seer will suffer the same fate as will now be endured by the Apprentice of Tempus. This has been agreed by the Master Acolyte,' he added, looking across at the serene, veiled face of the Acolyte, who had been listening and nodding intently throughout the Master Apprentice's speech, 'who has permitted me to assume the role normally allocated to those of the Temple. It is not deemed appropriate that the Master Acolyte, nor anyone else from the Temple, and obviously not His Holy Name himself, should lend a hand to this deplorable business.'

'And finally, to those concerned about the welfare of our dear Apprentice from Ceres, she has returned to the Haven there and will soon be well enough to return to her sacred duties in the Archives. Now...' Tempus felt the hand in her arm loosen, 'does the creature occupying the soul that was once destined to migrate to that of our Apprentice of Tempus have anything to say before its final sentence?'

Tempus stepped forward, only a few feet from the yawning darkness that was her fate. Since the Archives she had not spoken. The Master Apprentice had kept a cloth bound around her mouth and so she had preferred to maintain a running monologue in her head, her voice a coherent, auditory facsimile of the one that had so urgently spoken to Helen then. She had been isolated and, unlike the Seer, she had not even been questioned by the Master Apprentice, Master Acolyte nor anyone else about who or what she really was. Of course, she reasoned, that was because Mayer knew that her real identity had reasserted itself. To him, she was now a virus, just like the one from the real world. Mayer had had to place her in a decontamination chamber away from even those closest to him in this world of make believe.

But now this cloth was unbound, the Master Apprentice's hands unwrapping the binds of linen allowing her to breath fresh air once more. She parted her lips, readied herself to fill the valley and the void below with her cries of protestation, which, in her imagination, she could already hear, echoing across the great divide, all the way to BridgeWest.

She opened her mouth and started to speak but the words did not come.

Instead, a dry, strangled noise exploded her head. She tried again and only then realised that there were no words there. No sound. Instead, a slither of foreshortened muscle at the top of her throat twitched in desperation, not long enough to feel for her teeth and the absence between.

Her tongue had been removed.

And after a moment, she felt herself fall.

17

‘Sherbet’ had been the first and best fruits of Levy’s labour. NeuralNet had stopped research into it at least a year before. It had been just another rejected antidote, left to desiccate at the bottom of some test tube, but something in its formula had fired the imagination of Brownlow’s team of epidemiologists.

It wasn’t a cure as such, but it marked a major advance in the war against the rapid neural degradation which afflicted the human brain in the second and third stages of the disease. Animal trials were still ongoing, but Brownlow had convinced those above him to forge ahead. What did they have to lose, he had argued. As soon as word had reached the top levels of government that their proud coastal command post had been compromised by the most virulent form of the virus yet encountered, all bets were off. Mayer had launched a first strike against democracy. If he had his way, anarchy would ensue.

Naturally, there was no proof of his involvement. There were even rumours that Mayer was no longer in the country but holed up instead on some equatorial island he had bought, several thousand miles away from the nearest infection hot zone.

Levy had reported no untoward activity at NeuralNet. As far as he was aware the place was crawling with software engineers and not those skilled in the art of germ warfare. If Mayer had weaponised the contagion, then he hadn't done so from his corporate headquarters.

'He hasn't gone anywhere,' I said, turning to Winston, remembering the silhouettes I had seen on the balcony of the Abbey during my last visit. 'And neither has his daughter. What's her name? Helen, isn't it?'

'Yes. Helen,' he replied, stirring milky swirls around his coffee. I wasn't sure why. He hadn't asked for sugar. Two tables away, Henney and McKenna were chatting to one of Brownlow's people -some uniform who was being given the order to stand down his team at McKnight's old lab. McKenna had just lit up another`cigarette even though smoking was still prohibited in public places like a café. But who now would bother to enforce a law like that when the world itself had gone up in flames?

It was an hour before dusk and through the street window, on a park bench across a desolate, litter-strewn road, a casually-dressed middle-aged had just nodded off. He could have been alive or dead. Homeless, or resided in some forgotten, bijou flat around the corner.

This is what the disease did to you. It relegated everything and everyone to a flip of a coin. You either knew who you were, or you didn't.

'Aren't we going to need...more guns or something?' I asked. 'If we are going to do this alone?'

The scar on his cheek creased as he smiled, a row of well-maintained molars peeping out from behind a pair of thin lips. 'Don't fret, doctor,' Winston advised. 'We have a safe house nearby. We can pick up a few semi-automatic rifles on the way. Ammunition. Bullet proof vests. If Doctor Knight does take the bait, he'll not come by himself.'

I tried my best not to gulp. 'And Brownlow's ok with me tagging along?'

'I am not sure, Dr Bishop, how capable Mr Brownlow is of making any kind of decision at the moment. Our doctors are working on him around the clock. Him, and a few dozen others back at the bunker.' Something made Winston look away. I followed his gaze. A couple of hooded teenagers, decked out in matching tracksuits and brand-new sports shoes, were rifling through the pockets of the man on the bench opposite, filching anything they could of value. 'It'll be dark soon. I have a feeling you will be better with us than out on the streets unarmed. Don't worry. We'll keep you safe.'

Our first night passed at the lab without incident. A couple of addicts, on the prowl for anything worth ingesting or injecting, were disposed of by McKenna and Henney on patrol at the main gate. They allowed the youths to struggle over the high walled perimeter of the lab, waited for them to jump to safety, before tasering them, and hauling their unconscious bodies to an empty store inside where they were bound and gagged.

A few hours earlier, several dozen disgruntled, white-coated scientists had had to pack up their centrifuges under cover of darkness and were frog-marched out the back of the building into a small fleet of ambulances that left at designated intervals in order not to draw too much attention. Ambulances, fire engines and police patrols were the only vehicles allowed on the roads after sunset -an unnecessary government edict given the shortage of fuel in the country. If Knight and Mayer's people were in the area, and had the lab under surveillance, Brownlow and co. didn't want to make the departure of the military and scientific teams too obvious. It had to be a furtive enough withdrawal to lure the predator to its prey.

The lab technicians were scattered in pairs to different locations throughout the capital; each individual housed secretly with someone working on a different aspect of the research. Together, each couple lacked the data or understanding to replicate the entire work from scratch. Even if Mayer had managed to kidnap three or four artists, he wouldn't have had enough to conjure up the whole picture.

In a small, adjoining warehouse, next to the main annexe, several crates of sherbet had been deliberately left behind. Hopefully, Mayer would prove incapable of resisting the temptation of pinching the jar of sweets behind the shopkeeper's back.

The whole idea was a risk, of course. After all, Mayer's own research teams had given up on the chemistry that had led us, via Levy, to the formulation of Brownlow's potential breakthrough. But, given what we knew of the man, it was widely believed that his ego would simply not be able to countenance the possibility that his research had been stolen. And even if Mayer was convinced that sherbet was a false trail, could he take the chance that Brownlow wasn't working on something else?

It was all smoke and mirrors. I hardly knew myself that the drug presently coursing its way through my veins was doing anything more than amber or Knight's placebo. And yet, you place an army to guard a field full of carrots, the carrots very soon become as rare as diamonds to the outside world.

There were eight of us in total. Winston, Henney, McKenna and myself in one contingent; four of the original crew in the other: Avenell, Willis, Derby and Yates -four, uncrackable nuts, the last one Yates being, by all accounts, female, although she could have snapped me in half in less time it would have taken her to do likewise to an unwanted set of knitting needles.

For the next couple of days, we operated four six-hour shifts; at least six of us alert and ready for action while two others slept. We stayed away from windows and took care not to switch on any lights that could be seen from outside. The lab had a kitchen equipped with a microwave, fridge, kettle and so on and we had enough supplies to last us a week if necessary.

Brownlow, however, had given us only three days to wait for Mayer to make his move after which we were to pull up sticks and join a special task force that had been set up to continue the search for Rachel and Knight in our absence. In the meantime, all activity at NeuralNet was being closely monitored and relayed back to us via satellite phone.

It was an hour before dawn when Rachel and Knight finally turned up.

Even through the green-tinted landscape of my night vision binoculars there could be no doubt that it was them. They appeared out of nowhere; Knight, unmistakable, in spite of his baseball cap and trench coat; Rachel, dressed casually in jeans and a leather jacket, her hair pulled back tightly into a tail. She was wearing the glasses she normally reserved for reading. Knight was toting a canvas bag over one shoulder while Rachel appeared to be carrying something bulky on her back, like a parachutist walking on solid ground. They were both alone and seemed more anxious about who might possibly be behind them than anything or anyone ahead.

'It's them,' McKenna confirmed, from one of the monitors where CCTV footage of the street below was being relayed, a patchwork of images from various angles. 'They've just walked straight in front of one of the cameras. Weird,' he added momentarily.

'What is?' I asked.

'They're just standing there,' McKenna replied. 'I think they're waiting for us to let them in.' McKenna dug into his pocket for his walkie-talkie. 'Henney, you seeing this?'

'Yeah,' a crackled voice replied. 'What do you think?'

'You have a shot?'

'From this height, I could take out anyone within a thousand yards on all sides. Knight has a bead smack bang in the middle of his forehead as we speak. Stupid bastard doesn't seem to know. Or care.'

'Remind me who's manning the gate?

'Avenell and the woman. Derby's here with me. Willis and Winston are beddy-byes. How do you want to play this? He's obviously using the girl as a hostage.'

I looked again through the goggles that were

perched atop a tripod and aimed at a chink in the blinds onto the street below. Rachel and Knight had moved out of shot. I crossed over to McKenna. Over his shoulder I could see the grainy, black and white images of my former colleagues. Knight's face partially washed in the sodium glare of a streetlight, Rachel's in shadow. She was looking up and waving frantically at one of the cameras. She seemed scared, but something told me it wasn't Knight that she was afraid of. I looked closer. She was directing our attention to the electronic mechanism of the gate. Then another hand gesture. This time, a thumbs up.

'I think it's ok, McKenna. I don't think Rachel is in danger from Knight.'

'You've changed your tune,' he replied, shaking his head. 'He's playing us, Bishop. Mayer probably has a team around the corner. Just waiting for the signal.'

'Not according to Henney. He says there's nothing happening out there.'

'They're professionals, doc. They're not going to be that obvious.'

'Still, might be worth having the two at the front find out for sure. They're both armed. If Rachel is Knight's hostage, her safety is our primary concern.'

'She's *your* primary concern, Bishop. Brownlow wants Knight alive more than he cares for your girlfriend. Surely, you have realised that by now?' I had. And yet, it didn't matter. There was a mad man on the roof about to fire a volley of bullets into Knight and maybe Rachel too. I couldn't just sit back and let that happen. 'Besides, what about our people at the front?'

'They're not our people,' I stung back.

McKenna grinned. 'Well, that's more like it! Bishop sacrifices two pawns, eh? Is that how it goes? At least, your head's beginning to clear a bit at last.' I didn't answer. I just knew I didn't trust Henney's aim especially since I knew Rachel was surplus to Brownlow's requirements. 'Ok,' McKenna added. 'It makes no odds to me whether we take Knight out now or five minutes from now. Whatever happens, he's not leaving with the drug.'

McKenna held his radio to his mouth again. 'Henney, they're coming in!' He adjusted the dial to another channel. 'Avenell? Yates?'

'Yeah?' a husky voice came back.

'Open the gates and let them in.'

'Sir?'

'Just bloody well do it Yates!'

We watched on as a figure in a balaclava and body armour -potentially Yates or Avenell - turned a hand to a panel on a nearby wall. Within moments the gates started to open. From a corner square of our monitor, we studied the reaction of Knight and Rachel. An acknowledgement of gratitude to the camera from Knight. A palpable exhalation of the shoulders from Rachel. On another square of the monitor, the tense, rigid outlines of Avenell and Yates, rifles primed, their centre of gravity prepared for any eventuality.

Just like a piece on a chessboard, Knight seemed to disappear and reappear onto another part of our computer screen. It was all happening very slowly and without sound. A rifle juddered upwards and in response Knight and then Rachel raised their arms in a gesture of surrender. I took a breath. Beside me, I noticed McKenna's fists unclench.

We switched our attention quickly to the door of the room where we had set up our temporary base. Heavy boots resounding on a metal staircase outside. Finally, one long knock followed by three shorter ones.

'Henney, what's it like up there?' I heard McKenna say.

'No change. All good.'

'Ok, Bishop. You can play footman. Unlock the door.'

I willed myself to move, skates on thin ice. A thin metal bar released the door onto its hinges. I pushed and stepped back almost at the same time.

Rachel and Knight were in front. The hulking presence of Avenell behind, his gun barrel hesitating between Rachel's and Knight's head in turns. Then came Yates carrying their bags, unzipped and harmless.

I was not sure what I was expecting but it certainly wasn't what I got -Rachel lurched forward and held me in a tight embrace. Her warmth and scent enclosing me, a waterfall of summer fragrance. Over her shoulder, a sly smile on Knight's lips.

'Are you…ok?' I whispered.

Her head nodded in response.

'Alright, that's enough!' McKenna exclaimed. 'Avenell, sit them both down at the table over there. Let's see what they have to say for themselves. No need to tie them up.'

I felt Rachel leave me as Yates grip tugged her backwards. It was only then that I got a proper look at her. Apart from a dark pair of half-moons under her eyes, a pallid, drained complexion, hair that had said farewell to its sheen several days before and the incongruity of her clothes, she didn't seem too badly off. A glance at Knight was enough to tell me that instead of his usual pompous body language and the sardonic whimsicality he gave so often to life, he too had been through the ringer since our last meeting.

'Who were those two on the roof?' he was asking McKenna now.

McKenna had already laid down his weapon, sat down and rested the heel of a hobnail on the table. Knight was directly opposite. It was a rectangular table, built for a scientific exchange of facts and figures, the type of crafted wood that impressed at board meetings. He seemed relaxed. And why not? Avenell and Yates were on guard duty. I was unarmed. Besides, this was the bit McKenna enjoyed. The idle banter before the interrogation proper. And after the interrogation the joy of torturing someone. If he had had his way he would have just skipped ahead to that point. An imaginary set of pliers had already appeared to take shape in his hands.

'Err…I'm not sure you realise Knight how this is going to work.'

'Is Brownlow here?' Rachel asked.

'Shall I pop the bitch now?' Yates sniped from the corner of the room.

'No, at least not yet,' McKenna replied, smiling at me.

'It's Henney and a thug called Derby,' I answered, a wilful act of disobedience. 'Brownlow is back at the coast. Not well, by all accounts.'

'That's enough Bishop or you will be joining these two!' McKenna bit back, his smile gone. 'I don't have orders about you either way.' He turned back to Knight. 'Ok, Knight, you're working for Mayer. You're here for the drug. You're gonna tell me all you know about your boss' little operation at NeuralNet.'

'You have got it all wrong McKenna. Dr. Bishop! Please!'

I had never seen Knight look so earnest. 'How have we got it wrong, Knight?' I asked.

'I'm here for the same reason you are, Bishop.

The drug.'

'You followed us here, Knight?!' McKenna barked.

'Yes, we did. For a while there we thought you'd never piece it together.'

'Piece what together?' McKenna asked, his curiosity piqued.

'The fact that Mayer would want to get his hands on it. After I initiated trials into Levy's drug...'

'...What?!' I exclaimed. 'You developed it?'

'Yes. What, didn't Brownlow tell you? McKenna knew.' McKenna puffed his cheeks and shook his head.

'You knew about this all along, McKenna?'

'It doesn't change anything, Bishop. It just makes the betrayal even worse. Brownlow's not convinced by Knight's innocence so why should you be?'

'So,' I replied, trying to gather my thoughts, 'the Huntington's research...?'

'...You were right, Bishop. So was Levy. I breathed life into old research that I knew would never catch fire. Our real efforts couldn't be conducted at the base.'

'Because Brownlow suspected you of being a spy!' McKenna said.

'No, McKenna, because he suspected *everyone* of being Mayer's man!' He shot a glance at Rachel, 'Or *woman* on the inside.'

I turned to Rachel. 'You trying to tell me

Knight, Rachel is Mayer's agent?' Rachel's face returned my gaze. A weak smile playing on her lips.

'Of course not,' Knight said after a pause. 'I started the development of the drug long after Brownlow's suspicions of a mole. He had no choice but to trust me, though not enough *not* to monitor every move I made. I only just told Rachel about it in the last few days. I suppose when we vanished, he believed we were both culpable. You know, Brownlow, he likes to compartmentalise…'.

'So why did you disappear?' I asked.

'The spy, the *real* one, was onto us. Well, Rachel actually.'

'So, how did you work that one out?' McKenna snapped, his tone still unable to accept the revelations being made.

'A process of elimination,' Rachel replied. 'He must have known his time was up. That was why he released the new variant of the disease through the ventilation system.'

I looked at McKenna. 'It's air-borne?' McKenna looked away.

'Yes, of course. Didn't Brownlow tell you?' Rachel asked.

'No,' I replied, dumbfounded.

'The anomalous scans we had started to collect. You remember trying to show me the scan of that student. The patient…what was his name? Joseph?'

'Yes,' I replied.

'Brownlow did his best to contain the spread, prevent it from reaching the lower levels. Got himself infected in the process if what you say is true. Another reason why he wanted you and the others off-base.'

'So Brownlow's people...?'

'Anyone exposed to the new variant...I don't know, Patrick...a year, maybe more.'

'So, the question is...' Knight continued.

I stopped listening. Instead, I found myself a chair and sat down. My legs had begun to fold. All those people. Brownlow. The kings and queens. The politicians. Marie, our eager to please kimchi waitress. All fodder in some war they knew nothing about. 'You said *he* Rachel. Who is it?'

Knight interrupted. 'The questions you should be asking are: who else knew about this place and what it was really used for? And why is Mayer so interested in our research?'

'To your first question: Brownlow, of course,' I replied. 'To the second: you, Rachel, McKenna. Maybe Henney?' McKenna nodded. 'And the driver, Winston maybe.'

'Yes, Patrick,' Rachel replied, leaning forward on her chair. 'Winston.'

'Winnie?!! No way!' McKenna exclaimed, fumbling for his walkie-talkie.

'Winston?' I mouthed, a cold wave passing through me. 'But he's here.'

'Where?' Rachel replied, jumping to her feet.

‘Henney? Henney?’ McKenna was roaring into his handset.

‘He can’t hear you,’ a voice sounded from across the room. We turned to face Winston, his pistol aimed at McKenna. ‘I wouldn’t worry about your friend, Mr McKenna. He is no longer with us.’

18

She was back at the Haven, the room where she had awakened, where she had been administered her first amrita. The female present had been the Physician of Ceres. The man: the Master Physician, such was the significance of her arrival at the Island that it had required his presence also. But there had been another voice as well, one she had yet to identify.

But then, she had known nothing.

The Village of Ceres had been populated with strange inhabitants, a hive of likened minds and bodies who had seemed to be linked by some truth, or quasi-religious fervour. They had barely any need for language. The Weaver would greet the Wood Turner upon meeting on the path, for example, and if they moved beyond words of salutation, the dialogue would soon peter out as they completed one another's sentences. And thoughts. Two identical fruit that realised they were on the same vine.

Tempus was right. They were just their occupations, identified only by the labour they performed. They had no need for free time or recreation. The villagers in BridgeEast had no line of demarcation separating work from play. Observing them in their roles, each one could just as well have awakened after each Tide to perform that of their neighbour. Joylessly and without passion. There was no skill set or sense of pride in the completed task, merely the act of work for its own sake.

On a few occasions, she would select a couple out of the crowd and follow them, evaluating their gesticulations and body language for any sign of friendship or camaraderie. But to no avail. A replacement interlocutor would have gone unnoticed by the other.

Now, the roles were reversed. In reality, it was *they* who were in the dark whereas she had the key to the gates that could liberate them all.

If Tempus was right, then all was not lost.

And so Helen continued her existence, back and forth from the Archives, masking her awakening from everyone, keeping in lockstep with the dreamers, mirroring their expressions, imitating their nods of greeting and hands of farewell. 'Two suns twice the day'. 'His Holy Name'. The fireworks in her brain masked behind the dark windows of her eyes.

If Tempus was still alive, then all was still possible.

The Master Apprentice had stopped his questions but had refused to answer any of hers. Tempus was dead, he had explained, her death witnessed by the entire population of BridgeEast. And the Seer of Ceres had not yet repented. He was surviving on the amrita that gathered in pools by the eastern coast. If he refused to acknowledge his guilt he would undergo the same fate as his fellow conspirator.

Sometimes, Helen would divert her route back from the Archives to the Haven and make her way to the East Tower. If this world was a dream manufactured by her father, this Henry Mayer, then there had to be some way for him to monitor that world. But she had to be careful. She waited, lifting her head from the Sorrow below to the Tower in the West, examining the latter for any sign of visible change, any fluctuation in the darkness that would signal her time to act.

If Tempus was indeed no more…?

But she clung on, wide awake with her eyes closed, while others slept with their eyes open.

After one Tide, she returned to the Archives, to sift through once more the sands of her last remembered life.

It had begun as one of four children. Two girls and one boy. One of her sisters had been Akila's mother from generations before -she had sensed it immediately. Another, her grandmother from that time. Her brother in this life had perished in the first year of a terrible war. Back then, he had been Akila's father.

And yet, the benefit of these hindsights could not make any possible difference to her feelings now. Love was simply love: paternal, sororal, fraternal, maternal all washed and rinsed through generations of emotions.

Like Akila, and as with all her incarnations, male and female, the field nurse Anne King had not married. Helen had long stopped feeling remorseful about this. It transpired that hers was a personality and temperament at ease in its own skin, independent and self-contained. In need of no long-lasting commitment. The masculine and feminine versions of her soul had accepted this as truth.

She had passed quite a few lifetimes as a priestess, nun, acolyte and monk and an equal amount as a philosopher, alchemist, astrologer and witch. As she got closer to the centre of the Circles, she had been a scientist more often than not. A civil engineer. And finally, a nurse.

The brutality of the war and her role in it had been the defining period of the life of Anne King. Its cruelty and injustice, however, had later served to break her spirit. She had died before the age of forty, at the end of the same needle she had so often given to others.

Anne's anger had not been at the enemy. The fallen in conflict were just simple, working-class recruits, after all. Victims of the same absurd propaganda that had been no different to the fabricated lies proclaimed to the soldiers of the enemy. No, her fury had been targeted at the politicians, the media moguls and, most significantly, at the military elite who had gambled with the lives of millions.

And, in particular, Field Marshall Rupert Mayer who she now recognised as the pastor.

Replete with full moustache and ruddy, high cheekbones, steel-rimmed eyes pierced the hearts of the citizens below as Mayer's warmongering index finger accused the masses from the scaffold of a thirty-foot poster. This was the first time the Helen that watched on in the Archives had ever witnessed close up the soul that was her father. In every other lifetime his existence had been a mere presentiment, a feeling of presence weighing down on her, regardless of geographical location.

Previously, if their paths had ever crossed, his was always a back that had just turned to leave a room, a broad hat casting a shadow over darkened features, a smudge of face in the distance. Akila, Anne and so on had never met *him* (he was always male), but now here he was, plastered on every wall in the nation, cajoling the population to arms in an indefensible, indescribable war.

The round lens of his glasses magnified his stare, unnaturally blue eyes that followed you as you walked by. Intrusive and pervasive, cold and forensic, they glared from sockets as impenetrable as the bottom of dry wells.

Mayer's lips sneered, as if already finding your fear objectionable, his finger like a barrel of a gun aimed at the coward before a firing squad. Unlike his face, his hair was soft and fashionably groomed, parted in the middle and finishing at the ears.

Helen spent a lot of time alongside Anne, invisible to her, pausing the playback of that life sometimes to examine both Mayer and the impact he had on her former self. Anne, like most of the nurses, preferred a coil of black hair, tied up and pinned away from blood spattered hands and arms. She had small, inquisitive eyes, a charming nose, but an ugly mouth. Especially distasteful on the rare occasions her alter ego laughed. Perhaps, that was the reason she rarely did. At this period in her life, Miss King was in her early twenties, but already the bloodshed had already begun to take its toll. She was a compilation in human form of the dust she would soon become. Solidified and yet to be cast to the four winds. And something else. She was terrified of Mayer.

But unlike Helen, Anne did not know why.

And then, from the West, the signal Helen had been waiting for.

The Acolyte of Ceres, fourth of five, brought word officially from the Master Acolyte. His arrival in the Village had had the same effect as before -a mixture of awe and fear: the emotional aftermath of the visit extracting the villagers briefly from the monochrome of their existences, an interim of shocking vibrancy, the shades of which they would discuss for several Tides.

Helen was invited to join him on his carriage, the hooves of the desert-walkers ahead knowingly finding a path she had not known a few miles south of Ceres. They navigated their way between a grove of mangled trees, each one of which bore the husks of some dried fruit that she did not recognise. Afterwards, the trail widened to a new horizon, where other desert-walkers seemed to roam free, whole herds of them lazily grazing upon a plantation of grey stalks that grew to match their height. They seemed to nod at us as we passed, our vehicle progressing through their midst like a scythe through a harvest.

'What are they eating?' Helen asked.

'Mycelium. It is contained within the kernel of the plant,' the Acolyte replied, indifferently, the folds of his purple cassock gathered around his knees. He adjusted them self-consciously. Even though he didn't need to, he chose still to wear the sun shades that Helen had long since discarded.

'That is their food source?'

'Theirs and ours.'

'We drink amrita,' Helen replied, surprised.

The Acolyte turned to one of his two

attendants, cowled in red in the seat behind. Helen sensed his disapproval.

'It is all the same,' he answered, finally. 'Surely, you know that?'

Helen thought how best to reply. Any indication that she believed that both she, the Acolyte, his attendants, the desert-walkers and the skies above her head might all just be a figment of her or someone else's imagination would be noticed and vetted. Conclusions would be drawn. Were the Acolytes and their Master aware that they too were not real? Perhaps that was why the desert-walkers imbibed the same nutrients as the villagers at source. There was, in fact, just one source.

'How far is it to the Temple?' she asked instead.

The Acolyte appeared to trace the angle of the suns overhead and cross reference the result with the bored profiles of the desert-walkers to his right.

'Not far.' He took a sip of amrita from his flask and offered her some. Helen shook her head. She closed her eyes instead -not to rest -between Tides there was no need to rest. She closed them, she knew, in imitation of Anne and Akila and all the others, the way they did when she had noticed them in prayer to their God or gods. In moments of strength or weakness. She couldn't tell the difference.

When she opened them again, they had arrived at gates of the Temple.

'Welcome to the Temple of Medulla,' the Acolyte said. 'Here, take this,' he added passing her a veil. 'To conceal your face. The Master Acolyte will prepare you the rest of the way.'

'Prepare me?'

'Yes, Apprentice,' came a voice from behind, pitched between two tall, marble columns, themselves perched at the top of a high bank of steps. 'Thank you, Acolyte of Ceres. You and your custodians may return to your own quarters within the sacred grounds.'

'Yes, Master,' the Acolyte replied. 'His Holy Name.'

'His Holy Name.'

From behind the pillars, two figures in white suddenly emerged and skipped down the steps that led to the main gates of the Temple. They looked identical: bald, of indeterminate gender, garbed in tunics, with kohl in spirals upon their cheeks. In the centre of their foreheads shone a golden orb, its rays as sunny as their smiles. It was this that confused Helen the most. She had never before seen such a wanton display of bliss outside of the Archives. They were each carrying one end of a wooden mounting block which they nestled alongside the door of the carriage. She looked up at the Master Acolyte who raised his right palm slightly -an indication for her to alight.

'Do not worry about the twins,' he said. 'They mean you no harm.'

Helen had not thought they would, but the Master Acolyte had been subtle enough to introduce the potentiality of danger, a lurking menace that filled the air between them. She had never met him but something about his voice was familiar. According to the Master Apprentice, he had been present at the East Tower, a witness to Tempus' death. He was tall and thin and had had painted a thick line of charcoal over his eyes, the bridge of his nose and no doubt around the back of his head. A purple hood hid most of his scrubbed hair, part of a thin robe that ran all the way to his feet.

'Their names are Isis and Osiris,' the Master Acolyte continued. At the sound of their names, each twin extended a hand towards Helen, beckoning her from her seat. She duly stood up and allowed each twin to support her from the carriage. As soon as she had done so the desert-walkers veered and began to slowly trot off, the head of the Acolyte from Ceres within bowing his head in farewell. 'Have you heard of them?'

'Who?' Helen replied,

'Isis and Osiris.'

'Of course, ancient gods from the Archives. Akila…'. She stopped, wary of giving too much of herself away.

'Akila?' the Master Acolyte enquired.

'She was one of my previous *hosts*.'

'Ah, of course.' A short silence ensued, during which the twins advanced to the Master Acolyte, proffering their arms as a set of handrails on either side. The steps upwards were steep and perhaps they thought their patron would require assistance. A strange idea since everyone on the Island was of similar age and physical attribute. 'Now, come, Apprentice,' he cajoled, finally. 'The Advocate has been looking forward to meeting you.'

'The Advocate!' she stammered.

'His Holy Name!' the Master Acolyte corrected.

'This place. I think I know it,' she found herself saying a moment later 'From *that* time.'

'*That* time is *this* time,' he replied.

The Temple of Medulla was dominated by five central pyramids, as tall as the ones Akila had once seen on a family pilgrimage to Gizah. They were glass-panelled and capped with crystal. The reflection of the suns blinded her momentarily.

'Here, take my shades. I am used to the energy distribution.'

'Distribution?'

'Yes, the Pyramids fuel the five Villages and the Archives.'

Helen had not seen much evidence of this energy in the pre-industrial world of Ceres but said nothing, preferring instead to listen to the languid tones of the Master Acolyte as he droned on. The pyramids, he informed her, relayed power to their respective Village via underground lines. They formed an equidistant perimeter around a gigantic obelisk at the top of which was the head of a large bird. It had two beaks that faced in opposite directions, east and west. Helen adjusted her line of sight so that she could see its faces. It looked exactly like the face of the mara that had attacked the Master Apprentice and her outside the Archives.

'What bird is that?'

'An ibis,' he replied.

'It is facing both sides of the Island.'

'Yes, it is. That and much more.'

'What do you mean?'

The Master Acolyte looked away and walked across instead to the foot of the monolith appreciating the cool darkness that resulted from one of the two shadows at its base. One was directed to the East Tower and the other to the Inner Temple, the enormous domed basilica which was the private residence of the Advocate.

'Tell me, what does this remind you of?

'A clock without a face. A face without a clock.'

'Excuse me?'

'A clock without a face. A face without a clock. I've heard that before,' she added. 'Somewhere.'

'Did you?' He gave Helen a penetrating look, as if trying to measure her tone.

'Yes.'

'You must have dreamt it then. It's an expression not known beyond the walls of the Temple.'

'Is that where the Advocate resides?' she asked,

pointing in the direction of one of the shadows.

'Resides? Yes. You could say he *resides* there. But His Holy Name is everywhere. You do know that, don't you?'

'Of course,' she replied, feigning an expression of reverential awe.

'God has come down from the mountain,' the Master Acolyte stated calmly. 'Now, he has joined us in the garden. You understand the metaphor?'

'I remember it.'

'Good. Now look again.'

Helen turned to the dome once more. But it was no longer there. In its stead, a walled garden lined with slender trees had taken its place and in the background, miles in the distance, the golden silhouette of a mountain, topped by a plateau, upon which the towers of a glass city shimmered, contemplating the valley beneath.

'How...?' she said, loss for words.

'The Advocate has no one location,' he interrupted. 'The act of observation, however, can make Him materialise according to the thought patterns of the observer. The observer, in this case, is you. You expected a magisterial, opulent setting, like those enjoyed by the pontiffs of your previous life experiences. And then, I gave you another thought.'

'Are we in the Archives?'

'No, Ceres. *You* are doing this. But only because the Advocate wills it.'

'I don't understand.'

‘Consider the old religions. No amount of prayer or meditation could make their God manifest unless He willed it.’

Helen thought back to what Tempus had said. Her father, Henry Mayer, was the creator of this world. ‘Are you saying the Advocate created this world. The Great Unseen…’

‘The Advocate *is* the Great Unseen. Only the Acolytes are aware of this truth. But His Holy Name can be seen. He can take on form, just like he can create the extension of that form and place Himself in a mountain or the garden. Or a church. Indivisible from it in essence.’

‘But why are you telling me this?’

‘You know why, Ceres. Or would you prefer it if I call you Helen Mayer?’

19

'I'll kill you!' McKenna cried out, reaching for his pistol.

I watched in slow motion as the back of Avenell's head exploded against the wall behind. Yates, who was still holding Rachel's bag, had even less time to react. She took two bullets in the chest, the second of which propelled her body sideways, the contents of the backpack -an assortment of documents and dossiers -spewing outwards, fluttering like confetti, an endless, slow choreography of paper in the air, before finally coming to rest on the floor. She ended up, slouched in the corner of the room by a filing cabinet, her head resting against its side as if asleep.

'Ah ah!' Winston warned, his gun already primed on McKenna. In the time it had taken the latter to manoeuvre his legs off the table, and then launch himself forward to reach for his weapon, it was already too late. He had managed to grasp it, but not redirect it at his quarry.

'McKenna! No!' I shouted.

'That's right, Mr McKenna. Listen to the doctor. Or maybe, don't listen. It doesn't matter to me either way.'

McKenna's eyes were wet with perspiration or tears. Winston's face stared back coldly, a merciless indifference to what was going to happen next. He appeared to have no interest in either myself, Rachel or Knight. We were like an audience at the theatre, caught up in the moment, unaware of ourselves and transfixed by the action taking place on stage.

'You!' I exclaimed. 'You were Mayer's inside man!'

Winston ignored me, his attention firmly fixed on McKenna's right hand. 'What is it to be, Mr McKenna?'

'Fuck you!'

Winston bristled. 'Let go of the gun!' You have three seconds!'

'You watch too many movies, Winnie!'

'McKenna, just do what he says!' This time from Rachel.

A grin on McKenna's face. I knew what he was thinking. Just stay alive. The tables may turn back any moment. You never know. Besides, how else would he ever get revenge for Henney? He splayed his fingers suddenly, his hand webbed innocently a few inches above the butt of the gun.

'Now, just sit back, Mr McKenna, And relax. I never like killing in cold blood.'

Five minutes later McKenna was gagged, his hands and legs bound, the tension of Rachel's knots verified by Winston who positioned himself in a large chair at the head of the table. His gun changed tact, more interested now in Knight and me. The former was made to gather up the loose papers that had been spurned from Rachel's pack while Winston sifted through his own bag. It was Knight who had obviously been placed on laundry duty -both his and Rachel's together in a spin cycle of old and fresh clothes. They had obviously needed to travel light.

We then watched Winston pore over the details of Rachel's pages, his eyes narrowing over each word.

'What are those?' I asked Rachel.

She didn't answer. Neither did Winston. Soon he had finished, the sheets shuffled neatly and folded. He thrust them into his jacket pocket which he buttoned with his free hand.

An uneasy interim of silence followed, or perhaps it wasn't an interim. Maybe, Winston would kill us before we would ever have the chance to speak again.

'So, what exactly is going on?' I asked. Winston's face for the first time took on an expression of genuine surprise.

'You don't know?'

'Enlighten me.'

'Ms Hunter here was as good as her name suggests. She *hunted* me down.'

I turned to Rachel. 'That's what you were going to tell me at dinner that night? Winston was working for Mayer.'

'That and a lot more besides,' she replied.

'Like what?'

'We'll come to that doctor,' Winston interrupted, patting the front of his jacket. He glanced at his watch. 'We have enough time. Besides, it really doesn't matter now,' he added. I looked at Winston's gun and then quickly at the helpless McKenna. He was struggling hard against his binds with his last reserves of strength as though suddenly aware of the fate that awaited him. I turned back to Winston who was shaking his head slightly in amusement. 'Oh no, Doctor Bishop, I don't mean *that*. At least not for you.'

'If you're not going to kill me,' I exclaimed, 'then what the hell do you want from me?!'

'Your mind, doctor,' Winston replied, slowly. 'Mayer wants your mind. Or what's left of it,' he added smugly.

'I will never work for that mad man!'

'Not *consciously*, no,' Winston intoned, sharing a look with Rachel. He leaned back into his chair and tipped his head back momentarily in thought. 'But we are getting ahead of ourselves, aren't we, Doctor Hunter?'

Rachel looked down, her scholarly glasses concealing her reaction to Winston's words. I glanced at Knight. He seemed to be in the dark as much as me. For the first time, I felt a tinge of sympathy for him.

'So, to the night of Dr Hunter's and Dr Knight's departure,' Winston continued, beginning to enjoy himself, the way one did when unburdening oneself of a heavy load at the top of a mountain and about to appreciate the view. 'I realised that I had reached my end game.'

'How?' I asked.

'By design,' he replied.

Rachel looked up quickly, her eyes wide. 'What do you mean? By design?' she asked.

Winston smiled. 'I have worked in covert operations all over the world. Do you really think I would allow myself to be so obviously discovered by a *civilian*?' He held the last word like a bad musical note, a bitter aftertaste that rankled at the back of one's mouth.

'How?'

'Geography, Dr Hunter.'

'What do you mean?' Knight piped up, for the first time.

Winston ignored Knight, a bit player now in an altogether more complex game.

'I wanted you to hunt your prey but not serve it up.'

'You needed her off-base?' I said, the permutations suddenly unravelling in my head. 'For something she would do when she got out. Or something she would uncover. That dossier in your pocket, for example.'

'Precisely,' Winston chuckled. 'Precisely. Such a fine mind he has. Wouldn't you say, Dr Hunter?'

'You mentioned 'geography'. What do you mean?' I asked, saving Rachel the trouble of a reply.

'Consider, Dr Bishop, Brownlow's base. The different levels. Someone... the spy obviously, but not Dr Knight there...' he threw Knight another dismissive look, '...far too self-indulgent for the role. Though he was useful for a while. Not you, either, Dr Bishop. Far too honourable, though a worthy distraction for Brownlow. Not Mr Henney or Mr McKenna. Too...' he glanced across at McKenna, his torso expanding and contracting against the rope used to fasten him, his face apoplectic with rage, '...well, you can see for yourself. At any rate, *someone* releases a new variant of the virus. People start showing symptoms here and there, but not everywhere. Mr Brownlow, of course, succumbs but not our spy who strategically never seems to be at, or near, the location of each outbreak, which is unusual as his duties normally warrant his presence in at least some of them. Brownlow then hushes the whole business up to avoid mass panic. I imagine *that*, Dr Bishop, was some of what Dr Hunter wanted to share with you over soju.'

I threw Rachel a consolatory look. She was being humiliated and Winston was loving every second of it. It was all I could do to stop myself from wrapping my arms around her, giving her an alcove of shoulder in which to hide away forever.

'He starts protecting himself well before, of course,' Winston was explaining, 'and makes sure he is spotted doing so.'

'When you came with Henney to my apartment…' Rachel began to say, '…you were wearing a mask.'

Winston sniggered. 'Useless I know. Another placebo amidst all the others. A hopeless fashion statement worn by millions, but enough for you to pick up a thread. Or begin to sew one. Anyway, by the process of elimination, it could only have been me who had had the means to get his hands on the new variant. I spend more time above ground than under it. That was what I was banking on. Later, all I had to do was keep a careful eye on the good doctor.'

'So, the papers? What are they?' I asked, frustrated, and wanting to put a stop to his whining, self-congratulatory voice.

'Localis.'

'Localis?!' I exclaimed. 'I thought sherbet…?'

'…Mr Mayer's trojan horse. Mr Brownlow had his own with the Huntington research, after all,' he added, looking at Knight. 'You see, doctor, he knew all about Mr Levy. Knowing the existence of a spy in your organisation is just as good as having one in someone else's. But it's more than that. The truth is Levy has been playing the role of spy for years. We turned him years ago.' A heavy blanket of silence descended while we processed the implications of this. 'Besides,' Winston continued, with relish, 'Mr Mayer is not interested in your type of cure. Not when he already has one of his own.' The effect of these last words could be read in everyone's face. The silence continued until Winston, bored, decided to break it himself. 'Mr Levy himself mentioned the lack of virologists at NeuralNet. Software engineers, on the other hand...'

'...So, sherbet was the trail Rachel would pick up,' I replied, my head still spinning, 'because she knew it was where *our* thinking would lead us.'

'With a little persuasion from me, of course. But yes. I listened in to your plans for dinner and realised it was time to act. The benefit of Mr Brownlow's paranoid security protocols. Dr Hunter made off as soon as she saw me. I could hardly blame her.' He glanced down at his gun, appraising it anew. 'Guns tend to have that effect on people. You see I needed to get her off the base to track down Localis. I also wasn't too keen on her unveiling me to all the monkeys at Mr Brownlow's zoo.'

'What about me?' Knight asked.

'You?' Winston sneered. 'You are the hapless fool who just so happened to be with Dr Hunter at the time. Following her round all the time like a lap dog. But that fitted in perfectly too. You took the blame for her supposed abduction. You, Dr Bishop, were only too ready to believe *that* eventuality.' I looked down, ashamed of how easily I had been manipulated. Winston had made all the right moves and predicted every one of his opponent's.

'How did you know I would come here?' Rachel's turn to spare my blushes.

'Because of him, of course,' Winston replied, pointing at me. 'And the drug which Mr Mayer offered as bait. It works by the way. It'll not save the world, but it will buy it some time.'

'Why would Mayer give Brownlow the means to do that?'

'Because, Dr Hunter, Mr Mayer is not interested in *this* world,' Winston replied.

'I don't understand,' I replied.

'No? But you will. My employer, I am sure, will explain it all to you both in person.'

'Mayer is at the Abbey?'

'He never left.'

'But Localis is a simple tracking system,' I protested, 'providing early diagnosis of the virus.'

'It started like that, perhaps. But Dr Hunter developed it into something much more.'

'Rachel?' I stammered. '*You* developed Localis.'

'Patrick,' she began, tears in her eyes, 'it was before the pandemic. After university, I needed funding...it was before we met.'

'You...you...worked for Mayer?' I felt myself turn cold again, my mouth filling with metal. There was a coin sitting on my tongue, payment for every betrayal and rejection I had ever had.

'You remember that meeting, Dr Bishop,' Winston interrupted. 'It was at an AI conference, wasn't it? A symposium bought and paid for by Mr Henry Mayer.'

'Brownlow?'

'He never knew about my employer's interest in AI. He wouldn't have employed Dr Hunter if he had.'

'How long?' I asked Rachel, as though the room had darkened around us and we were sharing the moment alone, over candlelight and too much wine. I felt punch-drunk and only the ropes were holding me up, the same ropes that had immobilised McKenna. Even he seemed to have given up the fight, if not yet the ghost. He was sitting calmly, his forehead slick with sweat, his eyes fixed on Winston.

'Three years. I left before the Forgetting really took hold. Seems we both sold our souls to the devil.'

I sighed. She was reminding me delicately of my own indiscretion. Which was only fair. I couldn't really hold Rachel to account, but it is human nature to expect more of others than to do of yourself. One of the downsides of being in love. You place that love on an impossibly high pedestal and insist, unreasonably, it can survive the lows that life puts in your way.

'Devil?' Winston was saying. 'No, not the Devil. The opposite, in fact.'

'What is he talking about Rachel? What

exactly did Localis become?'

Rachel was about to reply but thought better of it. Something in her expression was trying to communicate an alternative message, a wavelength hidden beneath the one being broadcast. I sensed that whatever she wanted me to decipher was happening directly behind me. She had to be careful as Winston was watching us both intently and so I too had to play along. The image of the strangely subdued McKenna flooded my brain. He had been staring at Winston, but perhaps too attentively -as if he were trying not to stare somewhere else. It all seemed part of the same body language and I was being invited to translate. I tried to remember the layout of the room. Rachel and McKenna were both facing the door while Winston, in his desire to play the role of king on his throne, had positioned himself with his back to whatever else might be happening.

A millisecond later, I noticed Rachel adjust her face slightly, as if terminating the transmission of whatever it was she was trying to say.

'Come on,' I began, a carefully judged note of irritation in my voice, 'surely it doesn't make much difference now. Tell me, what *is* Localis?'

Her mouth opened but once more she paused. A drawbridge had been lowered from her high castle of secrets but had halted half way across the moat.

'It began,' she announced finally, 'as you say,

as simple tracking software. I developed the schematics early on. I wasn't aware of the work you and the others were doing at NeuralNet. Mayer must have spotted something in my work and developed your team around it. I only discovered the truth from you…that the knowledge of what Localis had become had led to the murders of Wilson, Armstrong and the others.'

'What had it become?'

'I couldn't be sure. Who knows how someone as twisted as Mayer could manipulate my research. That was why I needed to track down my notes. To find out for sure.'

'Where did you hide them?'

'With Imogen.'

'Imogen!' I exclaimed, shocked.

'Yes, I visited her once.'

'But why would you do that?'

'Once I knew Brownlow was bringing you on board because of your work at NeuralNet I knew something about my time with Mayer might surface. I remember you telling me about your sister. So, when Brownlow asked me to visit her…' I nodded. '…Your back story was being checked out, Patrick', she added, hastily, 'I took the opportunity to stash the blueprints there.'

'Blueprints?'

'Yes.'

'Blueprints for what?'

'A machine. Instead of the tracker being placed

into the body, the body was to be inserted into the tracker. It mapped the brain…'

'The brain is the map,' Winston interrupted, a note of solemnity like a far-off bell.

'But if you have this machine, then why do you need the blueprints?'

'There's only room for one God in Mayer's universe,' Rachel replied.

Winston smiled.

'What does that mean?' I asked.

Before either had a chance to explain, the shift in the atmosphere of the room which I had felt a moment before returned. I could see it in Rachel's widening eyes. A few butterflies flapped their wings in my throat, and then a tingling at the back of my neck. My instinct was to bale to the floor but how foolish would that have been if my primordial instincts had become too hyper-evolved, causing me to find danger everywhere and in everything. Time seemed to stand still. Winston's face seemed lost in thought, his pistol looser in his hand.

He might just have been about to explain what he meant by the brain being a map, but he never got the chance.

Henney, his shirt matted in blood, his face ashen pale, had somehow managed to stagger from the roof and was propping himself against the frame of the door. In his hand a gun trembled. In the time it took Winston to guess that something was awry and pivot around to the danger, Henney had somehow managed to get off one shot before his weapon dropped to the floor with a thud.

His aim had been true enough because Winston reacted, a wild, otherworldly scream before launching himself at Henney. His wound wasn't fatal, but it had been enough to disarm him, his own pistol careering across the waxed floor like a puck on ice. He dealt Henney a fierce blow to the side of the head, knocking the huge man sideways, before making his escape from the room.

20

She did not have enough of a tongue to sense the absence of one. In its place, a tadpole of flesh seeking a harbour among gritted teeth. In the beginning it had hardly mattered. Then, Tempus had kept her distance from the lost souls with whom she shared her domain, who meandered a mindless, insectoid course through the featureless tundra of BridgeWest.

Later, it was the very absence of speech that had made communication with them possible.

The West Tower, she discovered, was strongly fortified. Hundreds of terrified inhabitants, rags and bloodied flesh coalesced onto forked limbs, gravitated to its locked gates, sacrificing themselves at the bottom of the monolith, their insides ripped apart by the mara that waited for them there.

It was the Tower, along with its sister in the East, which somehow had to be destroyed.

It was of equal height, she assumed, to its partner on the other side of the Sorrow, though instead of brick, it gleamed like glass, a smooth patina of hard grey down which the long rain ran. Rivulets like tears, widening as they merged with others, fat streams slaloming to the sod of earth below. The gates themselves were distinguished only by the faintest of grooves, a fingertip beneath the surface, which traced an entrance perimeter to doors which no one had ever known to open. And yet, they had to have opened sometimes, for how else did BridgeWest ever populate with new souls, those to replace the mass suicide cults that either smashed their skulls against the walls of the Tower, or launched themselves, hand in hand, over the crag of cliff into the river below? Bones caked the base of the monolith all around, climbing a hundred feet into the air, a cracked veneer which some attempted to climb before hurtling to a different death.

The mara feasted on their prey with relish, at times carrying them away to eyries beyond the clouds. But mostly, they dined at the foot of the Tower, with slow claws, preferring to avoid the essential organs at first, keeping their victims alive for as long as possible. They never fought with one another for souls. Each soul had its own mara and a mara, ideally for its victim, could wait forever before cornering its prey. But who could survive BridgeWest for that long?

No one in the West really knew how their kingdom of the damned really operated. Or why. They were simply hunted and devoured, punished for crimes that they could not remember while across the river a seismic wave of frozen light marked the boundary of BridgeEast where others like themselves, it was rumoured, lived out whole aeons of total, unimaginable bliss.

Worse than this, more unimaginable to comprehend, was the knot in their brains which, if unravelled, might culminate in a belief which they simply could not afford to have under any circumstances -the lingering doubt that death was not the end and that they simply returned over and over again to the same hell, each time with their memories erased.

Was that why some of them appeared to identify more with one than the other, gathering in small collectives, protective of their mutual welfare? Had these clans met before, with different faces, and endured similar suffering? Was that also why their side of the Island never seemed to increase in population? No one had ever taken a census, but the numbers of the lost never seemed to change.

Nothing grew so farming too was out of the question. Neither could shelter be furnished from the meagre supply of lumber available in the form of trees. The standing stones on the Island were too cumbersome to lift which left only the coastal caves and the natural craters over which awnings of cloth, stolen from the dead, were draped to keep out the incessant wind and rain.

Tempus had found a cleft in a solitary rock

large enough for her to sleep lying down on her side. Like every newcomer, it took a while for her eyes to adjust to the darkness, and so for a long period after her arrival she had remained huddled and afraid, monitoring the shades in the blackness until such a time that darkness eventually began to seem to her like light. Some souls, more ancient than others, had evolved knitted skin where eyes had once been. Meanwhile above, two moons, half the size of the one she remembered from before, barely impacted on the blackness all around, one high and one low, in perfect imitation of the suns in BridgeEast.

BridgeEast. How long had it been? Months? Years? A century? It had been so long since she had thought in those terms. Without a ruler it was difficult to measure anything. Without scale, nothing had any weight. And what of Helen? She tried hard to hold onto the face of her friend and wondered whether she had made any progress on her own mission.

In the distance, across the great river, the East Tower still stood, defiant and imperious.

But she could not think of that. She had to place BridgeEast, and everything associated with it to the side; its Archives and feudal system of control, its Church without churches, its dazed populace of ant-workers, overlorded by a cult leader who had chosen the name 'Advocate'.

It was the dolmen, perched on a hilltop overlooking the valley and the Tower, which had first given her the idea. She had used it initially as shelter, but then as a vantage point, keeping an eye on the insanity below.

She had noticed the strange marking in the rock straight away. Her curiosity aroused, she had placed the flatness of her hand in the impression, feeling it fill the space like a glove. Someone, or more likely there had been many taking turns, had placed their hand on the same place in the stone. Each imprint working its heat into the rock gradually over time.

But how had this happened? And what did it prove? Merely, that chemistry and physics did not make sense in this place.

Perhaps it was the feeling of communal anguish the mysterious hand seemed to exude that had drawn her back to the dolmen, its salute of hope across the generations. The same hope that had laboured in the hearts of those who had taken the time to construct the dolmen. It had made the impossible possible as had the reaction of the mara to the dolmen.

Tempus, like everyone else, had used the standing stones throughout the Island to hide from her tormentor, but she had also noticed how the stones had also repelled it. It, and other mara, seemed to recoil if their talons got too close. This was obviously the reason why some of the newer Islanders had used some of the rubble lying around, and wrapping it in slingshots, flung them at their winged predators, keeping them at bay at least until their quarried supply ran out.

Tempus had made note of this and then remembered something else.

In the Archives, one of Helen's incarnations, the servant girl Akila, had worshipped a god called Nekhbet. The statue of a stone vulture had stood in the midst of a temple, surrounded by a circular colonnade. She had often wondered how the natives had managed to place the twenty-foot bird on its plinth. It must have weighed about a tonne and so she had asked Helen to go back to the point in Akila's past when the statue had first been erected.

The builders of the colonnade had measured out its diameter by using a length of vine stretched out from the exact centre of a circle. Other measurements then had been calculated to ensure each of the colonnade's high pillars were equidistant from each other. Large bricks of quartz were laid to mark the exact place they were to be placed. Then the pillars were rolled close to the construction site using a system of pulleys and rollers after which the quartz blocks were replaced by heavy, waist-high slabs made out of the same crystalline stone. All the while a sculptor was hard at work on the stone vulture that would occupy a plinth at its centre.

Following this, a long ceremony took place which lasted several days. This involved a large litany of high priests from the local region and other celebrants participating in a ritual, during which, Tempus assumed, the whole area was sanctified in some way. Fires were lit, animal sacrifices made, drums beat, mushrooms ingested and lurid, contorted dances choreographed.

Then something truly remarkable happened.

A strand of energy, clearly visible to all present, appeared through a gap in the stones.

What happened next had appeared to Tempus as truly wondrous. One of her own previous lives in the Archives had been spent as a worshipper of a sun god called Lugh. It had been millennia before her final life, but the woman, whose name had been Aoife, had been an important druid in a clan made up in part by members of her own soul group. As Aoife, she had helped to construct stone circles and dolmens just like Akila's. Although she knew that Lugh rarely visited her land, as his power and influence was stronger in lands further to the south, she had witnessed, on one occasion, a light channelled from beneath the stones that had made them levitate. In this state of grace, they became as light as a crow's feather, and could be easily manipulated into different positions as ordained by the leader of her clan. She had even witnessed some of her own druidic school walk through these stones to different worlds never to return.

As Aoife, and then Tempus, none of this had made any sense. A magical demonstration of the power of one god, later reenforced by similar miracles witnessed in other lifetimes by other gods. After experiencing the centre of the Circles, however, she had understood, at least partially, the science behind some of the things she had seen.

The energy source Akila and Aoife had both experienced, but never understood, had been attracted to an arrangement of particular types of stones in the form of a circle. It was a magnetic force that entered through a gap in the circle and then spiralled towards its centre as though descending down a rabbit hole. The stones, meanwhile, pulsated with concentric rings of alternating current resembling ripples in a pond. The energy was channelled onto the stone bird, rendering it as light as one of its feathers if it had been real.

If Tempus could align the stones of BridgeWest in a similar circle and then create of them a path to the West Tower, would she be able to channel a destructive force towards it? Would she be able to destroy the antenna which she had become convinced was one of the two transmitters receiving signals from the real world? Transmitters which were being used by Henry Mayer to broadcast a holographic reality from there to an imaginary island conceived by his own consciousness.

She could be wrong, of course. The Towers might simply be that of a bridge that linked the two parts of the Island, but no one had ever seen the crossing point high up in this world's atmosphere. And no one had ever journeyed from one side of the bridge to the other, at least not to her knowledge. So why then was there a bridge at all?

Mayer, however, had to be using some scientific means to manufacture the illusion of the Island. Even if the Towers turned out to be symbolic reference points only, metaphors for the real science that lay secreted away in the shadows, what else could she and Helen do? The structures were deified, incongruous to their surroundings, and for that reason alone perhaps their destruction would mean something.

And so, she had begun the slow, arduous task of gathering rocks into small knee-high piles while her mara watched on, its expression snide but at the same time appreciative. Here was a prey who had worked out its weakness, its eyes seemed to suggest.

One stone, then another. The smaller ones at first as her arm was still causing her pain. After a while, at the sight of her lone silhouette on the mountain top above, some of the more curious Islanders scaled the incline to see what she was doing. She gesticulated as best as she could at the stones, carved out a circle in the air, then a line down the hill towards the Tower. She then drew their attention to the mara circling overhead. It had stopped its offensive assaults, she tried to explain, because of the minerals in the stones that were somehow acting as a barrier to it.

Most of the new arrivals dismissed her with a wave of their hand, or a cackle of contempt, before returning to their endless sojourn by the Tower. A few remained, however, and immediately began to help. In time, others joined in and soon a small army of workers were busy using up all the rubble around and organising it into small mounds while others ventured further field for more.

Before long, a hundred or so inhabitants had broken through the security blanket of their own tribes and were now actively cooperating with those with whom before they had never even spoken. A chain of volunteers working in tandem down the slope towards the Tower.

The skies soon became laden with mara, angrily swooping and diving at their formerly cowered preys. Some ran, scurrying towards the Tower and headlong into the chasm beyond. But most remained, maintaining the assembly line of workers, and so the creatures changed tact, flying low to sweep over the columns of stones, toppling them with the vibration of their wings. But each time the stones fell they were rebuilt until such a point that even the mara gave up. They ascended to the heavens, a darker patch in an already dark sky, hundreds of them in conference, discussing their next move.

Finally, the circle and the path were complete. And yet for the first time since the beginning of the project Tempus felt real fear once more. What if it didn't work? It was pseudo-science, after all. And how would her followers react to their new, silent leader? Would they suddenly turn on her, blaming her for sadistically allowing a ray of hope to touch the despair that suffocated their hearts.

The odds, she knew, were not in their favour. There was no sun in the sky from which to draw the necessary energy. Just two pale discs of moon, two wafers of unlikely eucharist that would never be enough to kindle more than a spark of the fire that was actually required. And even if the West Tower actually fell, what impact would it have on the Island? Would Mayer simply rearrange the photons and have it miraculously re-emerge? Would he merely reset the simulation or move it onto another level?

But if it did form part of the Bridge, surely it would raze the entire structure to the ground, potentially taking with it its partner in the East? That would surely help Helen on the other side.

There were so many variables, and she no longer had a computer or team of fellow scientists upon which to rely. But she *had* been a scientist. If she was now some kind of semi-conscious avatar, had she really managed to tap back into the source of who she really was, enough for her to gain access to that obscure knowledge that was the provenance of so few? She remembered equations, formulae, flickering cursors and numerical columns of data. She recalled test-tubes, microscopic slides and the secret underworld of bacteria, the wriggling ink of minuscule life that even now scattered itself across the field of her vision when she closed her eyes to rest.

The sun, she remembered, was just one star in space and the moon was a lump of rock trapped in the orbit of the Earth. If this world was like her own, then the same ley lines of telluric current were running beneath her feet. She had read, that once activated, these currents gravitated back and forth from areas of equatorial light to regions of polar darkness. With the help of her crystal path, and the Tower itself, there was a chance that she could steer this energy in the same way atomic particle colliders premeditated the direction of airborne ions.

Tempus inhaled a deep draught of amrita and with two of the stones in her hands stepped across to the centre of the circle. She bade the assembly of about a hundred Islanders to form another a short distance from where she stood, outwards in a snakelike spiral, down the escarpment towards the Tower. Each Islander held in their hands their own stones which Tempus hoped would facilitate the energetic flow. Meanwhile at the foot of the Tower, those too cynical to have assisted in the experiment before, now stood to the side, each of them laying their hands on the surface of the megalith.

She wanted to say something, make some significant and uplifting address to the masses, but of course she couldn't. She felt the back of her throat gasp instead as she held up her stones with outstretched arms. The others followed suit, all the way to the Tower, a domino reaction to the person beside them.

Above their heads, a swarm of mara made a bee line to the megalith. Unable to nest there, claws slipping and sparking off the metal, they hovered a protective wall all around, no doubt to minimise, or block the scale of what was about to happen.

The wind, for once, quietened, and the black air settled. The scent of amrita was permitted to settle in the gaps between them all, filling their mouths and nostrils: familiar, though at the same time different.

Tempus, shoeless, felt something give beneath her feet. It tingled and warmed her soles and then became hotter, rising up her legs, torso, head and down her arms to the person beside her. She felt herself pulse, as though an old pain had resurfaced. But this was not pain. This was pain's opposite and for the first time since leaving the Archives she felt her body bathe in a soothing balm of joy.

She sensed this wave of happiness pass down the line. Perhaps it wasn't happiness. Perhaps it was merely the absence of misery but its effects travelled through the spiral, creating an intense ground swell of emotion; great sighs of audible delight, unnatural smiles cracking the porcelain of faces.

And then the joy turned to light.

And the light turned to fire.

21

For those of us without a military background, it had all happened too quickly. We were too civil to even think about scooping up the pistols on offer while McKenna, the only sharpshooter amongst us, struggled away in his electric chair.

Knight finally untied him and, with Winston's gun in hand, he hurtled out of the room before returning a couple of minutes later, dejection etched across his face.

He knelt down beside his fallen friend, but it was already too late for Henney.

'A car,' he seethed, looking up. 'Mayer must have had one close by. I heard its brakes.' He looked back at Henney's vacant death mask and very gently swept his fingers over his eyes. 'The chauffeur's turn to be chauffeured,' he added, the irony not lost on any of us. After a moment, he picked up Henney's discarded pistol, straightened to his feet, and pointed it at Rachel. 'Right, you bitch! Start talking or by all that is holy I'll put a bullet in the whole lot of you!'

'Is there anything to drink around here?' Rachel replied, coolly.

'Plenty of ethanol around, Rachel,' I added,

trying my best to defuse the tension. 'Though I would advise against it.'

We had coffee instead but first we got a sleeping bag and zipped Henney's body inside. While the kettle boiled, McKenna used the satellite phone and made a call to Brownlow. Someone other than Brownlow answered. McKenna pressed a button so we all could hear.

'Who's this?' McKenna barked.

'Atkins. New security chief. Who are you? How'd you get this number?'

'How'd you think, Atkins? First prize in the apocalyptic sweepstakes?'

'You must be either McKenna or Henney?' Atkins chuckled.

A brief pause. 'McKenna. Henney's dead. You think that's funny Atkins?'

'No, I just meant…'

'…Just get Brownlow, you bloody moron!'

'Brownlow's at Stage Three, McKenna. He doesn't know what year it is.'

McKenna whistled. 'Who's in control? Military?'

'Yeah. Arrived here two days ago. Fully suited up. Taking no chances. Some general and fifty or so others. Elite. General's name is Barrett.'

'Never heard of him.'

'He's a bloody psychopath. Issued a complete lockdown. Major decontamination.'

'How bad?'

'Top levels all infected. Each level below the

ones at the top less so. It's fast, McKenna. Faster than anything we've ever seen. Our man really did a number on us.'

'Get Barrett for me. Our *man* was Brownlow's driver. First name: Winston.'

'The driver? Holy shit! The old man never saw that one coming.' McKenna didn't answer. A short silence. 'Second name?' Atkins enquired, finally.

'What?'

'He have a family name, McKenna?'

'Probably, but I have no idea what it is.'

'I'll get Barrett to call you.'

'Just stick him on, Atkins!

'Can't do that, McKenna. Lockdown, remember?' McKenna took a breath and rolled his eyes. He hunched the phone between his chin and shoulder and managed to light himself a cigarette. He took a drag, closed his eyes and then opened them almost immediately. 'What level you on, Atkins?'

'Three from the top, McKenna.'

'You…?'

'*I'm* not going anywhere anytime soon, my friend.' Another silence filled the distance between them. When Atkins spoke next there were tears in his voice. 'David Atkins. Thirty-four. Married. To Janet. No kids, thank God. Address is 14 Peacock Gardens. I've been repeating this over and over again in my head, McKenna. Just to hold on, you know?' Something got caught in his throat. 'The address…if you get a chance?'

'Will do, Atkins,' McKenna replied, more softly. Atkins ended the call. McKenna turned to me and declared: 'Poor bastard!'

I nodded.

'How are *you* doing, Bishop?' he asked, with almost a hint of concern in his voice.

'Better. I think. Sherbet seems to holding things together.' It was his turn to nod. 'So, we wait to hear from this Barrett?' I asked, after a moment.

'Maybe…but in the meantime I want to know about this machine *you*…', he glared at Rachel, '…helped Mayer build.'

We managed to salvage a few out-of-date sandwiches from the fridge in the kitchen which with the coffee made for a melancholy supper around the same conference table as before. Knight tucked in with relish while Rachel sipped her drink, blowing into it occasionally due to the absence of milk.

All the time I knew she was buying for time, trying to arrange the words in her head before allowing them to escape her lips. Putting the notes of the melody in the right order. McKenna had taken a mouthful of his BLT and upon tasting had flung it against the window just over her head. A little act of intimidation. He knew very well that the truth was more often than unrehearsed, and he didn't to let Rachel off the hook too easily.

'So?' he snapped.

'Localis. What it was, we all know,' she began. 'What it became, I can only guess.'

'That's bullshit for a start!'

'How about you let her explain in her own way?' I suggested. I hoped my tone did not reveal too much of how much I shared his anger. Rachel, though, must have picked up on something sarcastic in my voice for she repeated: 'Yes, let me explain it *in my own way*!'

She gave up on her coffee, set it down and turned to McKenna. Her way perhaps of shutting me out. If she was to have it out with McKenna she wouldn't need my help.

'So?' McKenna said. 'I'm all ears.'

Rachel inhaled. 'I *now* believe that Patrick's team, Armstrong and the rest, were brought in to work on one project while being vetted individually as to their trustworthiness to work on another. That is, a covert side-line operation, with the working title 'Localis'. I have gone through my early research with Bill and can see how it could have been developed down another avenue.'

'What avenue?' McKenna said,

'Localis began as a software programme to map the brain. There was no reason why it couldn't also map other parts of the body.'

'Go on,' I encouraged, trying to involve myself.

She ignored me and continued. 'It's all in the

files. My original design.'

'Which Winston now has!' McKenna barked.

'You don't think I made copies?'

'Show me,' McKenna demanded.

She looked at Knight who had yet to join us at the table. He had the papers in his hand and with a nod from Rachel duly handed them over to McKenna.

'Even a professional won't delve too far into someone's three-day old underpants,' Knight said.

McKenna took the sheaf and started to flick through them, his face wincing the more he read. 'Lots of pretty diagrams. The equations, on the other hand...'

I offered McKenna my hand. He shrugged, passing me the documents. It was my turn to wade through the foolscap of rough notes. They were scrawled in black ink, with some parts underlined in red or circled with an exclamation mark for added emphasis. I could feel Rachel's eyes boring into me as I read and turned each page. After a few minutes of silence, during which everyone's coffee had gone cold and McKenna had smoked his way through half a cigarette, I lifted my head and turned to Rachel.

'You think Mayer actually created such a machine?'

'It would explain a lot. Maybe even the Forgetting.'

'What do you mean?'

'The destroyer and creator of worlds,' she replied.

'What the hell are you two talking about?' McKenna asked.

'We -that is, Rachel and I -have come to the conclusion that Mayer released the virus deliberately,' Knight announced.

'No way!' McKenna exclaimed. 'You sound like those bloody conspiracy nuts, Knight. You know the ones I mean. The ones banging on about how companies like NeuralNet are profiting from a pandemic that they themselves caused.'

'Well, don't they?' Knight challenged.

McKenna snarled at Knight and shook his head slowly. 'Not much profit to be made if everyone's dead.'

'Not everyone has to die,' I replied.

'What do you mean: 'not everyone has to die'? McKenna asked.

I thought back to my brief visit to NeuralNet and its ancient abbey; the shrouded silence of the place, a nightmare visited upon the waking world. Could it contain within its walls the technology required to achieve what Rachel, Knight and I thought it had? Like a cyborg cased within the hard shell of a decrepit, Victorian grandmother.

'I had been working on a different type of AI application,' Rachel began. 'It derived from earlier work completed on 3D mapping of the human brain. That then progressed to cover the entire human body. Essentially this provided us with the possibility of looking at disease without having to connect physically with the patient at all. You heard of cinematic rendering?'

'You trying to be funny?' McKenna scowled.

'No,' Rachel replied, puffing her cheeks. 'I'm not.' She bit her lip and tried again. 'Take your average CT scan.'

'Ok.'

'Now imagine a 3D CT or 3D MRI scan merged with computer-generated imaging technology. It allows you to see the *texture* of the anatomy. For example, render a person's skin more real. More porous.'

'Right,' McKenna. 'With you so far.'

'Now, let's think of what a hologram actually is. Back in the day, they were recorded optically. You split a laser beam with half the beam used to illuminate the subject and the other half used as a reference for the light wave's phase.'

'The what?'

She sighed. 'A photo encodes the brightness of a light wave but ultimately yields a flat image. A hologram encodes both the brightness and *phase* of each light wave giving a truer depiction of the object's parallax and depth. But the image of the object is static, incapable of capturing motion. I borrowed the concept of computer-generated imagery and merged it with the hologram to give it *life*. I did this by simulating the optical setup.'

'What do you mean? Life?' McKenna asked,

removing his cigarette from his lips. He held it up and scanned the room. 'Tell me I'm only smoking nicotine everybody!'

Giving up on McKenna, Rachel turned to me. 'But the process was computationally very onerous. Each point in any given scene has a different depth, so you can't apply the same operations for all of them. That increases the complexity significantly. Directing a clustered supercomputer to run these physics-based simulations takes seconds or minutes for a single holographic image. Plus, existing algorithms don't model occlusion with photorealistic precision. So, I took a different approach: letting the computer teach physics to itself.'

'Was that as far as you got?' I asked.

She avoided my eyes and focused on Knight instead. Her port in the storm. He knew the import of what she was about to say and was well beyond playing the part of judge and jury. Not that I wasn't either. I simply wanted to hear her say the words, trepanning them to the world beyond her own mind. The first step towards expiating her guilt. Guilt that she had never needed to feel.

'No,' she replied, lowering her head. 'Levy came to me with a directive from Mayer. He was fascinated by the implications of my research.'

'What happened next?'

'Money. Lots of it.'

'And?'

'He wanted me to build an actual neural network which would allow for real-time hologram generation. This would mimic how we, humans, process visual information. That required constructing a massive database of thousands of pairs of computer-generated images, each pair matching a picture to its corresponding hologram. By learning from each image pair, the network was able to tweak the parameters of its own calculations and enhance its ability to create its own holograms.' She paused and ran a nervous hand through her hair. She looked exhausted, shrunken. 'That's as far as I got,' she added.

'So, after you left, you think Mayer carried on with the programme?'

'Yes,' Knight responded, filling in for Rachel. I looked at him, impressed not by the man he had become but by the man he had always been, beyond his cheap bravado and the high walls of jealousy that I had maintained him behind. 'There were whispers of a machine that would interface this technology with humans. Like a virtual reality headset but for the whole body. But more than this, Bishop. Previously, that virtual world was a dead simulation, a carbon copy of something either real or imaginary. Regardless, the interaction was all one way. We now believe that Mayer has created the dimensions of an environment which is both alive and reactive. It not only simulates but stimulates, according to the individual or collective consciousness of its user.'

'You mean avatars, Knight?'

'Yes, but avatars who may or may not know they are avatars. Perhaps programmed individually with narratives within a holographic mainframe, like characters in a holo-novel if you like.'

'But how is that possible?'

'Psychedelics, possibly. Hypnosis. I am not sure. Heavy sedation, definitely.'

'But where is the proof, Knight? This sounds utterly fantastic!'

'The programme,' Rachel interrupted, 'or mainframe, computer, or whatever this is, would require a massive amount of computational power. What is the brain but the most sophisticated, biological operating system known to mankind? You remember those old experiments with rats? How electrodes in their brains were linked via the Internet. They were able even then to use the brain signals of a rhesus monkey to control robotic avatars. How far advanced do you think someone like Mayer is with his resources?'

'So, the very connection of the subject to the system maintains the system?'

'Yes, Patrick. Like a plug. Or a switch.'

'But what evidence do you have for any of this, Rachel?'

'The more subjects he has the more expansive the simulation. For all we know he has created a small country, maybe even an entire continent in the heads of his volunteers? Noting so elaborate as an entire world yet maybe. But who knows?'

'Volunteers?'

'Well,' Knight said, 'going around kidnapping random members of the public and forcing them to participate in a crazy, unproven neurological procedure would be difficult even for Mayer. Even if he could bribe a subject with more money than he or she had ever thought imaginable. The general population, even if they know nothing about science, realise how little we have explored the workings of the brain. All this nonsense about 90 per cent of the brain being junk etc doesn't help either. Tells folk we have no idea what the brain is.'

'But if they came to him…to extend their life during an epidemic…'

'…while some pie in the sky future cure is sought…' Rachel said, finishing my thought.

A canopy of silence descended over us. I stood up and crossed to McKenna, tempted to borrow one of his endless cigarettes. He shrugged. A shrug of indifference or incomprehension, I couldn't tell which.

'And then there's the puritanical side of things,' Rachel began.

'What do you mean?' I asked.

'You know the land and Abbey used to

belong to some cult or other?' Rachel replied. I nodded. 'Well, Brownlow knew from Levy that Mayer had resurrected the tenets of a pseudo-religion formulated by the original inhabitants of the area– a mixture of Gnosticism, Sufism and Kabbalah by all accounts. To this archaic mumbo-jumbo, Brownlow believed, Mayer has superimposed an exo-skeleton of technology. A sort of techno-cult if you will.'

'So, you think Mayer might be playing god?' I asked. 'Nothing strange about that. False prophets litter ecclesiastical history.'

'But prophets with their own self-generating universe?' Rachel replied. 'That's another thing entirely.'

'But Brownlow's information may be compromised,' I argued. 'Levy would have seen to that?'

'There's only one way to find out,' announced McKenna, lining up another cigarette with his lips.

'What's that?'

'I reckon we should unplug Mayer's little set up. If nothing else, it'd be revenge for Henney. Besides…'

'…Besides what?' I asked.

'Besides,' he took a draw on his cigarette, and puffed out a few blue haloes of smoke, 'if what you're saying is right and Mayer really did fuck up the world, maybe then there's a way for the world…'

'...to be saved?' Knight enquired.

'Well, to be unfucked at least,' McKenna replied.

22

The City of Glass morphed with the rays of the higher sun, long piano keys of ribboned light. When it had dissipated, the city was no longer there, its particles disassembled back to the ether from which they had come.

The Inner Temple shimmered in its stead, its gilt-laden cupola rounding to walls of transfigured brilliance, a solid glow of edged luminescence against a backdrop of paler sky. Four towers holstered the corner walls of the structure upon which the dome squatted, and atop a further thinner spire, an antenna broadcasting its signal to some other world.

'You know my name?' she asked.

'Of course, Helen. Or should I say Ceres?' the Master Acolyte replied. And then, curious, he added: 'Tell me, which name do you prefer?'

'I don't know,' was all she could say. The memories of her life as Helen Mayer were still lost to her, a life of smooth lines beyond her braille fingertips. She identified more with Akila, Anne King, more even with Ceres than Helen. And once again, the same doubts overwhelmed her. Perhaps Tempus was insane, after all. And everything she had been told was back to front, words that needed a mirror. 'Do you remember your last life?' she asked.

The Master Acolyte smiled knowingly. 'Of course, I do. All the Masters do…well, almost all.'

'Who were you? Did I know you? Was I in your soul group?'

'You knew me very well but I only knew you and the Advocate in my last life. It took me all that time to wake up to His truth. I worked against it. But His Holy Name was patient. I was an…' he looked away, as if distracted by some random memory strand. Giving up, he closed his eyes and a word in Helen's head suddenly reverberated, crisp and clear, in a voice other than her own: *apostle*.

She stepped back in shock. 'Did you…did *you* do that…?'

'Not me, child. The Advocate. Words can sometimes be so misleading. Thought form is actually far more precise.'

'Who was the Advocate in your last life?'

'His Holy Name was always the Advocate. In all of what you call *lives*. The Advocate was always His Holy Name. Now He is in his truest form. I was one of those blessed to be gathered around him at the end.'

'The end?'

'You still don't remember?'

'No, but the word 'apostle'. I remember it. But not…not…'

The Master Acolyte looked at her, a cloud of pity shadowing the sky of his supercilious features. His eyes squinted, the axis of his head tilting a little; a mocking, paternal concern that was really condescension. They had reached the outskirts of the Inner Temple where paths of loose diamond macadam verged onto gardens, filled with silken flowers whose petals, when stirred by the wind, ascended like butterflies, flying from one stem to another. A fountain was sprinkling them with amrita and, if she had been alone, Helen would have licked its residue off the back of her hand. A voice in her head, her own this time, warned her that this would not be appropriate in the sacred domain which she had just entered.

'It is what He called us, those who remembered who He really was. Those who had not forgotten. And those whom He gracefully awoke. But come. Revelation is near. The Advocate wishes to speak to you.'

'Why?

'You know why, Helen. As does Tempus.'

The walls of the Inner Temple were enamelled now in gold, but its colour seemed to hesitate as they approached. As if reacting to a change in the atmosphere, the gold dulled to bronze and then brown. The Master Acolyte raised a hand and it reverted immediately to its original hue, a form of alchemy overseen by the hand of a sorcerer.

'How did you do that?' Helen asked.

'The structure is held together by a photonic forcefield, Ceres. Tightly harnessed beams of decoded waveform information.'

'I don't understand what you mean.'

'You don't? Did Tempus spare you the details then?'

'What details? I don't know what you are talking about.'

The Master Acolyte nodded and walked on. The Temple ahead had no visible means of entrance but the Master Acolyte showed no signs of slowing his pace as he approached. In a moment, he would collide face first with its outer wall. Helen stopped, suddenly overwhelmed by the strangeness of it all.

She thought back to her first day on the Island when the memories of her old life had been at their strongest. And then there had been the Village, and after that, the Archives. But like weights on a set of scales, each time she had become more acclimated to the Island, she become less attached to what had gone before. Each step on her path ahead appeared at the expense of the one behind, and with that some sense of balance had been achieved. This, on the other hand, was happening far too quickly.

Tempus had convinced her that the Island was a sham but had she really believed her? If so, why was she so shocked to hear the Master Acolyte confirm its constitution of lies? And what would it mean for her future on the Island? Would she be simply allowed to carry on as an Apprentice, one part of her brain believing one thing and one part believing another? And what of Tempus' plan? The Acolyte had taken the fragile secret of their collusion and smashed it to smithereens as if it had been meaningless.

Aware that she had lingered behind, he halted his progress, turned and stretched out his arm. 'Do not be afraid, Helen. The physical world can no more hurt you than the world of dreams.' She shuffled a few steps forward and for some reason took hold of his hand like a child. Together they faced the wall and walked through.

When she opened her eyes again, she was alone. She glanced down at her hand, an after-impression of warmth like a glove on a winter's day. Its provider, the Master Acolyte seemed to have either vanished or transported elsewhere.

She recognised where she was immediately, back at the gothic cathedral where she had first witnessed herself as a young girl centuries before. Above her head, the same ribbed vault like the carcass of a gigantic whale, and under her feet, a chessboard of black and white tiles. She raised one shoe and, because it seemed the right thing to do, moved it from the white to the black square, careful not to thread on the line between. A child's game, she remembered. One she had once played. But when? And with whom?

And then she noticed she was no longer wearing her desert sandals. In their place, a pair of rudimentary, no-nonsense brogues. On her legs, thick dark woollen stockings had already begun to irritate her skin. She instinctively reached for the back of her head and grasped a bun of captured hair stabbed into place by a pin. Gone were her coveralls of cricket-white, replaced instead by an all too familiar livery of black pinafore and high-buttoned blouse. She touched next her chest, fingers expanding to explore its soft ampleness.

The church was empty; emptier than empty, as with all places that should be full. Mildew hung in the air like incense over dark, twisted pews and like curtains on a stage, a towering organ perched high over the altar, its triptych of soundless pipes awaiting the blare of a solitary key.

The pulpit too was vacant but Helen could distinguish, on the wingspan of a golden bird, the open pages of a massive book. She started to walk towards it, her heels clicking noisily in the vacuum, her new body strange and yet intimate, habitual, but as exciting as the touch of someone else's. The sight of pulpit itself registered similar emotions inside her. It was something quotidian but forbidden, an apple in her hand, but not one that could be eaten.

It was shaped like a chalice, with a sounding board above and could only be reached by a helix of small, wooden steps. Her hand gripped the security of its handrail and, feeling her legs about to give way, she forced herself upwards. She paused halfway, a moment of recollection from the Archives, as she peered downwards to a perspective of the church from the disembodied elevation of her previous visits.

This time though, she felt a wave of nausea threaten to capsize her as if over the rigging of a sinking ship. She tightened her grip, blinked once, and breathing heavily, lifted her feet once more.

Soon, she was standing next to it, able to distinguish the features of the bird upon which the large tome had been laid. It was turned sideways, fixing her with a dead stare as she inched forwards -the golden and imperious head of a large-beaked ibis. Something primordial inside her made her recoil; a reptilian, cold snap of blood and recollection draining her of strength and will. Gazing down at its open pages, she tried to decipher the strange, spidery verse that had been scratched onto the thick, musty parchment of the book. She heaved its cover into place. There, embossed in large, archaic font its title read: *BridgeWest, BridgeEast*.

'You finally made it all the way up there, child.'

Helen looked down. Below, dressed in a black soutane, stood the pastor, a rosary bead of buttons counting their way from his collar to his shoes. His hair, long and brilliantine, was parted at the middle, his face clean shaven, sharing the same cheekbones and eyes that had dominated the face of Rupert Mayer. A different nose perhaps, less defined. A firmer jaw but more sunken cheeks. But his eyes, Helen noticed, were two slithers of the bluest ice, ice that had been chipped off the surface of a frozen ocean, almond-shaped but with an intensity that could eclipse both suns on the Island.

Helen leant over the pulpit. 'You are…the pastor?'

'The pastor?' his voice boomed. 'If you like. But come down from there, Helen. There's nothing in that book that you don't already know.'

Helen retraced her steps, a slow, measured descent. Her head lightened, a taste of bile at the top of her throat. With effort, she found her feet on the chequered floor again, its dark and light ceramics suddenly merging into grey. She felt a pressure in the air, as if some new element had been released into it, making it difficult for her to breathe. The roof of the church swayed as the whale above seemed to lumber in its sleep. The pews on either side of the aisle seemed to come together like the wheeze of an accordion, feathers on a gigantic bird about to take flight.

The pastor took a flask from his pocket. 'Here, take this. It'll make you feel better.'

'What is it?'

'You know it well. On the Island, it is called

amrita.'

She accepted the flask readily and took a long draught, its cloying goodness entering into every yearning crevasse of her body. Suddenly, the world returned to its customary proportions of volume, distance and mass, its colours sharpening into focus.

'What do you mean 'on the Island'?' Is this not the Island?'

'This is *real*, Helen.'

'No, this is from the Archives,' she countered. 'I remember it.'

'But it is also real. The Archives are a mere projection of potentiality, an accruement of data based on what is known of history, geography, archaeology, anthropology and so on. We have tried to extrapolate the unknown from what is known. This place,' he swivelled a hand through the air, 'still exists however and has done so for several centuries. We were able to model *it* precisely and populate it with real characters based on authentic, genealogical records. For the rest we relied on a slightly more *fictional* approach.'

'So, this is my last life. The centre of the Archives.'

He smiled. 'You can see it that way.'

'Are you the Advocate?'

'I am Henry Mayer, your father.'

Helen felt the floor swell again and so allowed herself to be led to a pew. The pastor sat beside her, both of them facing the stain glass window that trapped the light from the physical world outside. She wanted to run, escape the stifling sarcophagus of the church into the warm, embracing sun outside, feel it kiss her skin once more.

Behind her, she could make out two huge doors, barred into place by an oak beam. Through those doors she could escape from this man, her alleged father, from Tempus, the Master Acolyte and the Island. But she felt weak. Too weak even to stand. She glanced at the flask of amrita in the pastor's hand, trying to decide whether she needed more of the refreshing elixir or less.

'You created the Island?' she asked.

'The Island? Yes.'

'Why?'

'You still don't remember? The world, the one beyond those doors and that window, is gone, Helen. I created a new one, a raft of an island for shipwrecked survivors to live while the world mends.'

She closed her eyes. 'There was a virus. Humanity…'

'…is in the dark. Everywhere the lights are going out, one by one.'

'Memories. People are forgetting who they are.'

'Yes, and the *memory* of that would be too much to bear for the inhabitants of my new world. That is why I created a world of avatars, with no awareness of their 'last life'. You helped me, Helen. Don't you remember?'

'No.'

'You will.'

'But I remembered my name.'

He tried to hold her hand, but she pulled it away. 'You are my daughter, Helen. I couldn't anaesthetise you completely. I needed you to remember some part of yourself. Your name was the least I could do.'

'The Master Apprentice told me that you were not part of my soul group.'

'A necessary lie.'

'Why?'

'I needed to keep watch over you. Throughout all your 'lifetimes'.'

'What about all the others? The weaver? The wood-turner? Why aren't they given access to the Archives? Who are they all?'

'They are from outside our *collective*, Helen. They offered themselves to me. Begged me to give them one last chance at life. Unfortunately, their neurology is too far gone to interact with the Archives. But you know all this...'

'...They *paid* you to help them escape death.'

He looked away. 'Yes, and their lives, limited as they are, are better than that eventuality, Better even than their own lives were. On the Island, they live out a quiet, pastoral existence, without disease, violence or murder.' Helen was silent. She looked at her father's eyes and tried to remember if they had ever looked at her with love, younger eyes on a younger face. ‘Besides,’ he begun again, ‘this is all just temporary until we find a cure.’

‘And the Masters? They are aware of all this.’

‘The Masters on the Island are friends, devotees, brothers who worked together with us to create the original system. As I am sure you know, they are aware of the truth of their reality. That is why they have the Archives, a distraction the healthy brain requires to prevent it from going mad. That is why we need to dream, after all.’

‘What is the system? How does it work?’

‘It would take too long to explain to you now.’ He smiled. ‘But not as long as it took you to explain it to me. Suffice to say, it is a neural network that wires our synapses to this virtual reality. I can override it, of course. Bring myself back to full waking consciousness. Bring others back as well.’

‘The Master Acolyte. You woke him from his slumbers?’

He smiled. ‘Yes. To prepare the way for your return.. It was the Master Acolyte who released you from your chamber and carried you here.’

‘My chamber?’

‘Yes,’ he replied, with a sigh. ‘But you cannot stay here long, Helen.’

‘Why not?’ she asked.

He stood up and stared upwards at the

fragmented light of the window above the church altar. He seemed to be sharing a moment of quiet contemplation, one god in supplication to another. 'Why not?' she insisted. 'Why can't I just leave here?'

'You are infected, Helen. Stage Two. That is why you volunteered for the Island in the first place.' He turned around. 'I'm sorry, child.'

Something inside Helen finally gave way. A whale and a bird were carrying her off through an ocean and sky of black and white squares.

23

It had taken a while to convince General Barrett that it was not a prank call, that the faces that populated his computer screen were not a who's who of the latest bunch of half-crazed zealots hell-bent on paradise, one Armageddon ride away from the nearest clifftop or the length it takes a bullet to measure itself against the width of a skull.

We had made our way to the offices of the Minister of the Interior, an arrogant pen-pusher barely out of his twenties who had risen through the ranks, like so many others before him, on the entrails of a *Youth First* policy which had seen our government, like most globally, transform itself into a kindergarten for needy, love-starved, tin-pot autocrats.

Knight had known Simon Gale at university, had once shared a girlfriend with him, as well as a flat and a fledgling drug habit. Later, he had got back in touch with his former friend when he first began to witness with astonishment Gale's meteoric rise to political power.

As a government minister, Gale had access to the Internet, which was how Knight was able to arrange a conference call with Barrett. Once online, Rachel took the lead, bamboozling the general with science while I addressed more judicial concerns; a list of Henry Mayer's present and past crimes which we hoped would persuade Barrett to sanction our plan to gain access to a few of his more disposable grunts for hire. The possibility that Mayer, a wealthy billionaire and philanthropist, might have precipitated the fall of mankind for no other reason than to line his own pockets, or play God, was too much for the general to bear. Barrett, in his early forties, was untested in war and only too keen to try and scribble his name on the pages of a history book that someday one lucky survivor might write, and a few more fortunate ones might read.

I didn't know what to expect from any of it. Winston, our man in the long grass, would have wasted no time in reporting back to Mayer. No doubt, both would be expecting some kind of major assault on the sanctum that was NeuralNet. Especially since Winston had let slip that Mayer had an antidote to the very virus he was alleged to have released.

Levy was probably long dead like all those involved in the project in its formulative stages. It seemed more likely that Mayer and his whole cult of religious renegades had fled the country already, ferried off in his fleet of a dozen or so private jets. No doubt to some island haven where they would simply set up begin their work anew. Somewhere else where Mayer could bribe the local hierarchies with precious metals or diamonds. Or better still, dupe a naive and desperate class of young politicos with the holy grail of a vaccine that would always be just out of their reach, around the next corner of a never-ending circle.

'I don't think so,' Rachel had replied when I had voiced my concerns to her about Mayer having left the country.

We were making our way to a rendez-vous point with Barrett and his men north of the city; McKenna assuming driving duties in the absence of Winston, Knight doing his best to catch some sleep alongside while Rachel and I conversed *sotto voce* in the back. McKenna was playing some appropriate, Ragnarök death metal at full blast so our attempts at discretion were hardly necessary.

'Why not?' I asked.

'I don't know, Patrick. It's the hardware. It can easily be taken apart and put together again, component by component. But the software...'

'What do you mean? Software?'

'The mainframe or whatever system Mayer has developed can easily be reassembled...'

'But...?' I encouraged.

She hesitated, looked down and pinched her nose between her fingers. She looked as though she were developing a migraine. Probably McKenna's bloody music. The idiot was tapping away at the steering wheel in time with a melody I was failing to pick out. ‘The subjects,’ she began. ‘The *living* hosts. If I am right and they are powering the hardware, removing them might have unfortunate consequences.’

‘But surely their consciousnesses can be uploaded onto a Cloud of some sort.’

‘Yes, but what about the organic interface with that Cloud?’

‘You’re talking about their brains?’

She nodded. ‘Patrick, you must remember that Mayer’s subjects are all at some stage of the virus. The remaining neural pathways may not survive the degeneration that would result by being disconnected from the mainframe for too long a time.’

‘So, he gets new subjects. What does he care?’

‘I have thought a lot about that very question.’

‘And how far has your thinking taken you?’ I asked.

‘There must be someone who means a lot to him, so much so that he can’t risk losing them. A partner, maybe…’

‘…or a daughter?’ I replied.

‘Yes,’ she said after a while. ‘He has a daughter, doesn’t he?’

‘Helen Mayer,’ I confirmed.

‘Helen Mayer,’ she repeated. ‘I remember the rumours about her during my time at NeuralNet as I’m sure you did. Mayer goes a bit off the rails after the death of his wife. Dementia, wasn’t it?’

'Yes,' I replied. 'Hence, his passionate pursuit of a cure.'

'No one ever saw much of the girl after that. Fancy education abroad, I heard. And then some kind of fall out with the father. I asked Brownlow what he knew of it.'

'What did he say?'

'Not much. Girl became as much a recluse as her father.'

'Did he ever say anything about this church of Mayer's?'

'Only that it doesn't have much of a congregation. It doesn't seem to operate like your standard messianic congregation.'

'How so?'

'Well, it's not interested in recruiting young virgins for a start. In fact, it's not much bothered in populating its pews in any way. Brownlow believed that it was made up of extended family members and maybe a hard-core rump of company loyalists.'

'Believed? He's not dead yet you know.'

She blushed slightly. 'Sorry. Of course.'

'I'm only teasing,' I replied, feeling myself redden. 'No branches overseas?'

'No, they are an *actual* chosen few. At least in number. Seems the area itself holds the key.'

'What? The land, you mean?'

'Yes,' she replied, then sidled closer to me. She had managed a shower and a change of clothes courtesy of Gale's staff and, if I wasn't too much mistaken, the faint allure of an old scent that she used to wear on nights out. 'I took the liberty of surfing the net a bit more when I found myself alone with Gale. With his permission, obviously.' She winked.

'Of course,' I replied.

'The Abbey was built atop a small network of caves. The remains of a church stand nearby. Records indicate it dates from the time of the Reformation and itself was constructed upon the ruins of an even older monastic settlement.'

'Interesting. Anything else?'

'Plenty. In the middle of the seventeenth century the church, which I think was Anabaptist at the time, suddenly became heavily influenced by the ideas of the Gerrard Winstanley.'

'Who was he?'

'A so-called *Leveller*. Ranted on about economic equality based on agrarian collectives. You know the idea. All common land shared out and farmed during the week. Praise be to God on Sundays. The colony was one of the few not to be shut down by the authorities. Might have had something to do with the topography of the area.'

'Again, interesting Rachel, but how does any of this help?'

'Well, the colony becomes sort of generational over the next hundred years or so and then at the end of the eighteenth century a new preacher takes over the reins of the church.'

'Let me guess, some ancestor of Henry Mayer?'

'Bingo. A Jonathan Mayer to be exact. Now he was a real firebrand. Became notorious for preaching hellfire around the whole region, stirred up a lot of unwanted attention for the community. According to newspaper reports from the time, he died when he was still in his forties. Murdered.

'Murdered?!'

'For conduct unbecoming of a man of God -if you get my drift.'

'Hmm, I see.' I puffed my cheeks. 'Murder though?'

'At a place called All Hallows Bridge.'

'All Hallows Bridge?'

'These days, a popular suicide hotspot. But a rope bridge back in the day which connected the mainland with a vertical column of rock stack.'

'Rock stack?'

'Bit of cliff left behind after wave erosion.'

'If you say so.'

'Anyway, Mayer was flung off this bridge by his own people.'

'Ouch!'

'So, safe to assume our Mayer believes the land now his own personal fiefdom.'

'Or kingdom,' I suggested.

Suddenly our car jolted. Rachel was flung towards me, her hands on my right side as she tried to steady herself. I used my arm to prevent my head from careering against the window of the door to my left while, in front, McKenna's hands worked feverishly on the steering wheel, first left, then right, then left again. Knight, still asleep, took a nasty blow to the skull against the windscreen and was now slumped forward. Unconscious, probably.

'What the hell…!' McKenna roared. 'Bloody maniacs!'

'What is it?!' I exclaimed.

'People! Hundreds of them! Blocking the way ahead! They've put bollards all across the road! There are fires everywhere! Hold on!'

'How's Bill?' Rachel shouted.

McKenna risked a glance sideways. 'He's breathing! He'll be fine!'

He slalomed a bit more before finally bringing the car to a sliding halt, the brakes screeching as he put the gears into reverse. He spun us around and navigated us back the way we had come.

'What are you doing, McKenna?' I shouted again.

'We'll have to access the motorway some other way,' he replied. 'No way, we are getting through here!'

Just then, Rachel's side of the car was splattered in red paint. A posse of middle-aged hooligans, their faces wild, were sprinting in our direction. Something heavy struck the top of the car. I felt Rachel's hand grip mine as the car lurched again. Then another impact, this time behind me. A hole had been punched through the glass in the back window and the rock that had caused it skimmed just past my head, rebounding against the chair in front and striking me just below the knee.

'Patrick!'

'I'm ok, Rachel!' I assured her. 'McKenna! Get us the hell out of here!'

Finally, we managed to break free, a dustbowl of pandemonium in our rear-view mirror.

'Jesus!' McKenna exclaimed, giving Knight a stiff prod. The doctor muttered something incoherent, a large welt already forming on his forehead. Blood was streaming from his nose, not too out of step with the skull and crossbones of his T-shirt. 'He's coming round.'

After a mile or two, he pulled over, giving Rachel a chance to bandage Knight up.

'What the hell was all that?' I asked McKenna.

'First Stagers, I reckon. They're angry, confused, and not too keen on letting folk from the north enter the city. A matter of resources. Heard a bit about it on the daily government brief. Happening on all points of the compass. A ring of steel around the capital.'

'That's all well and good, McKenna. But we were trying to *leave* the city.'

'Yeah. I noticed that, Bishop. That's what I don't get.'

'When are we due to meet Barrett's men?'

He pulled out a large sheet and flattened it on

the bonnet of the car. 'An hour from now. There!' He dabbed a finger on a spot on the map then shook his head. 'We'll have to go across country if we are to make it in time. You don't think...?'

'What?'

'You don't think Mayer...?'

'...Organised the whole thing to prevent us from reaching NeuralNet?' I replied, connecting his dots.

'Or delaying us, at least,' McKenna replied.

'Ask me that again when we get there. If there's a human shield around Mayer, then I'd say you're probably right. But at least that's something,' I added a moment later.

'What's that?'

'You're more of a conspiracy nut than I gave you credit for.'

Ten minutes later, Rachel had done her best to patch Knight up. The blood from his nose had been staunched at least. He switched seats with me, protesting all the time that he was fine, only for Rachel to overrule him. They sat in the back together; Rachel making sure he didn't nod off. By the looks of him, he needed a hospital. But then again, the entire nation needed its health service, a nationwide provision which had long since been overwhelmed by all the minor and major incidents and accidents associated with the early stages of the virus.

It was almost dusk by the time we arrived at our destination. McKenna had taken us on a scenic route, replete with abandoned combine harvesters and tractors, long fields stripped of crops, and meadows where scrawny cattle huddled in corners. On the way we spotted dozens of starving farmhands picking through empty furrows, all to the backdrop of a setting sun -it would have made a decent canvas I thought -a snapshot of the End Times if anyone had anything as luxurious as time anymore to yield to a creative urge.

The last time I had seen this bit of wasteland had been from Brownlow's helicopter just before my aborted interview with Levy, isolated and far removed from the world below. But the country had nosedived even further since then, especially since the release of Winston's new variant. It was all Brownlow's people could do to contain it and stop the spread inland. Barrett's extraction team, it seemed, was the penultimate chance for mankind. If we failed, what was left of the military would be our final resort. And if it was up to the army, I feared what damage would be done by the track of tanks on shelves of glass vials filled with any potential antidote.

The cloth sails of Barrett's windmill juddered as McKenna parked alongside, but not enough even for a quarter rotation. There had been no grain to mill, after all, and the lattice framework of the blades had already begun to peep through in places. Elsewhere, an amputated stump was all that remained of one propellor, its vandalised wing no doubt plundered for firewood.

The mill was centuries old, like the valley of farmland over which it perched, but its whitewashed walls still held firm in spite of the graffiti that tagged its southern side. Other indicators of recent use awaited inside – a few used condoms, a couple of syringes, some discarded pills, a sleeping bag with a broken zip and a slop bucket in the corner made up its miserable decor. Overhead, the broken gears of the mill's machinery ensured the sails would never produce a crust of bread again.

As a landmark it was perfect however and Barrett and his men had already set up base there; four of his jeeps idling nearby, their headlights assisting the general to inventory his stock of grenades, pistols, machine guns and night-vision goggles. His men, all jawlines and hobnailed grit, were in the process of blackening their faces, adjusting their khaki and sharing gum like a reluctant child shares sweets.

Barrett, several social rungs of the ladder above his men, had an accent that grated and an attitude that reeked of hot, sweaty, colonial nights spent getting bitten alive by ill-tempered mosquitoes. In another world, in another time, he would have barely made the rank of second lieutenant. Unfortunately for us some part of him already knew this.

He sniffed when he saw me approach, ignored

my handshake, and peering over my shoulder, addressed McKenna instead.

'You McKenna?'

'Yeah. Barrett?'

He winced. '*General* Barrett. And you would do well to remember that!'

'Oh, would I? Why's that, Barrett?'

The general paled and was about to take the matter of his rank further when Rachel intervened.

'We have an injured man. Any chance, general, one of your medics can have a look?'

'Medics? This isn't a Sunday School outing, you know.'

'He took a blow to the head and...'

'...Griffiths?'

'Yes, sir?' one of Barrett's men replied, the whites of his eyes emphasised by the boot polish around them.

'Take a look.'

'Sir?'

'Just bloody well do it, man!'

'Yes, sir.'

'Thanks,' Rachel said, as Knight was led to a large camouflaged canvas tent that had been erected alongside the lighthouse. It looked like a jungle version of a Big Top.

Barrett shook his head and made a sucking sound with his teeth. 'For the record, Miss Hunter...'

'*Doctor* Hunter,' Rachel stressed. She

exchanged a look with McKenna who was grinning widely.

'For the record,' he repeated. 'I am totally against bringing civilians into a theatre of war...'

'...A what?' McKenna spat.

'...but given the unique situation we find ourselves in...'

'...You mean, the apocalypse?' I suggested.

At this, a few of Barrett's own recruits appeared to titter. If the general heard anything, he chose to ignore it. 'You're Bishop, aren't you?!' Barrett snarled. 'Another one of these eggheads who got us into this mess in the first place!' I nodded and folded my arms defiantly. 'Just remember, keep out of our way. Once you locate the formula or test-tube or whatever it is you're looking for, you are all surplus to requirements as far as I am concerned.'

'You're a proper little charmer, Barrett, aren't you?' McKenna retorted. For the first time since I had known him McKenna actually seemed to be defending us, acting as if her were part of a team. No doubt it was merely a question of my enemy's enemy and all that. But still, I was pleased to hear it.

'Just you make sure, McKenna, where you point that thing!' he glanced at McKenna's sub-automatic pistol. 'If we weren't so short-numbered, I wouldn't have you on this mission at all. I know all about your record.'

'Jealous of it, are you?' McKenna sniped.

Barrett's face turned a convincing shade of merlot. Even a couple of his own men shuffled their boots nervously. I decided it was time to play peacemaker.

'This isn't getting us anywhere,' I intervened. 'Maybe it might be an idea to outline the plan of attack.' I threw McKenna a dagger of a look. 'I can assure you we won't get in your way and understand of course that our protection is not your priority.'

Barrett harrumphed but seemed appeased. He had an upper-class moustache which he wrinkled once and a pair of eyes a bird would have been proud of. His helmet squared his fringe which I imagined was part of a sculpted wave of chestnut pomade. 'Right!' he replied, a baton suddenly appearing from behind his back. 'Jones! Get the blueprint. Let's go through this for our new friends! And Bishop?'

'Yes,' I replied.

'I hope you're theory is right. For all our sakes.'

It was a two-mile hike, mostly downhill, to the NeuralNet complex; my night vision goggles furnishing the landscape with a phantasmal, other-worldly haze. Rachel, Knight and I, in ill-fitting uniforms, did our best to keep up with the others as we scurried through the brush and gravel of the incline, a huge melon of a moon hanging overhead no doubt betraying our progress to Mayer's men below.

I paused briefly and removed my goggles. Unlike before, the three towers of concrete and steel where both Rachel and I had laboured for Mayer seemed alive with activity, blocks of pocketed light smudged in the rain that had started to drizzle and was making the terrain beneath our feet hazardous to cross. Patches of sodium flared in places along the perimeter of the high electric fence that surrounded the complex, but to the east, what should have been the Abbey was concealed in darkness. Above, a row of three stars or planets were studded like coffin nails. I told myself it was the effect of this alignment that had inspired Barrett to halt the progress of his men, but really he was just annoyed at my inability to keep up.

'You seen enough, Bishop?' his voice sounded in the gloam.

'It's what I expected,' I replied, trying to sound convincing.

'Hmm.' He directed his goggles towards the main gates of the compound. 'Two guards on duty. Shouldn't be a problem.'

'There'll be more,' McKenna insisted, his words rasping on the cold night air.

'We stay together then,' Barrett replied.

I looked again at the star which helped to give away the Abbey's position and thought of astrological signs and tarot cards. And whether I really had it in me to play poker with the devil.

24

It was her father looking down at her. A mosaic of multi-coloured shards outlining his elongated form, arms cruciform and welcoming, the hem of his cassock splayed over invisible feet, suggesting flight. Above, an arc of five stars, capturing the jewelled light of a lunatic moon which beamed its madness through his face while the rest of the clerestory window bathed in shadow.

She jarred her head to the side, a faint unguent filling her nostrils. And he was there again, this other father, that one that had descended to Earth to save the world from its sins.

While she had slept, it had all come back to her. The intravenous rush of a truth drug sweeping the cobwebs away. She remembered everything now. Who she was, who she had been and why she had been a castaway on an island divided by a bridge. The footprints on its beach now spelled out her name: HELEN MAYER, an SOS to the real world, which couldn't save its own souls never mind anyone else's.

'You see now, don't you?' the pastor, her father, asked. She sensed cold fingers cradle her chin until she jolted her head back, turning her face once more to the deity staring down at her from its own personal heaven.

'You!' she mouthed, wearily. 'Why did you bring me back here? Why?' And then, as if answering her own questions. 'The virus!'

The god in the window stared down at her impassively. But the man beside her exhaled, and on his breath the recollection of fine wine. And with that memory, a wave of so much more. So much that it was difficult to process all at once.

Centuries ago it had been believed the stained glass above had been symbolic of the moment just before the *Great Descent*, when the Holy Messenger had first arrived in the world. That emissary's name had been Jonathan Mayer. But His testimony was ignored. His followers, beguiled by sin, had subsequently turned on him and so, more recently, God had sent another, someone who shared the same blood as the first. But vastly more powerful. An archangel, some claimed, capable of redesignating the energetic transfers of what most called money and drawing them to himself. The love of money was not the root of all evil, the new Mayer had declared. Money was the precondition that provided the space for love to flourish. This was what the first Mayer had failed to understand.

The second, however, fully aware of how the Universe really worked, created a business empire, the bedrock on which to found His new church. But soon afterwards, He had lain with another, a mortal female, siring a 'Nephilim' whom He called Helen. His disciples had been horrified. They declared him false and rejected His new teaching -the commandment that demanded fealty to His new born. They saw His *gift* to the world as weakness, blithely unaware of the Transition which had already taken place, that God had not sent his brightest angel to them. He had incarnated within himself the very spirit of God.

That essence was Henry Mayer, His Holy Name, and His daughter was the first of a royal lineage which would establish the New Kingdom.

This was the First Book of the Final Testament. It spoke of the eradication of those who had betrayed the Faith, and then the pilgrimage home, to the sacred soil upon which the first seeds had failed.

'You see the resemblance?' her father was saying now. 'It is remarkable, isn't it?'

'Is it?' she pouted.

'Yes, Helen,' he replied, somewhat irritated. 'That design was taken from the engraving. You know the one? The one completed just before…'

'…I remember,' she replied, straightening up, finding her legs and then the arms of the pew. It took an effort to manoeuvre herself into a sitting position, a cold sheen of perspiration on her forehead. She was aching all over, mostly her head and stomach, and where there wasn't an ache, her body tingled with electricity, her nerves like copper wires.

'The drug?'

'To bring you back, we had to sever the link. You can take it orally, of course, but while you are here you will suffer some withdrawal.'

'*While* I am here? Tell me, father, why did you bring me back? The interface…'

'…is working perfectly.'

'You've been maintaining it this whole time?'

He nodded.

'How long?' she asked.

He sighed. 'A year.'

She felt her spine run cold. 'A year? It felt like…?'

'How long?'

'Longer,' she replied, after a while. 'Much longer.' She folded her arms, in a bid to control a sudden bout of cramp inside. 'So, you finally found it? A cure?'

He looked away. A silhouette of a face on a coin. 'No, child. Not yet.'

'Then why…?'

'…The system is in danger?'

'But you said…'

'…Not from without, Helen. From within.'

Elias Levy shivered slightly in spite of his oversized coat, gloves and scarf. He hadn't refused the ushanka on offer. That would not have been wise. But he couldn't bring himself to wear such an absurd item even if he were alone. There were the cameras, of course, terabytes of useless footage, recording away for posterity the stilled images of rows upon rows of biopods, cubicles which harnessed the remnants of what had once been people.

Each chamber was a mesh of tubes and cables, tendrils and wires. There were monitors which confirmed the status of organs; cryomats which regulated the body's temperature. Ventilation pumps that facilitated oxygen flow; barbiturate caps that fuelled the brain and kept an eye on its metabolic rate. There were nutrient pipes and electrolyte patches that took care of alimentary and hydration needs; entry pins for hallucinogens and sedatives. In short, everything that Mayer's elite band of scientists had at their disposal to slow down a subject's life signs, placing it in a state of suspended animation just this side of death.

Levy couldn't begin to understand it all. And this was simply the biological interface, the inducement of a refined state of coma that could maintain a human being indefinitely, reducing them to a barely recognizable circuit board, hardly visible beneath the strangled cocoon of fibrous tentacles that entered each patient's pod through selected points from the outside world.

As far the rest of it, he had very little idea. The boffins called it *The Spider*. A mechanical arachnid that reached from floor to ceiling in the centre of a web of trapped flies. It pulsed a wireless signal of digital information which the fly on the fringes of the web decoded into a holographic field. That was how one of the starch-coated geniuses had explained it to him. Another had chosen a simpler metaphor. The volunteers were all 'skipping the light fantastic', having a collective, waking dream. And while they were dreaming, their neurochemistry sustained the very machine that kept them asleep.

But now there was no one left. The system itself was in trouble. He could read it in His Holy Name's face. It had something to do with that daughter of his. The High Priestess. The one who was supposed to lead them all to the Promised Land. But who herself, it was rumoured, had contracted the virus. The pestilence that the unbelievers had brought upon themselves, the plague that would cleanse the world like the Flood of old.

Why did she have to return, the prodigal misfit? And to save her, she too had been placed under His spell, like all the rest of the desperate pagans that sustained the machine. Surely, this was a sign that her human half had polluted its divine counterpart?

And since then, what had happened? There had been a drain on the mainframe. More and more of its computational reserves had depleted, so much so that He had asked His apostles, those closest to him, to sacrifice themselves for the greater good. They had all embarked on the same voyage to the Island, the land of make believe, the visual, drug-induced, holding pattern where they had been commissioned to not only watch over the Nephilim, but also to shore up the Spider that they themselves had helped to create.

And now he had led her back from the Island. Elias Levy, who had survived the Purge, whose faith had never once wavered, had been seconded to wake up the apostate from her sleep. Worse, he had been commissioned to the lower levels, to check on an Artificial Intelligence he knew very little about

He walked on, following his designated route, through a blanket of cold fog, lit up by tiny labels of red and green lights which flickered in time to a sound of a huge, trombone orchestra of air that inhaled and exhaled like a steam engine labouring on an uphill track.

This time he paused at the vacant cubicle that had been inhabited by Helen. How he had longed to disconnect her from the behemoth that was keeping her alive. To rinse away the blight that had infected the Church. But there were back up systems built into the core, he had known, and the only thing he would have risked would have been the irreparable damage to her cerebral cortex that she would have suffered in the interim. And His eternal wrath of course.

A few pods beyond hers were those of the former NeuralNet employees who had begun to ask too many questions, whose initiates had followed a creed they were not willing to accept. At least they were still alive, he thought, more fortunate than those who had met more permanent fates. A few of them had got very close to destroying everything the Master had brought to pass but, like all the other demons, His Holy Name had cast them out.

Levy stopped and pinched his signet ring, the way he did when he was nervous or ill at ease. The large, elaborate font of the *NN* had fooled everyone into thinking that he was simply just another employee, albeit a high ranking one, of the global corporation that was NeuralNet. But that was just how someone with an ordinary mind saw the world. The kind of mind that sees a Give Way sign and believes that this is merely an appeal to the vehicle he is driving and not some request to his Higher Self. He smiled and twisted the ring full circle. The double consonant was actually a single one, the *M* which demarcated the alphabet between the Alpha and the Omega and which stood for Mayer, the corporeal and corporate family name that was less a name now than a title.

The pod he had stopped at was one of a woman, someone he had once admired at a distance. The type that the devil had inundated with both beauty and intelligence and the strength of personality that bridged the gap between two. He had interviewed her many years ago, long before the Forgetting, and like so many others he had weighed her responses on a sliding scale between the company and the Church. Satisfying the first criteria was difficult enough; displaying the kind of markers that would conciliate the other was well nigh impossible, especially in the kind of agnostic, secular, male-driven world which made the skin of a woman like cat-gut and their hearts like so many pebbles on the beach.

But this one had been different. Or perhaps it had been *his* heart that had been stirred. There was a crack in the edifice of her soul, of course, but he had hope that this one could let the Light through before it rent itself asunder. There was an aura about her, the fragrance of a rose that had been rooted amongst the weeds, and carrying in the air she expelled, the hope that the world could be a better place. But, most significantly, she displayed the genuflection to the mysteries of life that scientists like her usually ignored. He saw her as his Diana, the huntress whose arrows could pierce the souls of all.

She had been the only one for whom he had fought. She would have made an exquisite acquisition, he had argued, but His Holy Name had thought differently. 'To see perfection,' he had said. 'you must be able to know all imperfection.'

'I don't understand,' he had replied.

'The new Kingdom will do away with the old. '*For He maketh his sun to rise on the evil and on the good, and sendeth rain on the just and on the unjust.*' You know this?'

'Of course.'

'It is false. Those who deserve it will have two suns and the heat from those suns will overwhelm them with light. The others will have only darkness. And the two will live side by side and know one another. Such will be the suffering of those in darkness'. And then He had added, for the first time in anyone's hearing, the epithet: 'Two suns, twice the day!'

They dined together, her mouth full of the flavours of a thick, vegetable broth; her taste buds working overtime to differentiate the carrot from the parsnip, the radish from the onion. It would have been too much of an effort to chew, her father had said, but as theirs was a plant-based diet, there was no danger that her jaw muscles would be overtaxed with something as foul as meat.

Afterwards, they withdrew to their favourite spot, the balcony on the top floor of the Abbey which overlooked the verdant darkness of the valley below and the purple cloth of loyal stars that had remained steadfast since in her youth, trapped in time from her perspective, even though they themselves had slipped out of time aeons ago.

'Strange,' she began.

'What is?'

'Now I see the stars, I feel as though I missed them. But I didn't miss them, as I couldn't remember them. So why do I feel such sadness that I am witnessing them now.'

He shook his head. 'That's your soul aching.' He stood silently for a moment and followed her gaze. 'And some people believe that there is no such thing as a soul.'

'I saw different stars,' she reminded him. 'When I went away.'

'Were those stars any more or less beautiful than these?'

'No,' she acknowledged. 'Besides…'

'Besides?'

'Who's to say that what we see at night, or during the day for that matter, is not just the projection of some great architect, one who has encased this world in a secondary sphere, a holographic grid lined up with transmitters emitting a false broadcast to receptors in our individual RNA.'

'Was that how you came across the principle, child?'

She shrugged. 'Had to do something during my forty days in the wilderness.' He frowned. She looked down. 'I am sorry, father. If I have achieved anything, it has been only as a result of your will.'

'And yet, you doubt my will now?'

'It won't work, father.'

'The world out there is dying, Helen. Our people are constructing scores of new pods. We will bolster the interface.'

'More donors won't save the patient,' she replied.

'What do you mean?'

'We will never have enough computational power to move beyond the Island. Soon, the bodies will atrophy and die.'

'They will be replaced.'

'Yes, but the scale will be the same. Unless...'

'...Unless...'

'...Unless we had thousands, tens of thousands of virus-free minds. To do that, they would all need to access the Archives which as you know is a tremendous strain on our resources. Their neurochemistry can cover some of that burden, but not all. And then you would need to outsize the System which will require a new influx of scientists working on it -which the world seriously lacks -and then you need to convince perfectly healthy people to volunteer for the programme in the first place.'

'Don't worry about the scientific community. Very soon the only science left in *their* world will be our science. And as for acquiring virus-free people, I have already begun the process of quarantining suitable subjects in every county where NeuralNet has influence with local government. They are being shipped in as we speak.'

'There isn't time, father!' she pleaded. 'The virus!'

'I am time!' Mayer roared. 'It is an illusion which I will control! Didn't all your stargazing teach you that?!'

She turned away, as she so often did when the monster inside her father clawed its way to the surface. His eyes bulging with anger, his mouth contorted, teeth that could tear through flesh. She took a step closer to the stone balustrade of the balcony and peered down into the abyss. How easy would it be just to throw herself over and enter into the dreamless sleep below, a sleep which she had begun to yearn for so much. The repose between nightmares. And then she remembered her friend.

'Why did she have to wake up?'

'Tempus?' he replied, composing himself anew. 'That is not the question you should be asking, child. They all wake up in the end. The real world bleeds through eventually. We cannot prevent the patient from coming out of the coma. That is why we have the final Circle. Once they remember their pre-life, our Villager tends to go insane. When that happens they are sent to BridgeWest. And then the brain finally dies. And so do they. That is why we need more people.'

'Why not simply unplug her?'

'Tempus overcame the programme...in the West. I want to know how. Otherwise, others will follow her example.'

'You want me to ask her?'

'I want you to stop her!' They shared the silence for a while. A cool breeze touched her face, real and pathogen free. At least for now. 'Will you do it child?' he insisted. 'We have come so far.'

Helen looked into the steel eyes of her father. And the Advocate stared back.

25

It wasn't much of a plan. And even if it succeeded we would still have to rely on the conscience of a man who up until now had shown very little moral capacity for anything other than his own insane impulse to recreate the world in his own image. As I gained my first sight of the Abbey, and the tower of the medieval church just beyond it, I visualised Mayer somewhere inside, a fragile test tube of antidote in one hand, a religious tome in the other. Smashing one to smithereens at our feet while lamenting us with apocryphal verse. And before we could stop him, producing a revolver from his robes and blowing his brains out. The bodies of his followers, gassed or poisoned, depending on their mass suicide of choice, piled up in the pews and all of them catching the nearest comet to never never land.

And that was if we managed to survive that long.

We were trying to save one world but I had to admit a selfish part of me just wanted to witness the technology that, if Rachel was correct, had the potential to create another.

'I hope you are right about this,' Barrett had asked.

'I am!' I had replied, trying to sound convincing. 'I think the labs are a decoy. That's why they're lit up like Christmas. Besides, there's something about the Abbey which ties in with his illusions of grandeur.'

As decoys went, it seemed a fairly obvious one. The Abbey and the chapel were cloaked in darkness, their gables barely visible upon the bluer edges of darkness. The moon had gone behind a bank of cloud and Barrett was keen to move before it howled its searchlight out through the night, giving away the element of surprise and our only advantage.

We were crouched in a copse of trees about fifty yards from the main gates. The main road bisected the distance between us, on either side of which lay two strips of reasonably manicured grass. At the end of the verge on the other side was a steep embankment at the bottom of which the wired perimeter began. The road was lined with lights, making it impossible to cross without being seen by the two guards on duty.

'Jones,' Barrett seethed, between clenched teeth.

'Yes, sir,' a young voice, not much older than twenty, replied. There was a bit of rustling behind me and the faint click of metal on metal. A bit of whispering from some of the other men, a deep breath and then two implosions of air that seemed to stretch trails of fine wind over our heads. I looked through my goggles at the guards who appeared now to have changed places with two shadows, fallen and inert at the feet of where they had previously stood.

'Not bad,' I heard McKenna acknowledge behind.

'Shit!' Knight muttered, next to me. 'This is actually happening.' I caught his eye. A bandana of linen had been sealed over the gash in his forehead. It was black, like his warrior paint, and made him look a lot tougher than he was. Rachel was standing next to him, but she needn't have concerned herself. Knight looked like he had recovered from his injuries. His breath smelled of cheap whiskey which one of Barrett's men had provided either medicinally or for Dutch courage. Rachel meanwhile looked right at home in her combat gear. I blushed inside, in disbelief that some animalistic part of me was even now craven to such notions.

There were ten of us. Barrett had handpicked five men for the incursion on NeuralNet. Griffiths, Jones, and three others whose names I had yet to learn and perhaps never would. Speed was of the essence, the general claimed. A small team would be less conspicuous, especially given the vulnerability of the prize on offer. McKenna was under orders to hang back with us until the labs were secured. Barrett had rewarded him with a spanking new sub-automatic machine gun. I, on the other hand, had secreted Henney's old pistol into the front pocket of my combat trousers. Our job, according to Barrett, was 'not to engage the enemy' but rather to keep our heads down and live long enough to identify Mayer's antidote, sampling the wares on offer after the deal had been struck. Like drug barons confirming the quality of the merchandise before money is exchanged.

If Winston was anything to go by, Mayer's men would be of similar stock to our own. But we were all disposable, I knew. Like razors that had lost their edge. There were newer faces now. Cleaner shaven. Others that had achieved what we hadn't be able to. I told myself that the success of our scientific counterparts at NeuralNet had been caused by the superiority of their resources. They had had time and an endless supply of money. We had had a broken government bankrolled by nothing but the failing human instinct to do the right thing. In the end, our share value had plummeted. It wouldn't have surprised me if Barrett was under orders to keep Mayer's white coats alive.

Such were my thoughts as we crossed the road: McKenna, Rachel, Knight and I making up the rear, harried on by our sheepdog Barrett. A five-minute scurry later we found ourselves in the courtyard outside the main entrance of the Abbey. We were now in two distinct groups. McKenna had been ordered back by Barrett.

He was to be our protector while the others ventured inside.

We followed McKenna in a slithery crawl towards a thicket of yew, their leaves still wet from the afternoon's rain. Across the dark bay windows of the Abbey, we traced the movement of Barrett's men who had already gained access to the building, the lasers of their rifles stroking red lines as they stopped and started from room to room. Near us, what sounded like a nightingale started to trill. Something rustled in the undergrowth in response. Possibly a fox or a badger. I pulled my goggles off my head and had a look around. Nothing. No cars in the car park. Nothing save for a couple of tangled-looking trees either side of the lawn which bordered the entrance.

After a while, McKenna's walkie-talkie spurted into life. A voice crackled. 'Ground floor secure.'

With that, McKenna give my back a shove and I sidled to my feet, the fingers of my left hand slipping easily into the sodden earth. We copied McKenna's approach, a low centre of gravity scramble, our boots doing their best not to disturb the gravel of the path that led to the main door. I wondered briefly how we had not tripped any motion activated lights. But then remembered what Barrett had said in the brief about one of his men being an expert in security systems.

Perhaps our electrical expert was the same

one who was waiting for us in the lobby, his hands semaphoring a stop signal. We halted and watched him raise an index finger above his head after which he turned and disappeared from view. I removed my goggles, allowing my eyes to acclimatise to the darkness.

It was the same sparse atrium as before. A reception desk and a low central table around which two white leather sofas had been positioned. A couple of fake potted plants stood either side of a narrow rug which rolled out a path from the sofas to an elevator -the very one that I had ascended to Levy's office in what seemed like a lifetime ago. If memory served, a couple of garish modern prints had also occupied the walls at strategic intervals, but the light now was far too poor to re-evaluate them.

I felt fingertips press against my hand twice. A consolatory heartbeat passed from one human being to another. I didn't need to turn to Rachel to know what she was thinking. The Abbey was indeed empty. Mayer's labs were where they had always been. And I had overplayed my hand, intellectualised what should have been rudimentary. The lights were on in the main buildings because that was where the science was being carried out; cold and calculating science with no time for artistic chicanery. Mayer's gambit had been to muddy the waters and he had done so by the simple act of emptying a car park of its vehicles. I had walked Barrett's men straight into his crosshairs.

McKenna shifted in the shadows. He made for one of the bay windows and took a look outside. As he pulled back its curtain, a strobe of moonlight unveiled a part of his face. An anxious face. He looked in our direction and shook his head. I breathed a sigh of relief. Just one sigh.

Above our heads a few older floorboards protested as Barrett's men ventured across, a little less stealthy than before as, surely by now, even Barrett must have realised that we were alone in the building. But he was doing it by the book. The book, after all, being all he knew. And Barrett was determined to read all the pages even if he knew the story didn't have a happy ending.

'You hear that?' McKenna whispered, suddenly.

'Barrett's men…' I began to explain.

'…No, not from up there,' McKenna interrupted. 'Listen!'

We leaned into the darkness, trying to pick out the sound of whatever it was that McKenna had heard. Somewhere, perhaps a mile away, a dog, or wolf, was wailing. I looked at McKenna but he shook his head furiously. I listened again. And then I heard it. The distinct sound of a whistle. But not just a whistle. The sound of someone whistling.

'What the hell?!' Knight exclaimed.

'Sssh!' McKenna warned.

We listened again. It was definitely somebody

whistling. I recognised the notation. A familiar tune. Something from my childhood. I couldn't put my finger on it. And then it stopped before I could.

'What did Barrett say about what lay beneath the Abbey?' McKenna asked, his tone measured and trying to maintain control.

'Nothing,' Rachel replied. 'There's not supposed to be anything down there.'

'The bloody idiot!' McKenna snapped. 'Mayer's men have a way in! There must be a basement or cellar down there!'

'Do you think...?' Knight began, genuine fear in his voice.

'...They're probably on the roof too!' McKenna continued, breathlessly. 'A pincer movement. We'll have to block them off. Knight, go upstairs and get some of Barrett's people down here! Now!'

Knight stormed off in the direction of the lift.

'Not the bloody lift, man! The stairs!'

Knight stopped in his tracks and hurtled off to the right.

'Right, you two! Stay behind me!' McKenna hissed. 'There must be an exit point around here somewhere.'

'Wait a minute, McKenna,' I replied. 'What was all that whistling about? If Mayer was launching a surprise assault from below, why would he let us know?'

'Cos he's a sick bastard, Bishop! What's wrong,

doc? You not read that particular memo?'

'Patrick is right,' Rachel said. 'Something's not right. At least, let's wait for back up.'

'No time for that. We need to move quick. That whistling was coming from straight beneath our feet.' He stamped his foot as if marking the spot on a treasure map. But then he stopped and tried his foot again. 'Quick, Rachel, help me pull up this rug! Bishop, push those sofas back!'

'What is it, McKenna?' I asked.

'I don't know,' McKenna replied. 'Something.'

I began to heave one of the sofas backwards.

'And turn on the bloody lights!' McKenna roared, tossing his night goggles across the room. 'I think we can safely assume we don't need to be walking on eggshells anymore!'

I fumbled my way to a light switch. The room blazed suddenly like a floodlit stadium. McKenna and I pushed back the sofas while Rachel overturned the rug. Under one, I noticed what appeared like the grooves of a hatch. Their tracks scoured halfway up the length of where the rug had been before coming to an abrupt end. A gold ring, fit for a bull's nose, lay at the other end in the second sofa's former position. McKenna knelt down and inspected its clasp.

'Move back. I think if I give this a twist…' Somewhere beneath, a spring sprung itself while somewhere else the crack of splintered wood. 'Bishop! Help me push this panel down. I think it's a staircase.'

I used all my strength to press down on what we had discovered were hinged floor boards. Finally, by some miracle, they gave way, a strip of floorboards lowering to a diagonal of small steps, the kind normally reserved for loft conversions.

At that very moment, the sound of gun fire broke out above. It seemed McKenna was right, after all. Mayer's men had been lying in wait on the roof the whole time.

'Stay behind me,' McKenna warned, his sub-automatic primed at the steps below.

The hidden stairwell had triggered lights in the space beneath it. There was a railing on one side as the steps proved to be steep and not very secure. They swayed and creaked as we descended. Perhaps it would have been better if we had taken them one body at a time but the rapid fire of bullets over our shoulders made us rethink that idea.

Finally, after a dozen stairs or more, we landed on solid ground. I was the last through and considered the option of pushing our slithering snake of a staircase back into place. McKenna, however, ordered me to leave it.

'It doesn't make any difference now,' he opined, the first indication of defeat on his lips. 'Let's go.'

'Go where?' Knight chimed in.

We were in a stone cellar; thick, clammy, ancient walls against which were pinned shelves of bibles. A dumb waiter greeted us to our left, its doors ajar, its stomach empty. Beside it, a log pile of rotting mulch, an iron hearth black with soot and a wine rack minus its bottles. I spotted a corner pantry to my right, its few sacks spilling sugar and salt onto a tiled floor, smothered in broken glass and old newspaper. A sturdy wooden table centred the chaos upon which I noticed an oil lamp, a few chipped plates and an ashtray half filled with cigarette ends.

McKenna picked up one of them and sniffed.

'Whoever smoked this isn't our whistler,' he announced. 'Its light went out long ago.'

'What is this place?' Knight asked.

'Didn't you say, Rachel, the chapel here was constructed on the ruins of an old monastery?' I flattened a hand against one of the walls. It felt old. Very old.

'Yes,' she replied, picking up some scrap paper from the floor and reading it. 'Look at this.'

'What is it?' I asked.

'Flight itinerary,' she replied. 'Whatever this place was, and I think it was a kitchen, became centuries later a storage space for contraband goods. From those air strips that used to work out of this entire area.'

'What's that?' McKenna asked, suddenly. I turned, my attention grabbed by a small door of peeling red paint. 'Looks like that's our way out,' he added. 'Probably to that church.'

'Might explain the bookcase of bibles,' I ventured.

Just then, an explosion above brought a cascade of plaster and dust down about our heads. It was followed by another loud outburst of gun fire. I rummaged hopelessly for the pistol in my pocket.

'Save it, doc,' McKenna advised, grimly. 'They're on their own.'

'McKenna!' Rachel exclaimed.

'One more pistol isn't going to cut it, doc!' he exclaimed. 'Besides, we have our own battle to fight. And it's on the other side of that door!'

26

It was said that new souls arrived at the Towers, their essences reconfigured from the aggregate of all their previous incarnations on the Other Side. Nothing remained from before but the end of a distillation process. No further evolution of the soul could occur. It had reached its zenith or nadir. Like a garment that had been rinsed and stained too many times. The Advocate had closed His book and His decision had been made, the soul transmigrating to its last destination, either east or west of the Great Divide.

All this was believed and yet no one had ever witnessed the arrival of an Islander. They simply appeared at the foot of one of the Towers and gravitated blindly to their respective Village or clan. In the East, they were appraised and allocated their role; in the West, they entered an anarchy of survival, immediately attuned to the mara that hunted them as prey, seeking some measure of solace with a faction of equally damned souls they somehow recognised from before.

But now something was happening to the

West Tower. Those nearer could have observed in detail the shift that had occurred to soften the structure into a sort of molten plasticity from which a strange, violet light seemed to birth. They could have if they had not scattered for cover like their mara above, a herd of them winging off in all directions beyond the clouds and out of sight. They could have understood if they had known anything about the mathematical code Mayer had used to underwrite his universe, the electro-magnetic field that code had created, and from that field, the photonic interface that locked in a person's consciousness.

It had become so much clearer to Tempus. With each passing moment, as the fissures in the monolith threatened to gape and explode outwards a firework display of light, the reverse was happening to her. She could feel the last frustrating fragments of her reality fly back together, an implosion of memory back to its source.

The Tower continued to heave from within, the outline of wider light forming the shape of a huge door. 'It worked!' Tempus wanted to shout. The words articulated as thoughts in her head. But to her astonishment they formed bubbles beyond her skull. She imagined them, floating side by side in the air in front of her, and with an imaginary pin she pierced them, releasing their sound, a tremendous, cavernous boom down the ridge.

She brought together the tip of her teeth to that of her tongue and wanted to cry.

And then she ran.

If there were others she did not see them, or they were a blur of shadows in her peripheral vision. The crescendo of noise had abated to a whistle and by the time she had reached the bottom of the Tower even that had dissipated. The braver souls of BridgeWest had not disappeared. Either by instinct, fear, or wonder, they had formed a semi-circle ten metres or so from the Tower's door.

It had not opened. But there was the definition of an opening, a tall oblong puddle of viscous blackness that was inviting her in. The molecular cohesion of the rest of the Tower had once more stiffened its resolve around and above it.

She turned and faced the audience of desperate faces that gazed up at her, each one scarred, bloodied, pocketed with filth but etched with an agonising hope that swelled inside them and which Tempus could feel. It was so palpable that it almost knocked her off her feet. How much had the Tower revealed to them, she wondered. Had they too awakened from their slumber? Enough to realise the scale of the task that Tempus had agreed to undertake? She felt a mixture of emotions: empathy, guilt, responsibility and anger.

But mostly anger. Only with it could she appease all the others.

And so resolved, she faced the door and stepped through.

Her eyes had become so unaccustomed to the light. When she dared to open them, she realised she had not returned home. The disappointment of this crushed her spirit. Had she expected it to be so easy? Instead it seemed to her the simulation had been reset. She was at the East Tower, standing before its high gates, in her familiar wardrobe of white.

After a moment, she sensed the presence of another beside her.

'Helen!' she heard herself cry. She rushed to her friend, a reflection of herself, a virtual twin, and held her in her arms.

'Tempus,' Helen replied, her body relenting to her friend's warm embrace. They separated and looked at one another. 'Or perhaps,' she added, 'now, so close to the end, we can *both* use our real names.'

'Yes,' she replied.

'Rachel.'

Tempus felt something give inside, the articulation of her name for the first time in so long, the whisper of a shell above the sound of a hurricane. 'You never once asked,' she challenged.

'No,' Helen replied. 'I'm sorry.'

'Why didn't you?'

'You said we met once. I assumed the meeting hadn't gone well. Seems I was right, wasn't I?' Tempus smiled. 'And perhaps, you didn't trust me. I don't blame you. I am the daughter of Henry Mayer, after all.' She looked around her, out across the Sorrow towards the dead wall that was BridgeWest. Where once its Tower had been was now just more adjoining darkness. The suns overheads glinted speckled light off the amrita below, its jellied surface stultified in the still air. But the sky was unusually dark, she noticed. Not night, obviously. But perhaps, in the real world, it might have been described as a few hours before dusk. 'I created all this,' she added after a while.

'I know.'

'With your help, of course. You created the machine, I gave the machine life. And Dr Bishop. Let's not forget him and all the others. You and Bishop at least didn't know the parts you played.'

'Patrick,' Tempus replied, his name like a foreign language on her tongue, the memory of whom she had wrapped in a chrysalis, the pain of that separation being too much to bear. 'Is he…?'

'No, he's still alive. He's somewhere out there.' She waved a finger towards BridgeWest. 'Or perhaps, he's here. A blacksmith or a weaver. My father has his own *individual* sense of irony. He chooses the programme.'

'He can do that?'

'Oh yes, Tempus. Yin and yang. Good and evil.

It's his thing.'

'*His* thing. But not yours, Helen.' Her friend looked away once more. 'You remember it all now?'

Helen did not reply. 'You did well. To destroy it,' she answered instead.

'It was what you wanted. I couldn't have done it without you.'

'No.'

'The East Tower hasn't fallen though,' Tempus sighed. 'The Bridge is still standing.'

'There is no Bridge, Helen.'

'No bridge?'

'That is what is meant by the Great Unseen. You cannot see it because it isn't there.'

'The Towers aren't connected?'

'No. At least not in this world.'

Tempus blinked. The high sun was troubling her as it did all new arrivals. Soon, her eyes would adjust. But she didn't want them to adjust. She didn't want to be in this world long enough to adjust. She felt panic seize her. She looked up and wondered if her mara was lying in wait for her, that it had somehow followed her across from the West. Then she met Helen's gaze. She seemed different. Resigned. Defeated. But worse than that. Her eyes betrayed sympathy. Like those of a mother consoling a child who has just had her heart broken.

'The Island,' she began again, following Tempus' gaze. 'Only the mara, the suns and the moons see it as it really is.'

'What do you mean?'

'Its geography. Its shape. You need perspective to appreciate it. A bird's eye view.'

'I don't understand, Helen.'

'The five Villages, Rachel. We were named as Apprentices of two of them. Ceres and Tempus. But what of Frontes, Pares and Occus? Are those names familiar to you?'

Tempus clawed a rake of fingers through her scalp and tried to think. Yes, they were familiar. But in what way? If she had a surgeon's knife she would have sliced open her brain, anatomised its contents, extracted the answer from the grey. Rendered it either black or white. And then it came to her.

'The brain.'

Helen smiled, sadly. 'The cerebellum, the temporal, frontal, parietal and occipital lobes. As I say, my father's sense of humour.'

'And BridgeEast and BridgeWest?'

'The hemispheres. The corpus callosum is the bridge between them, of course. If you have a proclivity to the left brain, you are more analytical, logical and so on. If you are more right brain dominant, you are more creative, artistic. You know all this, of course, but none of it really mattered to my father. He just enjoyed the symbolism.'

'The symbolism?'

'It ties in with how he sees his universe. Light

and dark. Right and wrong. I saw the design once. The map, if you like. Tempus, the Island is shaped like the human brain, right down to the topography of its coastline.'

Tempus shook her head. 'But why...?'

'The Great Forgetting in the world beyond begins there. In the dark cavern of the mind. On the Island, you also forget. Forget that you have forgotten.'

'But you never forgot, did you, Helen?! Tempus exclaimed, giving way to the anger coursing through her veins.

'I did forget, Rachel. Everything I told you was the truth. In the beginning I only remembered my name.'

'But why did your father send you here? I can see why he wanted to get rid of us. I know he's using us to maintain the system somehow.' Helen looked down. 'But why you? I knew that you both had your disagreements...'

'...I have it, Tempus,' she replied, softly, her eyes scanning the surface of the Sorrow. 'The virus. That is why I came back to him. He is trying to protect me.' Helen took a few steps across the gravel incline and gazed down the precipice into the river below. She stretched out her arms and sucked in the breeze. 'I wonder what would happen if I simply threw myself over the edge, Tempus? Would I die in this world or in the other? Would my father play God and send a mara to whisk me away to safety. I wonder...'

She moved closer to the fringe of cliff which bordered the two realities and which dropped to the amrita below. She levelled a right sandal on the flatness of air a footstep ahead, while using her left arm for balance. 'Or would I wake up in the centre of the spider's web again?' She inched her left arm upwards slightly, tipping herself forward, a bottle about to spill its contents over the edge of itself.

'Helen!' She felt two strong arms pull her back from the verge, strong enough to make her lose her footing. She fell backwards, her momentum also causing Tempus to fall. They found themselves facing upwards, to the line in the sky where the East Tower disappeared from view. 'He lied to you, Helen.'

Helen turned her head to face Tempus. 'I *have* the virus. Don't you think I haven't been tested?'

Tempus stood up. 'Your father is not interested in a cure. He doesn't want to save that world. He wants one of his own. You know that, Helen. That's why you thought about killing yourself just then.'

'I didn't...'

'...That's why your instinct was to help me before. You know this place is wrong, Helen. Evil...'

'Evil...?'

'...Tell me how to destroy it, Helen!' Tempus exclaimed, grabbing Helen by the hand. 'The West Tower wasn't enough, was it?'

'There are two servers…' she began.

'Servers?' Tempus sprung to her feet. 'That's it. The East Tower is the back up. Both Towers need to fall. Yes. Good. I understand. How do we do that? Will what I did before work?' Helen did not reply. 'Helen?!'

Helen brushed some dirt away from her arms. The gesture was a metaphor. She wasn't prepared to listen to her father being accused of safeguarding the antidote to a virus that had killed tens of millions. She was withdrawing from their alliance. Tempus felt desperation fill her once more. 'How did you wake up?' Helen asked.

'I…I remembered my pre-life, Helen. I am guessing everyone does so in the end whether they visit the Archives or not. Your father knows this so he makes the flaw in the system a strength. Or tries to. He embroiders it with religion. The Circles. The truth is no one becomes One with the Great Unseen. They just die.'

'I don't mean that. How did you wake up *enough*?'

'Wake up enough?'

'No one survives the West.'

'Neither has anyone ever destroyed the Tower. That was the plan, remember?'

Helen pursed her lips. And then a new thought appeared to rise to the surface of her mind. 'After the Circles, you came to me and told me my name: Helen Mayer.'

'Yes.'

'Why did you do that?'

'You were right when you said I didn't trust you, Helen. But the fact that you too had been brought to the Island meant something too. I wanted to escape. Maybe, you knowing your name might precipitate that.'

'Buy why did my father not prevent this from happening? Intercede. Prevented you from telling me.'

'Could he have?' Tempus enquired.

'He has his Masters to do his bidding for him. They kept a close watch on me the whole time I am sure.'

'Less so me, perhaps?'

'No, as Rachel Hunter, co-creator of Localis, you would have been high up on his danger list.'

'Maybe that was why the Master Apprentice brought us together then. To keep an eye on us both. Or…?'

'…Or what?'

Tempus thought back to her first meeting with Helen in the Archives. 'Or perhaps your father thought our combined sub-consciousnesses might come up with something to save Localis. It is dying, isn't it? The maras' intrusions into the East or a sign of that, aren't they?'

Helen nodded. 'The destruction of the West Tower has put the entire mainframe in jeopardy.'

'Then, let us destroy this one. We can return

to reality. Rebuild it. Improve upon it. We created this world. We can repair our own!'

'I don't believe you, Tempus! I can't!'

Tempus took a breath and approached Helen. She tried to grab her friend's hand but Helen snapped it away. Tempus sighed and closed her eyes. 'Helen it was your father, Henry Mayer, that created the virus in the first place.'

'No! No! Why would you say that?' Helen replied, reeling backwards almost to the edge of the cliff.

'Because it's true,' another voice replied.

Helen and Tempus looked up, shielding their eyes from the glare of the two suns above, the light from which served to conceal the advance of a luminescent figure, an angel without wings whose outline shimmered in the haze before finally emerging into view.

'Two suns, twice the day!' the Seer said, greeting them anew.

27

The door led to a tunnel. Its slick, whitewashed walls revealing in places the original brickwork -a mish mash of misshapen rock poulticed together centuries before. In keeping with the medieval ambience, a line of braziers tilted from the walls, their fires flickering shadows onto a broken path of slab and earth.

'This is madness,' Knight suggested, genuine fear in his voice.

'That's what Henney would be saying right now -if he was here,' McKenna replied. 'But he's not. And the reason he's not lies ahead. At the end of this tunnel. Believe me, Knight, I've been in tighter spots.'

'But they're expecting us!' Knight moaned. 'The fires are lighting our way!'

'Keep your bloody voice down,' McKenna snapped. 'Stay here if you like,' he continued, grabbing Knight's shirt. 'But make no mistake, a bullet's going to find you in the end.'

'Or worse,' Rachel said, from behind me.

'What could be worse?' I asked.

She didn't reply. Instead Rachel hugged herself

against the cold. I turned to examine the tunnel ahead. It was about twenty metres long, a straight channel to where another larger door awaited. Puddles lay strewn between like land mines where the rain had leaked from above. The air was dank and smoked our words as we spoke.

'Wait!' McKenna warned, letting go of Knight. 'There's a couple of small doors there, just off to the right. Hang back!' McKenna moved forward cautiously. He took a quick look through one, then another longer one. Satisfied, he sidled along to the other door. It must have been closed as he drove the heft of his boot through it. After a moment, he hissed: 'All clear!'

As we passed, I threw a glance into the rooms. Both had thick walls and what appeared to be a deep basin inside. One had a grilled floor; the other iron hooks hanging from the ceiling. 'An ice house to refrigerate meat,' Rachel explained to me over my shoulder. 'And a smoking room to flavour it. Our monks weren't vegetarians at any rate.' I nodded and pressed on, McKenna and Knight leading the way.

When we got to the end of the tunnel, McKenna lifted the latch of the door. It scraped noisily against the ground as it opened.

'Bloody hell!' Knight groaned again.

I was expecting a few shafts of light to filter through the gap but none appeared. Whatever lay on the other side of the door was in as much darkness as we were. For the first time in several minutes I heard more gun fire. A couple of shots and then silence.

'Here we go then,' McKenna said. 'For what it's worth, it *hasn't* been a pleasure!'

But on his face, there were the makings of a grin. The first time I had seen the bugger happy. I smiled too inside. I could have given the brute a hug of his own there and then. If I *was* going to die in the next sixty seconds, I couldn't have thought of better company. Even Knight's T-shirts of hard metal rock had grown on me. I searched for Rachel's hand in the shadows. And it was there. Waiting for me. My only regret was not having the chance to say goodbye to Imogen. But wherever her mind was now, I knew it was probably too far away for me to reach.

McKenna went through and we followed, finding ourselves next in a small closet of a room, dominated by the bottom of a spiral staircase. There wasn't much space and an image of a lighthouse came to me. A lighthouse without the light. McKenna puffed his cheeks and sighed. 'Hold on, people,' he said. 'We're not there yet.'

There weren't many steps to the floor above. After a few seconds, we found ourselves in the musty but scented air of the chapel's transept. We were in semi-darkness but just a few metres to our right I could pick out the nave of the church running perpendicular to our location. It was swimming in a stencil of variegated light. The rays of the moon were in there somewhere, a major part of the palette that washed across the pews on either side. We stepped towards it, our boots too heavy on the varnished, oak floor, McKenna working his rifle all angles, as if he had just entered an enemy foxhole.

Which, of course, we had.

I looked up. The ceiling was adorned with bas relief: alternating rows of what looked like moons and suns and noughts and crosses. And then, out of the stillness, the sound of someone whistling again. The same melody as before. Only louder. When it stopped, a voice boomed in the half-light.

'Surely you recognise it? Dr Hunter?...No?...Dr Knight? Now, *you* must know it, Dr Bishop? No? What about you, Mr McKenna? Even you had a childhood?' The sounds of our names echoed out from the four high corners of the church. They amplified anonymously from speakers which filled the air above our heads, an encounter with an invisible god. Which was probably the precise effect a maniac like Henry Mayer wanted to have on us. Up ahead, McKenna ducked, his outline making itself as small a target as possible. 'Don't worry, Mr McKenna. We have the chapel completely surrounded. As for General Barrett and his men. We only executed those who refused to surrender willingly. The others are merely wounded. The general himself is unscathed.' A pause ensued. 'His neural functions are still intact.'

'You're a bloody mad man, Mayer!' McKenna roared.

'Come into the light. I can assure you, you will not be harmed. No?' Mayer began to whistle again. That tune, I thought. Where had I heard it recently? And then the melody began once more. But this time, a different tone. Someone else was whistling now.

'Imogen!' I cried out, unable to stop myself rushing forward, past the crouching form of McKenna and into the river of light that ran along the nave of the chapel.

'Patrick!' I heard Rachel scream behind me.

I stood, facing the altar of the chapel, transfixed by the grotesque representation of Henry Mayer in the glass above. It appeared to float on a scattered rainbow of light, arms outstretched, the humanity of a sinner superimposed over that of a deity. Only it wasn't Henry Mayer. Not from any pictures I had seen of that man. But someone who bore a close resemblance to him. I felt my head lighten, my knees weaken, as just then it seemed the moon had travelled across the heavens to assume a position just behind the face in the glass. But it wasn't the moon. It was a manufactured spotlight, a navigation of rays from the raised gallery behind me. I turned around and looked up.

Winston, dressed in a hooded cowl, was staring down at me, a machine gun aimed in my direction. I turned around to face the altar again but the moon had gone. Instead, on either side, and all along the length of the pews, a procession of candelabra had wound a course, a votive mass of trembling light that danced shadows on the ceiling. To the left, in front of a microphone by the pulpit, the emaciated figure of Henry Mayer, his eyes like burning coals, the sneer of his mouth agape, his arms making the shape of an L as though he were conjuring demons from the large tome in front of him. Beside him, a face I knew better, even though it too was hooded. Elias Levy, incongruous in his robes.

And beside Levy, my sister Imogen, reduced now to a long, vacant, expressionless stare, that of a tenant who had long since vacated his property.

'Imogen!' I cried out again. But she failed even to turn her head, something invisible, hanging in mid-air was assuming all her attention. A fury I had never felt before rose inside me, both hot and cold at the same time, but I knew I could not yield to it. At least, not yet. Not until Imogen was safe.

'Your sister is fine, Dr Bishop. She is better, in fact, than she has been in a long while.'

'What have you given her?' I yelled, the control in my voice surprising me given the hell I was experiencing within.

'I have called it *amrita*. It appears in ancient texts -the drink of the devas.'

'If you harm her…!'

'…You do not have to worry on that account, Dr Bishop. On the contrary, one day those like your sister will live forever.'

'What are you talking about?'

'I will explain. But first, why not ask your friends to step out from the shadows? As I said,' he looked across at Imogen, 'there is no escape from here.'

The message was clear even if he had not said the words. Imogen's life was at stake. Weighed up numerically against the fate of the world it shouldn't have been much of a choice. But she was my sister. And she needed me. Even if she was well past knowing who I was. There were billions of human beings out there, I knew, that also need saving. But I didn't know them. I had no connection to them. They were the faces in the crowd that populated the periphery of my dreams at night. I didn't hate them, but nor did I love them. The truth was I felt as indifferent to them as to the trees in the forest. I had nothing against them. At least not until bare necessity required me to reduce one or more to chopped wood.

'Come out!' I shouted across to McKenna. 'And put your gun down!' I noticed McKenna flinch in the darkness. 'Rachel. Bill,' I added softly. 'You two as well.' They approached me like sullen children forced to return home at nightfall. 'McKenna,' I added, with resignation, 'drop the gun. There's no point.'

'No point?' he repeated. He smiled at me. 'You're right. No point.' He made to let go of his rifle but at the last moment swung himself out of the darkness, twisting his body towards Winston perched in the gallery above. 'McKenna!' I roared, but it was too late. He got one shot off, but not before he took two of his own in the chest.

'You bastard!' I screamed at Winston, diving myself for McKenna's rifle. Strange, I thought to myself, in the eternity it took me to reach his weapon. I'll sacrifice the world for Imogen, but myself for McKenna, the type of half-witted barbarian I used to despise. Perhaps, humanity was worth saving after all.

'I wouldn't if I were you, Mr Bishop. I have you,' Winston warned, 'right between the eyes. It would be a shame if I were to make a mess of that impressive brain of yours.'

'Winston is correct,' Mayer's voice bellowed from behind. 'McKenna made his choice, Dr Bishop.'

I turned around. 'I suppose you're going to tell me you made yours a long time ago, Mayer. The only difference is yours has meant the destruction of the entire planet.'

Mayer smiled, nodded to Levy, and made his way down from the pulpit. In the candlelight, he looked like a minister from centuries ago, a mad monk of a preacher whose idea of heaven was to bring hell to Earth.

'Yes, I have made choices. But they were forced upon me.'

'Who forced you?'

'In the absence of God, you have to become a god, Dr Bishop.'

'So, you create your own Apocalypse,' I heard Rachel say behind me.

'Not mine, Dr Hunter,' Mayer replied. 'His!' He pointed a finger at the stained-glass bay window. 'The one who guided my path. Jonathan Mayer.'

'Another mad man,' I declared.

'A visionary. His Final Testament. Soon *two* worlds will know of it. Its final pages warn of a pestilence that will ravage the Earth. Only the faithful will escape to the Island.'

'The Island?'

'Heaven on Earth, Dr Bishop. Paradise. The old world washed away to make way for the new.'

'Only that would take time. Wouldn't it, Mayer?' Rachel interrupted, standing beside me now.

He smiled, appreciatively. 'It was you, Dr Hunter, who gave me the inspiration. My daughter, Helen, carried on the work.'

'Your daughter? She's here? Where is she?'

'In the caverns beneath our feet. You will see her shortly.'

'So, you create a plague to facilitate the insane doctrine of one of your ancestors?' I asked.

'I was following the Word.'

'If that's true, then why make a cure?' I asked.

He laughed and took a few steps closer to me. I could see him clearer now, his hair wet and parted with some scented oil or other, his eyes cruel and despotic. 'There is no cure.'

'But Winston said...' Rachel began.

'...A ruse to lure you here.'

'Why?!' I demanded.

'For your minds, Bishop. You are already Stage One. How long do you think you have? You will make the journey to the Island first. As far you, Dr Hunter. You too will have a special role.'

'I'll never do it.'

'Maybe not, *consciously*.'

I looked at Imogen whose arm Levy was tightly holding. 'There is no cure,' I repeated to myself. The world, it seemed, was a stack of tarot cards, I thought, made up of random chance. They had once made a house, or a church like this one, but now were collapsing in on themselves.

'I told you the truth, Bishop,' Levy interjected, smiling. 'Remember? I told you there was no cure at least 'not in the way you think of one'.'

'What is the cure then?'

'The Island, of course,' Levy replied.

'That is correct, Master Acolyte,' Mayer continued, staring proudly at Levy. 'And here...' he continued, turning to Winston, who was approaching down the aisle towards us, '... behold, my Master Apprentice! We will create a utopia where no one will ever want or need anything again.'

'This isn't happening,' I heard Knight say. He began to laugh nervously.

'I can assure you *this*,' he stretched out his arms and breathed in the air, 'is the only thing that will remain of *your* reality,' Mayer said. 'Survivors will congregate at out gates and beg to be allowed inside.'

'What is amrita?' Rachel asked, her scientific mind reasserting itself even now.

'A drug, developed by our doctors, to sedate and sustain the illusion of the new world,' Mayer replied. 'It is fed intravenously into the body. A chemical which can prolong a person's body indefinitely.'

'You are a liar,' Rachel declared, stepping forward. She was so much shorter than Mayer and yet in that moment so much taller than he. 'All of this religious mumbo jumbo is just that. Mumbo jumbo. You had an empire, Mayer. And you cast it all to the dirt. For what? The ramblings of a wannabe prophet that just so happened to be related to you. No, I don't believe it. You had no predilection towards religion not until...not until the death of your wife.'

'Be careful, Dr Hunter!' Mayer warned.

'And she died of Alzheimer's, didn't she?' Rachel continued, unfazed. 'The only person besides your daughter you ever truly loved. And so, overwhelmed by grief, you searched for a cure. You became obsessed. A recluse. Even had a falling out with your daughter, the only other person you cared about. But, without realising it at first, you manufactured the opposite. A virus that *destroys* the neurochemistry of its victim. And somehow it escaped the lab. A pathogen that was latent, but...'

'...I will create a universe where death will lose its meaning!' Mayer roared.

'Yes, but all that came afterwards. After you picked through the strands of Jonathan Mayer's pseudo-claptrap and merged it with some techno-babble of your own invention. My version of Localis gave you the idea. Helen took over the baton. But then the Great Forgetting occurred and you realised you needed to find a cure.'

'I have found it!'

'A cure?! You're not even looking for one! You have devoted all your efforts to maintaining this system of yours. This Island. That's why your laboratories are empty. You have fallen victim to your own fairy tale. You even gave up your research into sherbet.'

'Sherbet?' he sneered. 'A failed drug. A toy. That's why it was given the name. But even it has its uses. It is the stimulus we use to counteract the effects of the amrita. It pulls the person out of their dreams.'

What the hell? I thought. Sherbet? Exactly how much of that stuff had I taken? Enough to rouse an elephant from its coma. For the first time, I had the inkling of some hope. That somehow I might wake up from this drug-induced nightmare. Brownlow had taken it too. I wondered, sadly, if the old man was still alive.

'If you didn't have a cure for the virus,' I asked, 'then why did you have Winston here release a mutated strand?'

'For the reasons he gave you. Don't worry, that particular strand of the virus has a shelf life. In six months, it will runs its course. In the meantime, it will drive others to Localis. Here, and throughout the world. But come, let me show you what became of your work, Dr Hunter. I think you will change your mind when you see exactly what my daughter and I have achieved.'

We were led at gunpoint to the sacristy of the church and then through another door which led to yet another staircase. At the bottom of it, an elevator ran several floors underground. Inside, I could almost touch Imogen, hold her in my arms, but Levy straightened his pistol at me, warning me off.

'*This* is Localis!' Mayer declared, when we exited the lift into a vast subterranean complex of cubicles and pods, computer terminals and state of the art mainframes. In the centre, a huge mechanical spider stretched its tentacles outwards in all directions. I could hear breathing -a ventilation system -and for a brief moment I thought it was alive. It wasn't, but it had a heart. I could see it beat once every couple of seconds, a light somewhere in its underbelly was flashing red. 'Helen believes we have imitated the Creator,' Mayer said, as we walked along one of the metal platforms that separated the lines of cubicles. 'A simulation within a simulation, perhaps? When a world achieves insight into its own base reality, it moves onto the next level. I will be the god of this new Eden. What is a virus, Dr Hunter, after all? But something that prevents the proper functioning of a computer. A computer 'sleeps' just as we do. It slows down with age. Just as we do. It has a memory. Just as we *did*.'

I was overwhelmed by the horror of it all. Rows and rows of bio bunks, thirty levels high, and in each one a victim, scarcely breathing, a razor's edge away from death, tubes no doubt fed into every orifice.

'And the programme? Rachel asked. 'This Island?'

'From my very own blueprint,' Mayer said. 'A model of the world Jonathan Mayer tried to build. We will start small. But the Island will grow.'

'What are those?' I asked.

'The Towers? They are our servers.' I couldn't believe what I was seeing. At the far end of the chamber, squinting lights like two mad computers playing chess with one another, were two enormous monoliths, almost thirty metres tall. 'Impressive, aren't they? They are like sisters. If one falls, the other will take its place.'

'They'll never last,' Rachel said.

'They will, Dr Hunter. They will.'

We had gone as far as Mayer had wanted to take us. He seemed impervious to the cold which had covered everything in a sheen of frost. A fog lingered around the spider in the centre and oozed outwards, tainting our tongues with the taste of dried ice. The biopods had a glass or plastic casing under a morass of wires and cables. I noticed that each time the spider oscillated its light a corresponding light responded inside the pod. What Mayer and his daughter had accomplished was nothing short of remarkable -a technology that really could play its part in renewing the world if it hadn't ended up in the hands of someone like Henry Mayer. But in a world that had stopped being a meritocracy aeons ago perhaps it was what we deserved. We were beside a cubicle now behind whose glacial window I identified the face of a famous movie star. In my world, his death had been publicised, at a time when death still had some meaning. Somewhere, in Mayer's universe, he had paid for less than a starring role. A fully immersive performance without acclaim and with an audience that didn't know they were an audience.

'This is my daughter, Helen' Mayer was saying now. 'In a while, she will be joining you all on the Island.' She had been standing in the mist that had gathered at the foot of one Mayer's servers. A perfectly healthy and apparently sane woman in her late twenties. A wave of auburn hair framing a face I hoped I would never forget. Hazel eyes, a snub of nose and cheek bones like brush strokes on canvas. She was of similar height and build to Rachel who stepped out from behind me. 'Stay back, Dr Hunter,' Mayer warned. 'Or Winston here may need to shoot you in the leg.'

Rachel and Helen studied one another, two geniuses that had taken different paths. If Rachel had been Mayer's daughter, no doubt she would have turned out the same way.

'I wanted to meet you, Dr Hunter.'

'Oh?' Rachel replied.

'Yes, to say thank you. Without your early work...'

'Forget it, Helen,' Rachel replied, harshly. 'You here to see us off?'

'It's the only way, doctor. Soon, very soon, you will see that.'

'I doubt it, Helen. I don't care how many drugs your father pumps me with.'

'We'll see,' Helen replied. She turned to her father. 'Both servers are performing within normal parameters,' she announced, mechanically. 'The West Tower is programmed to back up the East. We shouldn't have any more problems.'

Mayer nodded and watched his daughter return to her station by the Towers, her figure gradually becoming an apparition of beauty in the fog rather than the thing itself.

'Now then, it is time,' Mayer declared.

'Time for what?' Knight asked.

'Time for you all to depart. Time for time to have no further power over us. Winston, the pods are ready?'

'Yes, Advocate.'

'Begin with Dr Bishop's sister. She is the one with the greatest need.'

'Leave her alone!' I screamed at Mayer, lurching at Winston. Before I could defend myself, the butt of his rifle thudded against my forehead sending me sprawling backwards. 'Next time, you try anything like that, Dr Bishop, you will not need drugs to put you to sleep!'

I felt Rachel's arm on mine, tugging me backwards, as Winston lifted my helpless sister in his arms. Levy pressed a button somewhere and a hatch opened in one of the cubicles beside us. Strangely, for technology so advanced, it made a common sound as it opened, like a window whirring down on a car. I thought again of Brownlow, sitting in the back seat of his black saloon, the first time I met him. And all the times Winston had chauffeured him around before that. Winston stopped and looked at me, as though reading my thoughts.

'Oh, I forgot to tell you, Dr Bishop,' he said. 'I'm afraid our previous employer didn't make it.' He laughed. An ugly laugh which became an echo as Levy joined in. I freed myself from Rachel's arms, but the latter intervened, his pistol aimed directly at my heart. Winston smiled and placed Imogen carefully inside the biopod. He made some adjustments inside. She didn't struggle, no doubt her own heart already pumping Mayer's amrita around her shell-shocked body. Imogen's chamber closed and as it did so a series of syringes and tubes stabbed and writhed into and around her. A few moments later, a red light blinked once at the bottom of her casing.

My head ached and I could sense a cold wetness over my brow. I wiped it away. Levy grinned as I did so. 'Give the rest their injections now!' Mayer announced, victoriously.

Levy waved his pistol at Knight, manoeuvring him towards another biopod. Winston produced a small, steel canister from his pocket, the kind used to hold expensive, solitary cigars. He grabbed a handful of Knight's hair and jerked his head back. 'Get your hands off me!' Knight screamed, before Winston jabbed the metal rod into his neck and his body went limp.

'Now then, Master Apprentice,' Mayer instructed. 'Dr Hunter. But please be gentler. After all, we owe her so much. Besides, she will make you a fine Apprentice.'

Winston took hold of Rachel's wrist and before she knew it his needle had punctured her arm. Her body collapsed instantaneously. And with it the last of my soul. Winston laid her inert body gently at Mayer's feet. A sacrifice to his god.

'It's not going to work!' I roared, my voice carrying upwards, above the fog, up into the medieval chapel and through its rafters into the starry night beyond. The real stars. With its real moon.

'It already has, Dr Bishop,' Mayer replied. 'I am afraid you have no moves left.'

28

'Seer!' Helen cried, her first impulse to rush towards him. But she knew she couldn't, of course. Such a display of emotion would have merely aroused his suspicion.

'Ceres,' he replied.

The Seer looked no different to the last time Helen had seen him, on their way to the Archives, before she had first encountered the Master Apprentice. His clothes, however, were tattered and unwashed. By his feet, a woman lay, dressed in rags. She seemed exhausted, not fully conscious, and though Helen couldn't say for sure, she guessed the Seer had been carrying her. Standing next to him was a man dressed in dark navy. The colour of the Weavers.

'Weaver,' Tempus said, recognising the man. 'You are a long way from our Village.'

The man smiled. 'Yes, Apprentice.'

Strange, Tempus thought. Why had the Weaver smiled at her? She looked at him with fresh eyes. He was like so many of the male workers in BridgeEast, androgynous and passive, but without his sunshades his face took on a newer appearance. Then there was his voice. It seemed happy. But not just happy. His words percolated as though they carried with themselves some slow anticipation. 'Who is this?' she asked the Seer, pointing at the woman on the ground. The man looked at her, his eyes lucid and, if she was not mistaken, stained with tears. She had never met the Seer, except in the fantastic conspiracy conjured up by the Acolytes and promulgated throughout the Island. This was, after all, the man who was supposed to have corrupted both her and Helen. He was also meant to have been exiled.

'She is my…sister,' he replied.

'Your sister?' Tempus responded, taken aback.

'Yes, Rachel. My sister.'

Tempus felt her heart leap at the sound of her name. She took a step towards the Seer and scrutinised his face. A tear had just escaped the well of his right eye. She stretched out a fingertip, amazed by her own behaviour, and carefully removed it. She examined the minuscule diamond which caught the light of one of the suns behind her. 'You are…crying?'

'Tears of joy.'

'But who are you? How do you know my name?'

'You know who I am, Rachel. You know us all. Look closer.'

She stared at him again, through the wet crystal of his eyes. 'Patrick?!' she exclaimed, the word caught in her throat. He nodded. 'Patrick!'

They embraced, each one holding the other, as if they were both adrift at sea and afraid to be cast away to separate shores.

'But then, this is Imogen,' Tempus remarked finally, separating herself from the Seer's embrace and kneeling beside the woman. She placed a hand on her head. She recognised the symptoms. Imogen had spent time in the West. Too much time. 'And you?' she questioned, getting to her feet.

'Bill. Bill Knight.'

'Bill!' Tempus held him too in his arms, his body warm against hers. He wasn't really there, of course. Not her Bill. But then again, neither was she.

'But how is this possible?' Helen asked.

'I'll explain,' The Seer replied. 'But first, let us move away from here. I know a cave nearby. Quickly! Mayer's people could be upon us any minute!'

'You mean the Advocate?' Tempus clarified.

'My father,' Helen added.

'You know then?' the Weaver asked.

'Yes,' Helen replied.

'And the West Tower?'

'That was me,' Tempus said.

'I thought it was,' the Seer responded, managing another smile.

The cave was a mile away, embedded into the cliff, down a grassy incline. They sat on rocks around a fire, none of them scarcely able to believe they were there.

'Dr Bishop, where have you been?' Helen asked.

'You don't know?'

'How would I know?'

The Seer glanced at the Weaver. 'Perhaps from your father? You have been in contact with him?'

'Yes,' she replied, looking down.

'What?!' Tempus exclaimed.

'Just once,' Helen protested.

'What did he want?' the Seer persisted.

'He wants me to stop Tempus…I mean Rachel.'

'Helen, it's true what Rachel said,' the Seer continued. 'You father created the virus. He might not have done so on purpose but he did so all the same. You have to believe us.'

'Why is it so important that I do?

'Because you have to help us wake up. *Fully* wake up.'

'Even if I wanted to, how can I help?'

'We have to destroy…shut down the second Tower,' Tempus said.

'Localis is our only hope,' Helen replied.

'Localis is failing. You know this to be true. How else could the mara be making their way across from the West. That server has already gone offline. The mara are symbolic of the system breaking down.'

'Is that how you woke up?' Tempus asked.

The Seer picked up a stray bit of wood and tossed it into the fire. What Helen Mayer had achieved had changed science forever and he had never stopped feeling amazed. He felt his skin warm as the flames crackled into life once more. Even though he and the fire weren't really there, one gazing at the other. He sensed the discomfort in his lower back as he sat. If he were to grab a handful of dirt now, he wouldn't be able to count the grains as he let them slip through his fingers. 'I woke up before then, Rachel. Not long after I last saw you, Helen.'

'How?' Tempus asked.

'Sherbet. There was enough in my system to counteract the amrita, to build up an immunity to it.'

'Is that possible?'

'Mayer himself said it was the counteragent.'

'But why didn't you…?' Tempus' voice tapered off. She looked away and stared into the fire.

'…Why didn't I seek you out earlier?'

'Yes.'

'I wanted to. Believe me. But Mayer placed you in a different Village, removed from my influence. That's if he even thought it was possible for someone to wake up *and* wake others up.'

'But he allowed you to meet *me*?' Helen asked.

'Yes. Briefly. But you remember how the Master Apprentice, that is Winston, interrupted our journey to the Archives.'

'And so you have fooled Localis all this time?' Helen asked. 'Made them think you were still under its spell?'

'I am *still* under its spell, Helen.'

'So, what happened to you, Patrick?' Tempus asked.

'My supposed exile wasn't an exile, Rachel. I left Ceres to look for Imogen. I knew she wasn't in the East. I had occasion a few times to meet up with the other Seers and found Bill here working as a Weaver in Tempus.'

'And you left me there,' Bill teased.

'Temporarily, while I made my way to the West. The Advocate, Mayer, obviously found out about me going AWOL and fabricated a different narrative which he tied in with your own, Rachel.'

'How did you get to the West?' she asked.

'Suicide.'

'What?!'

'Death. Same way you did.'

'How is that possible?'

'You can't actually die, Rachel,' Helen interrupted. 'Not on the Island. But you can shock the system into changing programme. Usually, my father controls the location, East or West, for each the individual user. Those in the latter stages of the virus get sent to BridgeWest. It replicates, he thinks, their state of mind. That is: insanity. However, it seems, you can also cheat the programme into banishing you there. All these concepts run along the same principles. That was why when you were thrown into the

Sorrow you awoke in BridgeWest. But…?'

'But what?' Tempus enquired.

Helen turned to the Seer. 'But how did you possibly know that when you…?'

'…that when I killed myself, I would end up in the West? I didn't, Helen. But what had I to lose? I would have gone mad in any case. But time was of the essence.' A long silence ensued.

'So you found Imogen?' Tempus began again.

'Yes.'

'And you came back?'

'A lot of us were able to escape.'

'But how?'

'Through the same door as you did, Rachel.'

'But you did not bring down the West Tower in the process!'

'I have been awake a lot longer than you. I was able to control the energetic flow from the stones. Besides, you were trying to destroy the monolith.'

'So, the server has crashed?' Tempus asked, facing Helen.

'Literally,' Helen replied, looking upwards. 'Can't you tell?'

'The sky. I have never seen it so dark,' Tempus replied.

'Yes,' the Seer acknowledged. 'As though the world has been thrown off its axis or hit by a meteorite.'

'So what now?' Helen asked.

'You have decided to help us?' the Seer asked,

in return.

'Yes,' she replied slowly. 'Before it is too late for you all.'

'You think…?

'…My father is a vindictive man, Dr Bishop. Yes, he needs people to power his matrix. He would probably like you both to join him, help him restore Localis. But if his universe is coming apart at the seams, he will not think twice about destroying you and everyone else in it.'

He thought about how it would end. It was a race against time, the Seer knew. Would he simply vanish in an instant, his 'form' in this world, its entrapment of localised photons, winking out of existence, leaving behind a space which he had once occupied. Or would his programme degrade slowly? First an arm? Then a leg? Perhaps, ghoulishly, his head might vanish first? And would he awake, if only for a moment, as Patrick, back at the Abbey, his cold tomb under the floorboards of an abandoned church? A few precious moments in his own skin before his soul, if he had one, departed his body forever?

The alternative was life. But how to live? They were all just the equivalent of pop-up pictures, unable to leave their pages, while Mayer sat musing by the fireside, deciding whether to snap shut the book or not.

It had been Helen's idea. Her journey to the City of Glass and its Inner Temple. Whilst he had worked out another plan for them. Perhaps, she could even dismantle the hardware, the server itself, while they disposed off the software.

'But aren't we being observed at all times?' he had asked.

'Usually,' Helen had replied. 'But the sky in the East has clouded over. That too is symbolic. Perhaps, they are blind now.'

So, they had said their farewells, the Seer watching on as the two women embraced. They had formed an attachment, he had noticed. As Tempus and Helen they had been close. But as Helen and Rachel? He wasn't sure.

And what of Imogen? Even as this embodiment of her real self, she was close to death. Would she even survive the transition? At least, if they made it back, he would be able to bury her remains. In a proper graveyard, near a proper church, not Mayer's obscene version of one.

They stayed a little while longer in the cave after Helen's departure. The Weaver and Tempus, two off-duty doctors, flasks of amrita sustaining them like drips in a hospital ward. While he collected rain. Yes, it had even started to rain. And the rain too was amrita, which he collected and placed on Imogen's tongue. That too an illusion from which that they couldn't break free -the instinct to satiate a thirst which was generated by proxy.

When they ventured forth once more, he

thought night had actually fallen but it was the mara, a plague of them having infested the storm skies above BridgeEast. In the distance, he could hear the sound of screams as they plummeted for their easy pickings -the guileless populations in the five Villages having not learnt the art of self-defence.

The East was becoming the new West. Only Knight, as a Weaver, had not experienced the suffering they would encounter. The landscape reduced to a wasteland of the dead, rib cages and flesh-stripped limbs scattered as far as their eyes could see, blood-soaked earth splattered by new rain that would never wash it away. The mara, unperturbed. feeding on the marrow of bones. On the cusp of the five horizons, the Seer imagined a pentagram, each side marked with a rising turret of smoke where each of the Villages had been.

'Where are ours?' the Weaver asked once.

'Our mara?' Tempus replied. 'I don't think we have one any anymore. At least, I do not see mine. That is a good sign. We have woken up from the nightmare.' She stopped and looked up at the sky. Biblical proportions of the beasts were appearing and disappearing behind the clouds. 'I can be incredibly stupid at times though.'

'What do you mean, Rachel?' the Seer asked.

'The mara,' she explained. 'Here, in this world, they are night terrors. A mare is a demon. Hence, the word. *Nightmare.* 'Soon it will all be gone,' she added. 'Everything except the Tower and the City of Glass.'

'So, let's go,' the Seer replied. 'The Tower is our only hope. The City is Helen's.'

Before it had been Levy, masquerading as the Master Acolyte, who had guided her there and so she was unsure whether she could return alone. Whether it had been something he or her father had done that had expedited her passage back. Perhaps, though, the Inner Temple was a portal that was always there. Or maybe it had been designed to recognise life patterns belonging to those of her father's inner circle.

In reality, it was her astral form reconnecting to its physical host, a biological imperative activated in her brain which had rung an alarm clock to her dormant motor functions.

The journey had been eventful, but none of the events had involved her directly. It was so different now, a stroll through a four-dimensional film set where action sequences were being played out and the actors unaware of her footfall through the different scenes.

By the time, she reached the Archives, they too had been destroyed. The dreams within, those gossamer layers of false sub-realities which had been Mayer's gift or curse to them all, had surrendered to the horrors of awakening. A herd of desert-walkers were ambling back and forth through their open gates, searching for something upon which to graze.

She thought of Akila and the lifetimes of imposed happiness and grief she had enjoyed and endured and a new, violent outrage burned inside her.

Carrion and those that would soon be carrion were all that remained of her father's paradise. Even the mara overhead had begun to feast on one another. A harsh rain was transforming the earth to sludge, an overdose of amrita to the addicted who no longer required it. More symbols, she thought, signposting His Holy Name's Final Book of Testament. But this was all meant to have taken place in reality. How fitting the Apocalypse forewarned centuries ago by Jonathan Mayer was playing out upon the crumbling stage of Henry Mayer's arcadian dreamscape.

The cries of the lost were carried on the rising wind and she did her best to shut them out. They were just voices in her head and she was not mad. The voices were not really there. Those that projected them had had their life terminated in another hell, a technological prison of amnesiacs and holographics. Their souls laminated, their hearts cellophaned, their bodies encased in plastic.

The suns were gone, behind a dense wall of vapour and, as the temperature plunged, the amrita had turned to snow. It christened her steps as she walked, her prints forming a lonely trail through the valleys, camouflaging her approach, a good angel, attired in white, determined to defeat a fallen one.

Finally, she arrived. The City of Glass was ghosting between alternating versions of itself. One where it retrieved its previous sparkling resplendence. One where it had been reduced to a shattered mirror of everlasting misfortune. And one where it simply wasn't there. She watched it flicker, a match on the verge of going out. But beyond its dying flame, the Inner Temple still stood defiantly, its dome like an igloo, frosted with ice.

She found the entrance in the wall which Levy had shown her and without hesitating walked through.

29

Tempus had been wrong. Her mara had not been overcome. It was there, guarding the gates of the Tower, and beside it two others; a trinity of evil in the midst of a multitude above, circling the monolith where the bodies of the death had formed a membrane half way up on all four sides. At their feet, another mara, crouched and inert. Imogen's beast of burden, as weak as her, having nothing to prey upon.

'I don't feel well,' the Weaver announced.

'You'll get used to it, Bill,' the Seer replied. 'There, in crystallised form, is the sum root of every sin you have ever committed. That's the very stuff that keeps you awake at night. Your mara is there, next to mine. And I guess yours too, Rachel?'

Tempus nodded.

'It's as if they know,' the Weaver suggested.

'They do,' the Seer replied.

'Why do they want to stop us? It's Mayer, isn't it?!'

'No, Bill,' the Seer answered, shaking his head slowly. 'Not this time.'

'I don't understand why they haven't left.

They have nothing left to kill except each other,' Tempus said.

'And they will,' the Seer agreed. 'But you know what Mark Antony said?'

'He said a lot of things, Patrick.'

The Seer smiled. 'True enough. But *one* of them was: *The evil that men do lives after them.* The mara will disappear, but not in the time left to us.'

'How long do you think we have?' the Weaver asked.

'This world doesn't have long,' the Seer replied. 'But then Mayer might flick the switch on it himself. Who knows what will come first?'

'So how are we going to get inside?' Tempus asked.

'What is the opposite of evil, Rachel?'

'Good.'

'And love?'

'Hate,' the Weaver replied.

'No, Bill, it's not. It's fear.'

It was different than before. This time there was no one to carry her to the chapel above, lay her down as an oblation to a false god.

She was inside Localis, like a butterfly still trapped in its cocoon. On every part of her body, she felt a distributed weight or a pressure point of pain. Her brain ached, an over-ripe fruit about to pierce through its skin. In her mouth, and elsewhere, tubes sealed her connection from whatever it was that lay beyond the confines of her body.

She blinked open her eyes and through a narrow band of plastic was able to make out the red mist of a light in the darkness. The afterglow of the Spider still spinning its web, slower and smaller circles.

She freed one hand and, in the limited space where she ended and the chamber began, managed to disconnect herself, one severed link at a time. A different deactivation sound heralded her release from the web.

And finally her body lightened. The genie was escaping from its bottle, she thought.

She fumbled for the emergency self-release mechanism that she herself had devised and the lid of her coffin opened slowly.

It was only then that she heard the cacophonous wail of multiple sirens ringing out. She removed herself from her alcove and looked left and right down her aisle of chambers. Almost all of them were flashing red, the covers of their sarcophagi unhinged at the same angle.

On unsteady feet, she reached for a panel on the wall beside her and locked in a combination of numbers which brought the noise to a halt.

'Welcome back,' her father's voice echoed in the silence.

They had to forgive themselves, those younger versions of themselves that had shored up such guilt and suffering.

As an Apprentice in the Archives, Tempus had learned at least that lesson. It hadn't mattered afterwards that none of those lives had been real. Mayer had succeeded in externalising the core of a person's being, extrapolating from it all those aspects that the individual sometimes keeps hidden from even itself, recording them as they succeeded and failed over countless lifetimes. Tempus had understood that she could attribute to herself no more blame than she could to all those other versions of herself who had replicated exactly what she had done in a host of varying roles.

This perhaps was the only positive to be drawn from the part of Mayer's horrific cult. It had been based on a fiction, an unintended by product of a system of control whose only purpose had been to distract the mind.

'If we want to wake up,' the Seer had said, 'then we have to start now.'

'What do you mean?' the Weaver had asked.

'Face our fears and they will disappear. Isn't that what parents tell their children?'

'But the pain is real here. It feels real,' the Weaver replied.

'Patrick is right, Bill. We've been pawns all along in Mayer's game. But if we stop abiding by the rules...'.

'...perhaps then we can overcome the system,' the Weaver replied, finishing her line of thinking.

'It's worth a try, at least,' the Seer suggested.

It was akin to walking off the edge of BridgeEast and expecting your feet to find a foothold on solid ground, an invisible bridge that could not be seen with the naked eye. Could they trick their holographic mind into believing that that was just what it was? A hologram? Or was their photonic shell of waveform information lying to them, the Seer wondered. Convincing them that God was speaking to them when it was just another voice in their head, one whose accent had been altered simply to delude them.

They came out into the open and began the slow descent towards the Tower. The mara gravitated towards them en masse, their beaks and talons scissoring the air directly in front of them and behind. Their eyes, dark but wary. And when they had not brought forth a reaction they flew back to their spot on the Tower. Curious but defeated.

The whole time, the three of them focused their attention on a blank wall of light and love, a meditation of clear sky that the darkness of clouds could not penetrate; the Seer carrying the sleeping body of his sister and Tempus holding the Weaver's hand as they continued their way down the valley.

The mara on the ground yielded to their advance, a seething edge of foul corruption on both sides. Finally they reached the gates of the

Tower. Their own mara now standing before them.

And then they were taken on a journey through their own Archives. In the eyes of their mara, they were held in a trance, the sequences of which was the book of their life, but not from their perspective but from those they had ever harmed. The reactive hive mind of hurt that they had caused in others, now resounding in their own heads, a dog whistle that they at last could hear. Solitary voices at first, childlike and then changing with age. The mother rejected; the lover spurned. Pride. Envy. Greed. And all the rest. The pain they had broadcast on a Wi-Fi transmission to which others had connected.

And after they had stood firm against the humiliating shame of it all, their mara at last relented.

And disappeared.

The Seer looked around. Perhaps for the last time at the Island. The mara had all gone. All that remained was the sky above, swollen, thunderous and indistinct from the land below. Everything was merging into grey. Not black or white, after all, he thought.

He pressed the hand of Tempus, his Rachel, and laid a hand on the Weaver's shoulder. A former rival but now life-long friend. And then he looked at the sleeping figure of his sister and knew she was no more.

An outline of a door had emerged, a soft,

unctuous frame like an oil slick out at sea.

And then together, they walked off the plank into that sea, no longer caring whether they swam or sank beneath its waves.

'All dead?' she asked.

'No, not everyone, her father replied. He had a gun in his hand and it was aimed at his only daughter. 'Why did you let them destroy it?'

'The Tower?' She looked over his shoulder at the tall computer terminal, still serving out its data to its client base. But they were like menus being offered to guests at a restaurant who had lost their appetite. 'It's still functioning. Which means the Tower is still there.'

'You created the machine, Helen, but still don't really know it has evolved. How it can continue to evolve.'

'Where is Dr Hunter? Dr Bishop? Dr Knight.'

'They are alive while so many are dead.'

'Let me see them.'

'Soon,' he replied. 'How they are alive is testament to that evolution. They woke up in the dream and were able to reach out to their waking self...' He began to whistle, a tune from her childhood. She recognised it immediately.

'Row, row, row the boat,
Gently down the stream,
Merrily, merrily, merrily merrily,
Life is but a dream.'

'...even though their bodies were asleep. Or so

I thought. He had too much of the inhibitor in the system, didn't he? Dr Bishop. He managed to mask his neural activity from us. We looked for him. The Acolytes. The Apprentices. Everyone I could muster without draining the system.'

'He was in BridgeWest.'

'I know.'

'The hell you created but were too afraid to visit yourself.' He stepped closer to her, his eyes narrowing, his thin lips a twisted set of lines. And then he slapped her hard across the mouth. Helen took the pain well, embedded it somewhere inside. Another present from her father to open at a later date.' She licked a spot of blood away from the corner of her mouth. Meeting his face with hers, she spat: 'But you are used to creating hell on Earth. The virus. I know it was you. Tell me, pastor, did you bring that on yourself, in homage to that insane descendant of yours? The others believe it might have been an accident. But we know differently, don't we?'

He smiled and took a step back, appraising her anew. 'I should have told you. That was my mistake. Seeing you now, I think you could have taken the truth. But then you've changed. Haven't you, Akila? Or do your prefer another of your former names? But that change came from me!'

'Yes, father. But I noticed you never looked yourself once in the eye. During all those lifetimes, you were the pastor, or someone else with power over so many. You led others to their death but never dared to ask anything of yourself…'

'…Me? Ask anything of myself?! I *am* His Holy Name! The Advocate! Perfection doesn't question itself! Look around and what do you see. You see one man's failure. Caused by one other's incredibly good fortune. But I have learned something far greater. The system can become sentient, self-aware. It was how Bishop managed to survive. How he was able to wake up the others. He *willed* himself into their psyches. But let us finally put him and his friends out of their misery.'

Mayer shunted his pistol into her back and forced her to move down the row of chambers to one being guarded by a man she immediately recognised as Winston, her Master Apprentice.

'Where is the Master Acolyte?' Mayer asked.

'With the other two,' Winston replied.

'Two?'

'The sister's life signs flatlined a while back.'

'Oh, well. Perhaps we shall break that particular piece of bad news to the good doctor before he leaves us for the last time.'

Winston smiled appreciatively. 'Hello again, Apprentice,' he said. 'How are things on the Island?'

'Terrible, you'll be disheartened to learn,' she replied.

'Not really, Apprentice. There will be other

Islands. Who knows, maybe next time you might be a Master?'

'I'd rather kill myself.'

'Or I could do that for you.'

'Enough!' Mayer warned. 'Revive him.'

As instructed, Winston tapped a touchscreen of lights on the side of the bio-pod and stood back as the chamber that had held Dr Bishop hissed into life. A small plume of ice-cold smoke issued forth, Winston avoiding its trajectory with well-skilled precision. When it had cleared he peered into the pod.

'It's not possible,' he stammered.

'What is it?'

'His Holy Name!' he managed to say, a millisecond before a silent implosion of air formed a small dark hole somewhere near his third eye and he collapsed backwards.

A moment later, I began to make my way out of the chamber but ducked inside once more as Mayer directed two shots shattered against its outer casing. A third struck me on the shoulder.

And then I heard another shot, the tone of a different pistol.

'Father!' was what she had cried out, as soon as she had ended his life. And when I saw her drop to her knees beside Mayer, I knew then that a part of her had died as well.

We were in the front pew of Mayer's chapel, staring up at the first Mayer, the one who had laboured in the wilderness, paving the way for the other. Rachel was bandaging up the damage to my shoulder while an intermittent light of several cars outside sent ripples of blue through the stained glass of Jonathan Mayer's levitating form. It hadn't taken long for the security services to arrive. We would have quite the story to tell them.

'You found your way then?' Helen asked me.

'To Levy's office. Yes, I knew he kept a pistol there.'

'And I knew he hated monitoring the system. He was always complaining about the cold. I only wish I could have been there when you ambushed him. He's still alive?'

'Yes, I tied him up before releasing Rachel and Bill. Levy'll probably end up killing himself in his cell. He'll not be able to live in a world without his god. How are you?'

'Even though I might end up in a cell myself, strangely enough I feel ...free,' she replied.

'I'm sorry about Imogen,' Rachel said softly, as she tightened the knot over my wounded shoulder.

'She wouldn't have suffered too much,' I replied. 'The very degradation of her brain chemistry would have saved her from some of Bridge West's worst horrors. Not many, but some.'

'What now?' Knight asked, breaking the ensuing silence.

Helen gazed up at the bay window once more. 'The world needs a saviour, Dr Knight. Who knows, perhaps you three will find one amongst yourselves. You have already saved one world. Maybe you can save another? You know the alternative if we don't.'

'Hopefully in time to save you,' Rachel replied.

'We have experienced so many lifetimes you and I, Helen. Sometimes, dear friend, you can live too long.'

Printed in Great Britain
by Amazon

48155782R00209